The Devil
and
the Deep Blue Sea

The Devil and the Deep Blue Sea

Lynn Stansbury

Writer's Showcase
San Jose   New York   Lincoln   Shanghai

The Devil and the Deep Blue Sea

All Rights Reserved © 2001 by Lynn Stansbury

No part of this book may be reproduced or transmitted in any form or by any means, graphic, electronic, or mechanical, including photocopying, recording, taping, or by any information storage retrieval system, without the permission in writing from the publisher.

Writer's Showcase
an imprint of iUniverse.com, Inc.

For information address:
iUniverse.com, Inc.
5220 S 16th, Ste. 200
Lincoln, NE 68512
www.iuniverse.com

This is a work of fiction. Names, characters, incidents, dialogues, and places are either products of the author's imagination or are used fictitiously. Any resemblance to actual persons, living or dead, governmental institutions, business establishments, events, or locales is entirely coincidental.

ISBN: 0-595-17444-2

Printed in the United States of America

*For John, sine qua non. And for Galu Magalei,
because I always said I would.*

Prologue

Dr. Ray Begley spent the hour before his death in a bar in the only hotel in American Samoa. Begley was here in the middle of the South Pacific because of his wife. Which is enough to make any man drink. He was in this bar because it was walking distance from his beach-side house up to the hotel overlooking Pago Pago Harbor. And since the Territory had yanked his driver's license as well as his medical license, the walk had to be short. But it was also the only bar on the island fit for a white man.

"Not that you'd know it tonight," he said. The Samoan bartender flashed him a toothy smile. Begley looked out over the lounge. A week or so ago, he had lost his glasses somewhere, but he could see well enough. Both groups of patrons around the two low cocktail tables had gone native, white hotel guests mixed with copper-skinned locals. The bartender brought him his second drink.

"Hey, Dr. Ray, those guys over there from L.A. Go talk story. Cheer you up." Begley glanced at the group against the back wall. One of the men looked familiar. Without his glasses, Begley wasn't sure, but he didn't care enough to go find out.

Laughter drifted to him from the other group. Aussies or New Zealanders. He could hear the buzz-saw accents. Kiwis probably, since their pet Samoan was Welly Tuiasosopo. Begley knew the shape of the sonofabitch even without his glasses.

"Whaddyou think?" Begley said to the bartender, "Think that asshole over there calls himself a doctor really was born in New Zealand?"

"Sure, Dr. Ray. That's what his name means. Ueligitone. Wellington."

"So what is he? Fake Samoan or fake Kiwi? Like being a fake doc, I guess."

The bartender smiled again and wiped the bar. He was hovering, Begley knew. Trying to keep him out of trouble. Made him want to misbehave.

"I mean," he said, his voice getting louder, "What's a Samoan Medical Officer anyway but a jumped-up medic. How the Kiwis let him get through a surgical residency, I couldn't tell ya. If they did. And goddamned Hutchinson treats him like he was Royal College of Surgeons already." Hutchinson. Damned Hutchinson had been director of the hospital all of a week when his testimony to the legislature had gotten Begley's medical license suspended. In L.A., Begley knew people who could settle his score with Hutchinson hard and fast, for the right amount of money.

"Hey, Dr. Ray. Easy on the language. Why don't you go to the gents', cool off some."

"If I wanta talk to my mother, I'll call her." But he slid off the stool and stalked toward the door.

In the narrow hallway outside, he leaned against the wall for a moment, waiting for his legs to steady. The door behind him swung. Welly Tuiasosopo stepped around him toward the restroom. The Samoan was a head shorter and eighty pounds lighter than Begley. His skin was dark and his black hair and bushy moustache were wiry. He grinned up at Begley.

"Surprised they let niggers like you in here," Begley said.

Welly's face went mockingly solemn. "Maybe because my patients live."

"Or Hutchinson covers up for...." Pain exploded in his belly. He was being lifted, head and body slamming against the thin wall. The little Samoan's face was a shark's grin.

"Pick your fights carefully, mate...."

The bartender and a bouncer came through the door from the lounge. "Hey, out 'o here wit' t'is stuff." They were polite, like they were talking to chiefs, but they were both huge men.

Then Begley was alone outside on the gravel drive in front of the hotel. He wasn't quite clear how he had gotten there. He was certainly drunk.

Somebody should take him home. Hotel staff had done that for him before. Well, fuck them anyway. He stumped unsteadily toward the road.

"Hey, Dr. Ray. Hold up. I'll walk with you."

Begley turned, squinting against the hotel lights. He snorted. "Thought that was you. What the hell you doing here? Told my wife the other night I thought I'd seen you up here. Didn't believe me."

The electric power shut off. In that first moment of dark and silence, the footsteps of the man approaching him crunched eerily on the gravel. But the power went out at least twice a day. It wasn't scary, just a pain in the butt. One more proof what a dump this place was.

The man linked arms with him. Begley stumbled and pulled back. "Hey. Hold up. Hotel generator'll come on in a sec. Keep us from breaking our necks." Just to their left, banked volcanic boulders made a short, nasty drop into the bay. The man hadn't let go of him.

"But, Dr. Ray," the man said gently, "That's the point."

Begley jerked his arm away and whirled clumsily, trying to run.

He never took the first step.

I

Two hours later, the power was still out.

Detective Lieutenant In-yong Han locked the door of his house and walked out to his car. He had any cop's gut distaste for darkness, but the power failure itself was ordinary enough. He heaved his scene-of-crime kit into his hard-top Suzuki jeep and swung himself in after it.

Han was in American Samoa on loan from the City of San Francisco Police Department as a sop to local commercial fishing interests. These were mostly Korean, and he was Korean. Or at least he spoke and looked Korean and apparently that was enough. But he was also the only forensic investigator on the island. And across the darkness of Pago Bay, a dead white man—the ubiquitous Samoan word was *palagi*—had washed up on the beach at Utulei.

Han sat for a moment. The night air was warm and wet. The starlight was so bright that he could see the waves rise and break on the reef, and the Southern Cross hung just above the horizon. He started the jeep and pulled out toward the police station. It was barely six miles around the bay from his house, and normally he ran the distance, at least in the cool of the morning. His wife had needed the jeep because of the baby, and he needed to stay sane. Now his wife had taken their daughter and gone back to California. But he did have the jeep.

Under his tires, snails the size of oranges exploded like popcorn. A giant toad made a *thunk* like kicking a football. Around the point from Han's house, Pago Bay opened out to his left. The far edge of the bay was laced with lights. The village of Utulei had power when the rest of the island did not because it was the territory's administrative center. The hospital, the farthest cluster of lights around the bay, and the cannery, on this side, had their own generators. There was no town, just the string of bay-side villages: hospital at Fagaalu; government in Utulei; stores, post office, and bars in Fagatogo. And the police station. The road wound along the beach and then back among the palms and mangos and banyan trees. Thirty miles an hour was break-neck speed—his own neck or half the pig, chicken and small child population of any given village—and worse at night. It was slow going.

Ten minutes later and half way down the north-east arc of the bay, the power was still out. Lanterns glowed dimly behind the glass louvers of *palagi*-style houses like Han's or swayed from the rafters of the traditional open-sided family pavilions called *fales*. A lot of people were walking along the road, moving in and out of his headlights like schools of fish. Too many people for this hour. Samoans don't do things at night. At least not that they admit to. He saw no other cars.

Whatever was going on, Han didn't think it had to do with a dead *palagi* in Utulei.

Han drove past the cannery buildings in Atu'u. They looked deserted. But out on the open road again toward Pago, up the steep slope to his right, lanterns flashed in the trees. At the cannery docks on his left, the tuna fleet was moored gunnel to gunnel. Shadowy forms scrambled across the catwalks. Ahead of and beside him, people were trotting down the road, fishermen now, Koreans in their ragged clothes.

He leaned out of the jeep's window and barked in Korean, "Police. What's up?"

"Meeting. Samoans beat four guys off the *Cheju Star* and took all their pay. Police never give a shit. We don't have to put up with this shit from these savages!" The men dashed beyond his lights. Again, he thought of fish: flash and disappear.

He could hear more shouting ahead. He was coming out onto the smelly mud flats at the head of the bay. On his left, the pagoda-like structure built as a rec center for the fishermen was lit with hand-held lanterns. A crowd spread around the steps to the entrance, blocking the road. Han pulled up.

A man climbed onto the building's low stone parapet, shouting at the fishermen in Korean, "We don't have to take this!" Han recognized him, an ex-fisherman called the Tuna Pimp. He was called the Tuna Pimp because, they said, he sold tuna. Han didn't know if that was local jargon for drugs–after two months here he was still working out what people were telling him and what they weren't–though he had seen surprisingly little signs of street shit. "We have our rights!" roared the Tuna Pimp. "We may be foreigners, but they need us. They have to protect us!" The crowd roared back at him. The hair on the back of Han's neck prickled.

He grunted in disgust and threw the jeep door open. But he was too late. The Tuna Pimp's audience surged away from him toward the center of Pago village. Han leaned out the door and shouted, but the sound was lost in the general howl. The jeep was Han's and unmarked. He had no siren, no bull horn, no spotlight, not even a gun.

The fishermen ran by, cursing and laughing and pounding on the hood of the jeep. Han leaned on the horn and eased the jeep forward. The scattering of men at the back of the crowd shifted aside. Something was happening up ahead. Even over the noise he was making, Han could hear the shouting grow louder as the leaders moved into the village. The jeep's lights were useless. They stabbed straight into the mass of moving bodies. The mob stopped. A roar like a mountainside falling through a forest rolled back through them.

Later, counting all the ways he had been a fool, Han wondered why it hadn't happened before: the crowd nearest him turned on the jeep. A man with a hammer beat out the headlights. The car bucked as shoulders lifted under it. It hung for a moment then toppled to the left.

Han came up through the passenger window as the jeep hit the driver's side. The jeep slid down a shallow bank and rammed a low shed, Han leapt like a cat onto the corrugated metal roof of the shed, and the shed collapsed onto the jeep. Jarred off his feet, Han rolled down the back-sloped roof, hands and legs flailing for a hold, then off the edge into the mud and sand behind the shed.

Skin and clothes in ribbons from the roof, he rolled to his feet—not much worse off than a botched helicopter drop—and scrambled to put a few more sheds between him and the jeep. The fishermen weren't after him particularly, but the asshole of that mob was not where he wanted to be. Half crouched, he felt his way along the swampy paths between the jumble of sheds at the waterside. If he could work his way to the left around the mob along the bay shore, he might be able to get into the main part of Pago village ahead of them, face them, talk to them. He shifted along among the backs of the buildings as fast as he could, grateful now for the dark.

But the shadows moved. And spoke. In Samoan. Han could hear the fishermen off to his right. They were drawn up again and moving forward into the main street of the village, chanting. But now he understood what he'd being seeing for the last twenty minutes: the Koreans were surrounded by an army of young Samoans.

At last there were sirens.

He got to the edge of what had been the village green. Now it was just a weedy patch of rough ground between the road and the sharks. He was a little ahead of the fishermen. Sweat or blood or both ran down one leg and his hands were on fire. He could see two squad cars winding along the shore from Fagatogo. Headlights, roof lights, sirens: probably the only two functional police vehicles on the island.

The two cruisers crossed the bridge over the little stream marking the far side of the village. They pulled up, side by side, spotlights on the Koreans. The fishermen stopped also, bunching, spilling out into the open toward the bay. The doors of the cars swung out. Four officers emerged like a drill team. They were all tall, chests like oil drums. Han started out across the open toward them. It was risky: Han had yet to see a gun here, but a Samoan with a rock was more accurate than most shooters and damned near as lethal.

The officer in front roared, first in Samoan, then English: "What the hell's goin' on here? You get back to your boats!" The attitude was unmistakable: the assistant chief of police. His vast and important family had recently invested him as Talking Chief Sapatu, one of the senior titles of his village. His ego hadn't needed the help. Odd for him to be out at night, but he would have been at the station, waiting for Han. Even Sapatu had to pay attention to a dead *palagi*. He cradled a shotgun in his arms. The fishermen grumbled and shifted.

"Wait!" Han's voice was drowned by the sound of a gun firing.

Like any good soldier, Han hit the ground.

He looked up to see cops wading into the crowd, clubs swinging. The first rank of fishermen crumpled. Han rolled to his feet but was almost knocked over by someone running past him. A spattering of rocks hit the mob like hail. Two more fishermen collapsed into their fellows. And then the Samoans poured out of the darkness and into the fight. Most were dressed just in the native kilt of bright cloth twisted around their hips. Screaming, they hit the Koreans like a tidal wave.

The Koreans broke. They ran any way they could, between the buildings, back down the road into the mob of Samoans that had closed behind them, across the beach toward the bay as if they could fly across the water to their boats. Trying to get out of the way, Han was bowled over again, struck from behind, and went down like a stone in deep water.

2

For a Friday evening, the hospital's emergency room was quiet. Ann Maglynn, the evening doc, finished her charting and went over to stand at the screen door of the ambulance entrance. Three minutes to midnight, end of her shift. Her day had started at four in the morning, and she was tired. At least they were fully staffed tonight. Ann's medical specialty was public health, but the territory's health care system was usually so short of docs that working a couple of evenings a week in the ER guaranteed her a place to live and the gratitude of the head of the hospital. Being Samoan-speaking ex-Peace Corps probably also helped. Tonight, though, she was going home and to bed and no one was going to call her at three o'clock in the morning with a question she couldn't answer.

A screen door slammed, and the hospital's night guard, a recently retired career soldier, paced across the ambulance quad toward the ER. Even with the quad light behind him, he was unmistakable: square shoulders, white shirt, black kilt–the tailored form of *lavalava* called "with pockets"–rubber thong sandals. In defiance of all Samoan cliches, Sarge was also short, skinny, efficient, and disinclined to take orders from people he didn't respect. Because of this, Ann guessed, his family was never going to invest him with a chiefly title. But the hospital generators ran, as did the hospital's two ambulances and the Public Health division's two jeeps, and no drugs got stolen from the hospital pharmacy. Sarge nodded to Ann as he passed outside.

Somewhere in the web of screened cloisters connecting the four low parallel pavilions of the hospital, another screen door slammed. A long, thin figure glided along one of the breezeways like a ghost: Neil Hutchinson, head of the hospital, Director of Health for the Territory. Not a good sign that he was here at midnight but not unusual. He would have been a good internist anywhere, but here, he was so far the best that everything really awful got to him eventually.

The current disaster was the wife of a prominent church pastor. Neil knew them from years ago when he was here as a medical student, as he told it, losing his heart and his virginity to the South Seas. The old pastor's wife had come in to the outpatient clinic a couple of days ago with her diabetes and a fever and vague belly pain and been seen by Ray Begley. The Territorial legislature had put Begley on probation–again–because of his drinking, and he was only being allowed to see general clinic walk-in patients and only with supervision, meaning Neil or another physician reviewing his charts at least daily. This was a major insult as Begley was, supposedly, a board-certified anesthesiologist somewhere. Begley had gotten around the ruling for a couple of days by having his wife Gloriana, who was also a doc, sign off on his charts. In the mean time, Begley sent the old pastor's wife home three days in a row with Tylenol and reassurances. By the time the old pastor got his wife to Neil, the old lady was so sick that not even Welly Tuiasosopo's surgical miracle of keeping her alive while he got her rotten gall bladder out could save her.

And then there was the Nightingale business. Two days before, Hutchinson's wife, Adele, also a doc, had diagnosed acute salmonella meningitis in a four-year-old. She had bullied the Off-Island Care Committee into calling out the Nightingale, the U.S. military Pacific long-distance medical air evacuation team, to fly the kid to Honolulu–sixty thousand bucks a flight when the off-island care budget was thin enough to see through–because the next commercial airline flight wasn't until Sunday. To the *palagis*, the non-Samoans, this was a natural: an innocent kid at a mortal but curable moment, the spectacle of American power and money swooping down to the rescue. To establishment Samoans, it was a criminal waste of money on society's least valuable element. *Children are not yet members of the family* went the proverb. The child's parents probably had their own opinion, but they were a young couple without rank and therefore, in village opinion, without good sense. And the noble old pastor's wife lay gravely ill and deserved a trip to Honolulu.

Down the back hall from where Ann stood, Neil came through from one of the connectors.

"*Talofa*," he said. Like the Hawaiian, *aloha*, it was both the word *love* and a greeting.

"*Talofa lava, lau susuga*," Ann replied, smiling as he came up and, in the classic Samoan way, upping the ante: *much love, your honor*.

"How's she doing?" Ann knew the old pastor's wife was dead. She could see it in Neil's face.

"Pulled the plug ten minutes ago."

Ann nodded. "I saw the old pastor come in tonight. He doesn't usually take the night watch." Custom and necessity left a lot of bedside nursing to family on the regular nursing wards. That didn't work for the ICU. So families spread their woven palm-leaf mats in the corridor outside and camped, waiting out the time to death or recovery with their London Missionary Society Samoan translations of the King James bible on their knees.

"He was a prince," Neil said. "Like always. He apologized. To me. Apologized for betraying his own dignity. That he was glad, in the end, they hadn't been away from home when she died."

"In other words, that he didn't blame you or Adele for not sending them to Honolulu." Neil nodded but didn't say anything. He was very nordic, pale lank hair, eagle-beak nose, fierce blue eyes. For a moment, the blue eyes swam. But he wouldn't want that acknowledged.

She waited. Then said, "Were you able to get to the reception?"

Neil was a perpetual Eagle Scout: he really did believe that being right was enough, along with honesty, cleanliness, and working four times harder than anybody else. Politics, he just didn't get. In this case, politics was going to a reception at the Governor's house and being nice to the politically well-connected lady who had thought she was going to get the job Neil now had. And who also happened to be Gloriana Shutz-Begley, Ray Begley's wife.

"Briefly. It's a good thing Begley didn't turn up. I think I'd've killed him." He took a breath and tried on a tight smile." As it was, Gloriana tried to grand-dame Adele: *I know that your husband is working terribly hard. So glad that you could make it.*"

"I'm sure that was helpful." Adele Takeda Hutchinson was Hawaii Japanese. She was first in her medical school class, premiere in her pediatrics residency and had just passed her Board exams in neonatology before Neil took the job as Director of Health for the American Samoa Government. Her opinions on Gloriana's management of the island's well-child programs would blister paint.

"Well, it was at least distracting. Otherwise, I might have strangled Gloriana as well."

A ripple of fear like a chill passed over Ann and she shivered. She was just enough older than Neil and Adele to think of them as young and idealistic. She didn't like to see them so angry.

"I hear the governor's talking mediation." She was being unnecessarily oblique. They both knew that Neil's ex-Army commander–Ann's ex-lover–was coming in on Sunday's flight from Honolulu at the governor's request. Though, Ann guessed, they all, including the governor, had vastly different expectations of the result.

"What's to mediate? The governor hired me. The legislature confirmed me. They wouldn't touch Gloriana with a ten foot pole, no matter who the hell she's related to. Some of that's because she married Begley and they wouldn't touch *him* with a ten foot pole, but she's still incompetent...."

But you shouldn't have gone after her right off, Ann thought. Time and the back door would have worked. Now it's all armed camps and negotiation.

"...And she still refuses to account for big chunks of money she's had access to through the health promotion grants..."

Ann happened to know, just because both sides seemed to talk to her, that the amount involved wasn't that much. Given an un-insightful person in a position seen more as a perk than as a career, it was about what you'd expect in travel and other minor goodies. But Neil wasn't the sort of person to accept that kind of argument.

He hadn't answered her about the mediation. Before she could ask again, he said, "Have *you* talked to Gar?" Colonel Doctor Garfield Munro was why both of them were here, but they tended to avoid talking about him if they could. Or at least Ann did.

She shook her head. "Gar is the worst person to be coming as a mediator. You know him: he's just one more power-broker wanabe, honing his skills for Washington. What else do you do in Honolulu when you get bored with living in the most beautiful place in the world?" There were two kinds of Army docs in Honolulu, the ones using the army medical center there as a spring-board to Washington and the ones who wanted to get out of the Army and spend the rest of their lives in Paradise. Neil was definitely one of the latter.

"They only took me because Gar proposed me. Gar's who they really wanted."

"Clearly, one should be careful what one wishes for."

Tires squealed in the parking lot. They both looked out through the screens.

A small pickup jerked to a stop outside. Two Samoan youths burst from the cab and began yelling. Sarge's torso passed as a white blur as he bore down on the truck from around the end of the building, barking questions. The boys began pulling bodies out of the truck.

Ann would always remember it just like that. They were instantly overwhelmed. The five gurneys in the ER were filled and the table and the spare gurney in the crash room and the space on the floor and out the back hall as one pickup after another filled with wounded men pulled in.

Neil stepped among the bodies like a stork, trying to triage, trying to move the less injured out into the waiting room to make working space for those tending the more injured. More docs began arriving from the residential compound, at first sleepy and incredulous, then inappropriately noisy and jocular, as American physicians often are in a crisis. But there were never enough of them. A single badly wounded person can easily occupy three physicians. Here there were three or four wounded men for every doc: wet, sandy, drunk, bloody, limp, and underfoot.

And then an ambulance returned with four more wounded men, including two men in the grey shirt and black shorts of the Territorial Police. One of them had a bullet wound in his chest and the surgeon Welly Tuiasosopo at one end of the stretcher. The man on the stretcher was Assistant Chief of Police Sapatu. Welly's grin radiated moon-like against the night.

"Found a friend of mine in a spot of trouble, so I hitched a ride. Not this sonofabitch. Guy over there: Korean cop. Good chap but got a hole in his head and less skin than God gave 'im. This fella here is my cousin...." He nodded down at the uniformed man on the crash bed. Nurses were setting up IVs, trying to get a blood pressure. "We only just got 'im through his chiefly installation. Now I gotta take the bastard to OR and try and save the family the price of all that party. Eh, Neil, put in central line if you can. Who've you got for assist? Anybody but Begley. Two drunks in OR no good."

Neil was putting in an IV in the man's arm while Ann went for his jugular. "Haven't seen Begley for a day and a half. Not since he turned over the old pastor's wife to me. It'd be too much to hope he's drowned himself. Not Ann; I want her here on dirty wounds." Ann grunted neutrally: getting away into the OR would have been a nice escape. She secured her line and opened it up wide; fluid poured in. The Samoan policeman was breathing but not much more. He looked like a beached whale on the cart. Neil picked over him delicately.

"I don't see anything other than the chest. You better take the Texan. At least he's a surgeon, and you'll need all the help you can get. John's over in x-ray already if you want to get films."

Just then, the Texan strolled through the back door in a purple and green print *lavalava*, Hawaiian print aloha shirt, white socks, and Tevas. Welly flashed him his best demoniac native grin—it couldn't have been better if he had a bone through his nose—and hauled the man off down the long back hall with Sapatu's stretcher between them.

The *can do* aura left with the surgeons, and another van pulled in. So did the police chief, the Korean sub-consul, and the mayor, the two most senior talking chiefs, and the pastors of all three protestant churches of the village of Pago. And they all wanted to talk to Neil immediately and at once. Ann turned her back on them and moved into the main ward. The ambulance crew had shoved the gurney with the Korean cop between the two end beds in the row. More Koreans—she had yet to see an injured Samoan other than Welly's cousin, the Assistant Chief of Police—were lying on the floor around the gridlock of stretchers so that nobody could attend to anybody. With the aid of Sarge and a nurse, she got the bruised and drunk sorted out from the genuinely injured, levered some space between the three stretchers and settled down to work.

It was now half past one, and her left brain had abandoned her. She had no words left to channel or codify inpouring sensation. The smell of deoxygenated blood: she would remember it as an ill-kept meat-market. But now it was just cool, shocked flesh and grit and sea-water. And more smells: booze and vomit and dirty people. And noise: voices and engines and the startling snap of the crash room screen door slamming and the grating of sand underfoot on the floor.

From time to time, Neil Hutchinson passed through the ER, trailed by the chief of police and the Korean sub-consul blaming each other for what had happened with icy politeness. Followed by the six elders of Pago village who alternately clucked over the bad behavior of mischievous boys and denied that anything had happened. And everybody blamed Neil for what was going on because he was still paying attention to it.

Ann was halfway through the last of the five lacerations on her two remaining fishermen when the Korean cop woke up. Disoriented and combative, he tried to climb off the narrow end of the gurney and almost flipped it. Fortunately, Sarge happened by and tackled him across the chest, thrusting the man back onto the mattress and the gurney's wheels back onto the floor. The cop muttered something and waved one arm around but subsided.

Sarge said, "Where's the Director?" Ann shook her head, and he went off. She finished the overcast line of suture, pasted the wound with antibiotic ointment and laid a Telfa pad over it, and left the rest to the nurse finishing the same chores on the man one bed over. She stripped off her gloves and went over to the policeman.

She had gone over him when she had sorted out her catch the first time. He hadn't made much sense then either, but he had been rousable and without major signs of a broken skull or increasing pressure in his head. He did look like he had been through a shredder. His shirt and shorts were torn, and wherever skin was exposed, it was scraped in broad patches. He had two good sized cuts, one on the back of his head and one on his thigh. But beyond keeping an eye on him, she hadn't been able to do much more than wash off the grit and sew him up.

He lay on his back studying the ceiling.

"Do you remember your name now?"

"Han," he said tonelessly. "In-yong. Sergeant ...Lieutenant."

"Do you know where you are?"

His eyes moved again. He started to shift himself with one elbow then fell back. "Hospital."

"Do you know where the hospital is?"

"Fagaalu." Fagaalu was the tiny village behind which the hospital was located and so a fairly subtle identification. She asked him the date and he gave her the day before.

"Close. It's actually...." She looked at her watch. "About two hours into the next day. Do you know what happened to you, how you got here?" He thought about that for a while.

She knew who he was: you couldn't work in the ER and not know the only competent cop on the island. Something else they shared was graduate work at UC Berkeley, though neither of them had known it at the time. But she had also been there the night he had brought in his wife after she had overdosed on Valium. Like Adele Hutchinson, his wife was Japanese. But Japan Japanese, not American. In general, Ann knew, Koreans feel about Japanese like the Irish feel about the English, and the feeling is pretty well reciprocated. So she had been curious about them. Carrying his infant daughter asleep on his shoulder, he had been helpful, intelligent and as tightly shut down emotionally as submarine hatches on a deep dive.

He said slowly, "I was called to come in to the station. I must have...been in an accident or something." His voice was deep, the cadence more Hawaii than California, the accent crisp, almost British. He looked at her, and she knew that he recognized her now. She also knew that his wife was gone. Maybe for good, people said. "Did I wreck the jeep?"

Even in his present condition he was good-looking. He was tall for a Korean, his hair cropped in a military flat top. But he had the square-jawed face, wide flat shoulders and narrow hips she thought of as classic Korean, more kin to those who had crossed the Bering Strait eight thousand years ago than those who had stayed behind. On the rare occasions she had seen him smile, his long, mobile mouth would turn up at one end like a cat's tail.

"I don't know about that. But there was a riot. Samoans and fishermen. You don't remember any of that?" He studied her face again.

"No."

There was a little sound in the doorway and she looked up. Adele Takeda Hutchinson stood there in a brilliant pink muumuu. Her long black hair was twisted up on her head; her face, shocked and pale and exquisite, like a Hokusai drawing. The delicacy was an illusion, Ann knew; Adele had a temper like a steel blade.

"It's horrible," Adele breathed. "Hiroshima must have been like this."

"Seems unlikely," Ann said. "They say the ratio there was one doc to five thousand."

The only good thing about this night, Ann thought more than once, was that she was not Neil Hutchinson or the tuna fleet representative. The latter gentleman turned up about three and stood, looking stunned, just inside the crash room door. He was spotted there by the chief of police and the Korean sub-consul who went for him like sharks for blood in the water.

Just then, someone turned up from the kitchen with an urn of coffee on a cart. Neil appeared also, trailed by the delegation of elders from Pago village. Despite this encumbrance, he was able to cut the two Koreans off into the waiting room. There they could harangue each other and the less injured fishermen at length and keep themselves away from the chief of police who looked like he was about to violate every Samoan social norm and lose his temper. Abandoned in the middle of the ER, the chief of police suddenly noticed the delegation from Pago clustered at Ann's end of the room. Being a paramount chief from Manu'a, the three little islands to the east from which Samoa's most exalted titles arise, the chief of police lit into the six old gentlemen from Pago in forceful and un-high-chiefly language which at least got them off Neil's back.

Smiling to herself, Ann finished patching up the Korean cop and wondered what her chances were of grabbing two minutes to herself to get to the bathroom. She still didn't think that there was anything wrong with this guy that cleanliness and attention to detail wouldn't cure, both of which he seemed more than capable of handling himself. But he had been unconscious and then disoriented when he was first brought in. With no one at home to look after him, he deserved a night in the hospital. But she was going to be able to organize all that better with her bladder empty.

A few minutes later, she emerged gratefully from the little lavatory in one of the quiet clinics and was hailed down the corridor by Sarge. Behind the guard was the earnest and worried face of a youth in police uniform.

"This boy," said Sarge, "Has brought in a body."

Jesus, Ann thought, who *hasn't* brought in a body tonight?

"Alive or dead?"

She had begun to hope that they were going to get through this night with no deaths. Of course, if Assistant Police Chief Sapatu made it. There had been no word from the OR yet, but Ann guessed that was where Neil had got to and why Sarge had come looking for her.

Sarge nodded. "Dead." His voice had an odd inflection.

"Samoan?" She had still seen no other injured Samoan other than Sapatu.

"*Palagi.*" One of Sarge's eyebrows went up and down. Ann followed docilely, hoping that whoever this dead *palagi* was, she didn't know him–or her–and neither did anyone else. Sarge opened the morgue door.

Unfortunately, the man on the slab was Ray Begley.

Begley was another beached whale. But the diseases that had turned him yellow in life now colored him green in death. He was cool to the touch without being chilled. He might have been any of the men whose skin Ann had touched in the last three hours. Except of course that he wasn't breathing. And the back of his head was flat. So flat that his chin tucked back oddly against his neck. The skin of the skull was broken in places, extruding bone and bits of flesh coated with a thin layer of clean white sand.

"Damn," Ann said.

She turned to the young man in uniform. In Samoan, she said, "Where did you find him? Was he in the fight?"

The boy's mouth opened. Ann thought he was going to fold up on the floor and cover his head in recognition of extreme authority.

Sarge's voice was dry. "This Western Samoa boy, doc. Good boy. Does what he's told. *The road to leadership is through service.* They tell him guard body til someone come. Only never come. Lotsa noise, lotsa siren, lotsa ambulance go by, but not for him. T'ree hours there on beach he waits. No lights. Flashlight goes dead. He begins to worry about *aitu*, you know, ghosts, and maybe *palagi* ghosts worse even than Samoan ghosts. He has van, he thinks he will run away. But he's good boy: bring dead *palagi* to *palagi* doctors."

Ann said gently to the young man, "*E malo.* Is good. Is right thing. Who said to wait?"

"Sapatu."

"That doesn't help," Ann said in English. And then in Samoan, "Who were you waiting for?"

"Progress?" the boy said hopefully, in Samoan.

"Not a lot," Ann said, in English.

"No, my lady," the boy said triumphantly. "Not *palagi*, Korean."

Ann stared at him. "Progress. *Solo.*" She giggled, wondering if the good Lieutenant Han knew about these word games with his name. "Okay. You stay here now, wait, guard this man like before. I go get your detective. No *aitu* here: all the time light, noise, too many *palagis*. Okay?"

"Okay."

"*Praise to patience.* We return not long."

Headed back to the ER, Ann could feel the corporate adrenalin ebbing. It was quarter of four. Sapatu was still in surgery. The two men who needed the ICU were there. A dozen others were being admitted to wards for observation. The walking wounded sat on the benches in the waiting room with coffee, rolls, blankets, and the seemingly endless scolding by the sub-consul and the fleet representative. In the ER, all the beds in the main room were still full, but the floors and the crash room were clear. A near-silent handful of docs and nurses moved as if underwater, finishing up.

Adele Hutchinson was perched on a high stool beside the third ER bed, a bright little butterfly in her pink muumuu, working on a long cut across her man's back. But her voice rang in the falsetto sing-song of Hawaiian pidgin. So she, at least, was still pumping adrenalin and having a good time. "Eh, Annie...you know who we missing? Gloriana and Ray. Too dirty for them, maybe." Adele giggled, snipping the last suture. "Or maybe Ray get party-time tonight, yeah?"

Ann smiled briefly but said nothing. Lieutenant Han was sitting sideways on his gurney, legs hanging over, shoulders hunched a little as if pain were hung off them on poles. He looked to be deep in thought or wondering if he was going to puke. Not mutually exclusive.

"How are you doing?" Ann said.

He snorted softly. "Like the man says, it's the mileage that gets you."

"I'm going to put you in the hospital over night—or at least what's left of the night. But first, I need to show you something. Do you think you can walk? Or should I find a wheel chair?"

He looked at her carefully. And then one corner of his mouth curled up like a cat's tail.

"I knew there was something I had forgotten."

3

Han pulled a stool over to the morgue table and sat down. Begley. The doctor told him the man's name was Begley. One of the doctors, one of the hospital staff. Han knew the name was important but couldn't remember why. He sent the doctor off to find the director of the hospital. He thought about puking and decided it would hurt too much.

He looked at the dead man's head. You could get that watermelon-dropped-on-the-highway look without being murdered. But you needed motorcycles, fast-moving cars, or multi-story buildings to do it, and there weren't any here.

Murders, there were. In two months, Han had already investigated three murders. And had discovered why the locals had no forensics, other than the lack of dependable refrigeration. All three victims and all three perpetrators had been Samoan, each pair from the same village. The killings had been all been witnessed by most of their respective fellow villagers. All had been something to do with somebody not getting a chief's title they thought they deserved. Everybody knew who did it and why. All three killers had been or would be convicted despite legal proceedings that made *Gilligan's Island* look like a courtroom drama. All three were in jail and would stay there. Nobody gave a damn. The news in the papers, the gossip around the villages, was how the families were resolving the strife that had produced the murder. Han assumed he wasn't the only one wondering what the hell he was doing here.

This guy was the first dead white, the first dead *palagi*, Han had seen. Newcomer *palagis* did get mugged once in a while, just enough to keep the rest of the white community on edge. And groups of young Samoan males couldn't resist jumping a stranger encountered alone. Han's relative immunity to attack in his daily runs along the shore road had to do with the increasing recognition that he was a cop, not a fisherman, the discovery that he was a lot of trouble to catch, and the damage he had done to the first ones who had tried it. But this guy wasn't a stranger. And Han bloody well had to get this investigation right.

He looked down at his hands where they lay like two dead fish on his thighs. *Fuck.* His face twisted into a smile. *At least say it right*, the Oxford-educated uncle who had raised him would say, pushing his little nephew's lower lip up against the boy's upper incisors to make the *f* sound, so foreign to Korean, *otherwise you are merely ridiculous.*

Han pulled a couple of latex gloves out of a box by the sink in the end of the table. He couldn't pull them onto his raw hands. So he folded them into a pad and touched the arm nearest him, lifting it, the curve of his fingers hooked under the curve of the corpse's fingers. The fingers and the wrist were stiff, the elbow and shoulder progressively looser.

A voice behind him said, "So, is it starting or stopping?" Han hadn't heard the door open. Hutchinson: the director's name was Hutchinson.

"Starting. In this climate, you don't look this pretty for long."

Hutchinson snorted. "I don't know shit about forensic pathology. So what kind of timing does that give you?"

Han moved one shoulder. It hurt. But at least it moved. Like the corpse's. He looked at his wrist, but the face of his watch was smashed.

"What time is it?"

There was never any point in looking at wall clocks. The frequent power outages rendered them essentially random.

Hutchinson looked at his own watch. "Five of four."

Han sat for a while. Like crabbing, he thought. You pull up memory like crabs out of deep water, gently, so they don't let go of the bait before you can net them. "I was called at eleven-thirty last night. So he was dead by then."

"Could you fall and do that?" Hutchinson said. "Wonder what his neck looks like."

Han felt a couple of more pieces of his mind hook up again with an impact like a train coming together. Begley: politics. He couldn't let Hutchinson touch the body, at least not without witnesses and documentation.

"Do you have a pathologist?"

"No. I may be getting one on Sunday's flight, believe it or not. Or you could ship him on the turnaround flight back to Honolulu. Body bag, ice, some kind of casket...." Hutchinson was talking to himself.

Han's guts rose. He reached out one leg and then the other, rotating the ankle like a dance movement. His guts sank back to where they belonged. Hutchinson's face came into focus.

"You okay?"

"Yeah. Where's the woman doc? The red-headed one. The colonel's wife." The Japanese woman doc was Hutchinson's wife. Kind of a link between them, having Japanese wives.

"You mean Ann? She went to try to find a bed for you. We're a little short tonight. What do you need?"

"Witnesses. One of your docs, isn't he?"

Hutchinson turned down a plastic crate with one foot and sat on it. "I inherited him."

"Guy wanted your job, yes? Drunk? Married to the governor's old girlfriend or something? That it?"

"Close enough. Though I don't think Ray could have believed he'd get my job."

"You kill him?" It was very quiet. Water dripped in the sink. The generator rumbled outside.

"No. But I watched a friend of mine die tonight because of Ray Begley. She was old; she was frail; she might have died anyway. But right now, it's real hard for me to be sorry that I'll never have to see that sonofabitch again."

The door to the morgue flew open and a tall, blond woman swept in. She was angular as only a thin middle-aged woman can be, the electric blue silk of her evening gown catching on hard edges of her body as she moved. She shrieked, "You've killed him!" And fainted onto the damp concrete floor, cheek pillowed on one forearm. Neither Han nor Hutchinson moved.

A man, a blimpish *palagi* with long thin legs, came next. He knelt beside the woman. "Gloriana! Gloriana! Are you all right?" Han recognized Leon Fischer, the attorney general of American Samoa, said to be an old law school buddy of the governor. Fischer looked at Hutchinson, *"Do something, man!"*

Hutchinson got up from his crate, knelt by the woman, rolled her onto her back, lifted her legs and placed them in Fischer's arms. The woman's eyes popped open. She flailed at the two men, coiling away from them like a cobra. She sat up, thrusting wings of blond hair back behind her ears with long brown hands. Her eyes were the same startling blue as her gown.

Looking at Han, she said imperiously, "Who are you?" Her voice was accented but not Samoan. Something European. German maybe.

Fischer answered first. "This is Detective Lieutenant Han, Gloriana. He's the best man we have in the Territorial force. On loan from the San Francisco Police Department's Criminal Investigation Division. If anyone can find out what happened to Ray, he can."

Han was impressed. As a Samoan introduction, it was flawless. Bypassing Han's somewhat disagreeable or at least incomprehensible Korean connections—Han wasn't always sure he understood them himself except that it had something to do with how he got paid—Fischer had set him up as a superior commodity owing directly to *we*. The woman began to cry.

"My poor Samoa. We need doctors so badly and to loose the finest...."

Hutchinson sat back on his crate. Fischer was trying to get the woman to her feet without hauling her up like a puppet. She was having none of it, twitching her shoulders away from him with each touch, eyes buried in Fischer's handkerchief. Her long thin face reappeared abruptly, blurred eyeshadow making her look like a blue-masked raccoon. She pointed to Hutchinson.

"Don't let him touch Ray. He'll change the evidence. He'd do anything to...."

"Gloriana." Reality appeared to be kicking in for the lawyer at last. "Don't. I'm sure Lieutenant Han is...."

Han held up one hand.

"Excuse me." He looked at the woman. "Who are you, please?"

Her face went slack with surprise. "*I* am Doctor Schutz-Begley." It came out *shoots Begley*. Han thought: God, if only she had. Preferably in public. With lots of witnesses.

"You are related to the deceased, then?"

"I am his *wife*. Really, this is too much...." She turned to Fischer.

But Fischer waggled his head. "He has to do this, Gloriana. It's a formality, but it has to be done." Gloriana's mouth pursed and her tears welled again. She allowed Fischer to lift her to her feet. She drooped against him, the effect marred somewhat by her having to bend around his paunch.

Han let his voice rumble smoothly. "I realize this is a very difficult time for you. But I must have a formal identification. The deceased is your husband, then?"

Gloriana looked at Fischer, then at Han, then even at Hutchinson. Everywhere except the body on the table. Again, Fischer seemed to have the most stake in the overt process. "Gloriana. You have to look at him." At last, her eyes flicked briefly to the body. But she didn't say anything.

Finally, Han said, "Can you identify the deceased as your husband, Raymond Begley?"

Face pressed into Fischer's front again, she nodded briefly and muttered something.

"Excuse me?"

"Villiam...William. William Raymond Begley."

"Thank you." Still entwined, Fischer and Gloriana took a few stately steps toward the door. "Wait, please."

They stopped. Fischer's face was suddenly tight. Han ignored him.

"Doctor Schutz-Begley. Let's clear some things up while we can. When was the last time you saw your husband–alive?"

Gloriana's face contorted. "This is outrageous! My husband has been murdered and I, *I* am being harassed by a...."

I vont to be alone Han thought ludicrously. Fortunately, Fischer moved in again to preserve the proprieties.

"Gloriana, this is his job. I do think, Lieutenant, that we could move somewhere more appropriate. The Director's office perhaps."

Hutchinson said, "Lieutenant Han will be admitted to the hospital as soon as he's finished here."

Gloriana and Fischer looked at Hutchinson as if they had forgotten that he was there. They also looked puzzled, as if being asked to forgo a preference for the relief of another was very odd.

"We can finish this interview at some more appropriate place tomorrow," Han went on. He sounded dogged even to himself, but he guessed this was his best chance at either of these two. "But it would be very helpful if you could tell me what you can of your husband's movements yesterday. Particularly, when you last saw him alive."

Gloriana stiffened in the circle of the lawyer's arm. "I don't...follow my husband around. I am at work all day."

"Did you have dinner together?"

"No. That is, we were supposed to dine with the Governor, but Ray...was ill. I went alone. That is, with Leon."

"But you saw him. After you got home from work. Before you went out."

"Yes. Of course."

"So. What time? Maybe six o'clock? Six-thirty?"

Fischer put in smoothly, "I actually was with Ray for a few minutes. I live just a few doors down the beach. Gloriana wasn't quite ready yet, so I sat and chatted with him a bit."

"And that was?"

"Oh, maybe seven-twenty, seven-thirty. We were up at the residence just after seven-thirty. It's just a few hundred yards up the hill. Just around from the entrance to the hotel." He said it like a tour guide, as to one who would never have been invited there. Which Han hadn't been.

"And you left him there alone?"

"Our house girl was there," Gloriana put in. Rather quickly, Han thought, given her previous reticence. Fischer glanced at her but said nothing. "She was to finish her work and go home."

Han nodded. "Please write down her name for me and where I can find her. You didn't see your husband again, then, when you got home?"

"I...we..." Gloriana's eyes filled again.

Fischer said, "We were still at the Governor's when the call came...." His voice trailed off.

"What call?"

"That Ray had been found. Found dead."

"That's what you were told, that he had been found dead?"

"Yes."

"*When* did that call come?"

"About...about two, maybe."

"And it was you who took the call, Mr. Fischer?"

"Yes, as a matter of fact."

"Who did you talk to?" Han came alert like a hunting animal. Real information, pieces of the puzzle: it was what he got high on. What his Catholic Samurai wife called his besetting sin.

"Sasa." Sasa, *most sacred*, was the nickname for the chief of police. Han didn't think Fischer would have used it with other Samoans present. And it took some balls to suggest that the most exalted high chiefly title of Manu'a and Chief of the Territorial Police Department, after a riot in which his own first assistant–also an important traditional chief–had been gunned down, had paused to call the governor's residence to tell the attorney general that Dr. Begley had been found dead. But it certainly wasn't impossible. In fact, the more Han thought about it, the more likely it seemed.

Suddenly, he wished the little red-headed woman would come back and put him to bed. And maybe cradle his head in her lap.

"One more question, doctor," Han said. "Why did you say your husband was murdered?"

Gloriana stared at him. Finally she said, "Because he was. Wasn't he?"

"Is that what you were told?"

"I...." she looked at Fischer, her brows pinched together. "I don't...." This time, a puddle of tears worked its way through the eye shadow and ran as a blue trickle down one side of her face.

"Really, Lieutenant, I think we really must...."

"Mr. Fischer: did you tell the doctor that her husband had been murdered?"

"No. I told her that he had been found dead. She was of course very upset...."

"I understand. Dr. Schutz-Begley, who do you think might have murdered you husband?"

"Really, Lieutenant," Fisher started again, "This is hardly the time...."

Han ignorned him. "Doctor?"

Gloriana opened her mouth and closed it again. She didn't quite look at Hutchinson. She began to weep again. "I don't know. I don't know who could do such a terrible thing. He was a great man, and people are always envious. Especially in Samoa."

"And now, Lieutenant, really...."

"Thank you. You have been very helpful."

They seemed to take a few seconds to realize that they had been dismissed. For a moment, Han thought that they were going to argue. Then they swept out together.

Han said, "She's not Samoan."

Hutchinson reached out one hand and rocked it back and forth. "Hard to say. I've been told her family is mainly in Western Samoa. The Germans held Western Samoa until after the first World War. There're a couple of prominent German-Samoan families. No Schutz that I know of." He shrugged. "But she did her undergrad medical training in Germany. So maybe Shutz was somebody she picked up there. Anyway, she's got a teenaged daughter who's not Begley's...." Hutchinson's trailed off. He suddenly seemed very young.

Han grunted. "So. Did she kill him?"

"God. I'd have to be grateful. Seems unlikely, though. She's tall for a woman, but she doesn't lift a finger she doesn't have to, and she just made the big six-oh. Hard to see her being able to swing anything big enough to make that dent in Begley's skull. Or making the effort."

Han nodded. He also recognized Hutchinson as a very clever man.

"How about the house girl? Would she do it? On a direct order, say?"

"Maybe. A superior's order is supposed to be the most powerful motivator in Samoan society. But even Samoans have their Nuremberg."

"The chief who ordered his men to kill and roast the beautiful child so that he could eat her. So they did it but then killed him in disgust. I've heard that story. Look," Han went on. "We need help. You're a suspect; I can't use my hands. We need a photographer, a tape recorder or someone to take notes, a couple of dependable people who can move the body around and serve as witnesses."

"My wife?"

"No. Too close to you; too much gossip about her and the Schutz-Begley...." Han grunted. "What a name. Get the red-headed one–whatever you called her–the colonel's wife. And your security guard, the one they call Sarge. What about a photographer?"

"I can do that." Hutchinson got up and started for the door but then stopped. "By the way, I don't know where you got your information, but she's not the colonel's wife. She's his ex-mistress, and she doesn't like to be reminded of it."

They were an odd bag of deputies.

There was Hutchinson with his array of camera equipment that he wielded with deft familiarity. He would have a hard time, if the photos didn't come out, convincing a jury that he hadn't known what he was doing. But Han really didn't think Hutchinson was a likely suspect. For one thing, Hutchinson's itinerary for Friday evening suggested the complete lack of privacy usual in Samoa: clinic, hospital, governor's reception, hospital, and then more hospital. If it checked out, the closest thing he'd been to alone, give or take a couple of trips to the bathroom, was the ten minute drive to and from the governor's reception in the company of his wife. But given the gossip and given what he had seen tonight with Begley's wife and the attorney general, Fischer, Han also guessed that Hutchinson was going to be tried and convicted in inner government circles before Begley was completely stiff.

The red-headed doctor–her name was Ann Maglynn–and Sarge handled the body. Another odd pair. In aloha shirt and floppy white trousers, the woman looked like a little kid in hand-me-downs from a big brother. Her short dark red hair stood up in spikes from her sweeping the sweat impatiently off of her forehead with one arm as she worked. Sarge was a malevolent gnome, growling as he moved the corpse. Han thought he was cursing. But about halfway through the process, Han realized the old guard was praying.

Standing to one side as Ann and Han worked Begley's clothes off, Hutchinson said, "No watch; no wallet. Maybe he just got mugged."

Han said, "You've been here longer than I have. Anyone ever been killed in a mugging?" Ann and Sarge both shook their heads.

Hutchinson said, "No. Roughed up some. Good for a band-aid here and there."

Ann pulled off one of her gloves and pinched up a bit of Begley's damp shirt. "Certainly feels like seawater; smells like it." The shirt and pants were scuffed with green and brown–dirt or moss or algae–and ripped and abraded like the man's exposed skin. Both doctors thought that the left shoulder and hip were both dislocated and the left leg broken as well.

"Beaten up, then?" Han said "Not just bashed over the head?"

"Well," Hutchinson said. "He certainly *is* beaten up. Did it happen as part of the same assault?" He shrugged. "The pathologists in Honolulu should be able to sort some of that out....You're not going to try to ship him to San Francisco?"

"No. The Territorial Police has official connections in Honolulu."

"Funny, though," Hutchinson went on. "He didn't fight. Look at his hands. They're scratched up, like the rest of him. But nothing on the palms or fingertips; nothing specific on the knuckles."

Han looked at his own hands.

Hutchinson said, "How'd you do that?"

"Tried to hang on to a corrugated tin roof," Han said. A minute before, he couldn't have told them that. He poked back into his returning memory, wondering what else of use might be there. Something about a gun shot. But if so, it didn't have anything to do with this.

"Whatever happened, the head had to be the main target," Hutchinson went on.

"So," Han said. "Maybe a mugging that got out of hand. Maybe being hit by a car?" He looked at the doctors. They both shrugged and nodded.

"Be kind of a freak though," Hutchinson said. "Having the head end up like that."

Han said, "How about bashed first and then tossed out of a car?"

Hutchinson shrugged again. "Maybe. If you carry big heavy flat things around in your car to bash people over the head with when they're sitting in the passenger seat and you're in back with somebody else driving. I mean, you wouldn't want to do it if he was driving. Particularly along the coast road. Not to mention the mess in the car." Not, Han thought, that people think of things like the mess, usually. It just happens and then there's the mess. "Well, I guess they could have been pulled over somewhere. Bash him, push him out of the car. We could x-ray him. Won't tell you pre- or post-mortem, but it would give you some sense of the force involved."

"How about water first, bashed later?" Han said.

Ann shook her head. "I think he'd be dirtier. And he has to have gone into the water after he quit bleeding, because his wounds are clean other than the sand. Beyond that...." She shrugged. "I mean, considering you as an example...." Her eyebrows went up.

Han thought about the coast road. There were places where you could get seriously damaged rolling down lava boulders into the water. Hutchinson had a car, Han knew, a jeep like his own. So did Gloriana Shutz-Begley, a huge old black Mercedes in which she was driven around like a queen. He looked at Ann.

"Do you have a car?"

She shook her head. "I use a Public Health jeep when I have official business."

"Okay," Han said. "Just get him iced down as soon possible. Forget the x-rays. Don't handle him any more than you have to."

They were shifting Begley's corpse into a big green plastic body bag when the door to the morgue slammed back again and five more bodies were brought in. Four were fishermen, drowned in the bay fleeing the mob. The fifth was Assistant Chief of Police Sapatu.

Welly Tuiasosopo was pushing the gurney carrying Sapatu's body. The surgeon stood beside Han, waiting for space to work. "Wound wasn't that bad," he said. "Had a fucking heart attack."

On his first day in Samoa, Han had met Welly in the emergency room over the bodies of six mutual victims of broken beer bottles. "Hell," the surgeon said, "I never ask 'em what happened, and it's my own language. They tell you what they think is due to your position. If they've gotten your rank right, it's the truth. You could polygraph 'em and they'd look straight. Believe what you can see and touch and do yourself and let the rest go." It was close enough to Han's religion.

Han knew that Welly drank too much and screwed around too much and lived for the day when he could get together enough money to return to New Zealand and sit the written exams for the Royal Austral-Asian College of Surgeons. He had already passed the practical; the final step would free him forever from life as a Samoan Medical Officer. Han didn't drink or screw around at all but thought of Welly as the only sane person he knew here.

"A bad night for my village," Welly went on. "With the Nofonofo title still open and now Sapatu." As he spoke, Ann Maglynn had stepped back from Begley's body and was peeling off her gloves. He said to her, "And the Tapuafanua passed away tonight. One of my aunties told me. When I called about Sapatu." Ann stared at him, her brow furrowed.

Welly shrugged. "He was an old man. He had to go sometime." Ann shook her head and abruptly left the room. The little ripple of emotion was lost in the rustling of body bags. Family arrived to claim Sapatu's body.

"Jesus," Welly said to Han. "That was fast. Thought I wouldn't have to deal with any of these guys for at least another four hours."

Han had never been to Welly's home village on the other side of the island. It was hardly a mile straight across but hours even by car on winding mountain roads. Presumably these were some local deputation. Welly herded them outside to explain as best he might what had happened and why Sapatu also was now a specimen for the pathologists in Honolulu.

Han's head pulsed. He was suddenly sick with the smell of death and seawater. Ann reappeared with a wheel chair. She helped him off of the stool and into the chair. But his attention was entirely taken up by the mingled softness and structure beneath her clothes and the scent of soap on her skin as she slid her shoulder under his arm and half lifted him into the chair.

Somewhere across the hospital, the Samoan ward nurses smelled much the same. But they were not so gentle. Meaty bolsters, they flung him into bed, implying wordlessly that he should behave himself, private room or no private room. They needn't have worried.

4

Welly Tuiasosopo walked out the hospital drive toward the shore road. Under the trees, it was still night. If he went home, his wife would want to hear about everything, and he didn't want to talk. If he went to his girlfriend's, she'd want to screw. Funny when you get to where a cigarette and a night's sleep are worth more than a woman's ass.

He heard a car and turned. A pickup with a couple of boys in front and two more in back was coming out the drive toward him. He flagged them down.

"Fagatogo, eh?" he said. He didn't know this particular set of boys, but the island's population of thirty-five thousand people stayed stable mainly by rotating excess males through the Army and the Samoan communities of Hawaii and California. The kid in the passenger seat got out and climbed into the back, leaving the preferred seat for him. Half the territory owed him their lives one way or another and would have gone out of their way to take him where he wanted to go. The other half would have just as soon hacked him up with a bush knife and left him in the plantations. He didn't worry about them much. The brothers of all those girls deserved whatever hide they got out of him, and the rest were family fights he couldn't do anything about anyway.

The truck bumped on down to the shore road. Even over the engine, Welly could hear the birds raising the dawn with their clatter. Heavy-bodied fruit bats flapped and jostled for resting places in the big trees. He stuck another cigarette in his mouth, fighting the panic that dawn always brought him. He was just another fruit bat, he thought, in from a night's hustle.

Left from the hospital drive, the coast road wound around a bare and rocky headland for a mile or two, then into Utulei. Dawn light swelled up out of the sea on the edge of the world.

They passed no other cars. Work started early on the family's ground oven or in the plantations on the mountainsides behind the seaside villages. All the shit the chief and the old women could heap on you. In this pre-dawn hour, the boys would be piling up their sleeping mats, re-tying their *lavalavas*, stumbling out of their communal *fales* to splash water on their faces and bare shoulders. And somewhere down the river of time when power doesn't pulse in the hand the way it would if you were young, maybe there'd be a title. Or maybe just a glorious fight like last night. Hard to blame them. Welly spent most of his time patching them up after their fights, but he wasn't invested in it any more. He was trying not to think about Sapatu.

The village of Utulei was quiet. Too early for bureaucrats. The truck bounced along between the rows of ramshackle tin-roofed apartments under the beach-side palms. The apartments had been built first for the Navy and then for the technicians who came to replace them. The *palagis* still fought each other over the ones along the beach. Gloriana had sold her soul for one for her fancy *palagi* stud from L.A. Silly old cow thought she was one up on Hutchinson, having the house on the beach. And now her fancy *palagi* stud was dead. Just went to show something. Welly wondered idly what Gloriana would do now. Go back to Western Samoa, maybe? Somewhere back in the more distant genealogy, their families were connected, before the imperial *palagi* division of the islands at the end of the nineteenth century. Maybe that was why he never thought of her as *palagi*. Just another mixed up Samoan like himself, trying to hustle two cultures at once.

On his third cigarette and feeling better, he wondered if he should have said something to Han about him and Begley in the hotel bar. Well, somebody would, soon enough. Stuff like that got around fast. Han was going to be slow off the mark on this one, poor sod. Good he wasn't hurt too bad. Good he got Ann to put him together again. Welly considered Ann's bony little body. He wouldn't have minded giving her a go. But she'd never let him close enough to try.

Beyond the entrance to the hotel, they passed through the tunnel of huge mangos and banyans below the governor's house. Then down into Fagatogo. Just before the village green, he nodded to the driver and hopped out into the road. The truck roared away in a good imitation of people with somewhere to go.

The slanting light of the sun, still below the horizon, fired the water-laden air pinky-silver. He walked around behind the rickety clapboard shell of the police station. Maybe there were a few more cars, a few more people, a few more signs of activity than usual around the station. But the police's troubles didn't concern him. He didn't think of his cousin, the late Talking Chief Sapatu, as a dead policeman, just as a surgical mishap. And a family problem.

Behind the police station, he hiked up a steep dirt track under tall trees. He could smell wood smoke, hear a radio. A child disappeared into the broad green leaves of a backyard taro patch with a flash of little round bare buttocks, followed by the sharp voice of an old woman and the flutter of a brightly printed lavalava. He stopped for a drink of water from a communal spigot beside the track, looking down into a bare yard among wooden shacks stained with red from their rusting sheet metal roofs and the green and grey molds of perpetual heat and humidity. Chickens flapped and scratched across the yard; a pig squealed. You could almost hear things rotting.

The track led over a fold of volcanic rock then dropped down into the main part of the village. Even in the half-light of dawn, Fagatogo was its own uniquely ugly self, the sweaty chest of American Samoa. Welly slipped in behind one of the bars and tapped lightly on the bare plank shutter of the middle crib. A sleepy voice asked him what the fuck he wanted and he ought to go home to work like a decent man. He grinned at the fractional opening between the shutter and the wall.

"Eh, Susi, a bed and a drink. No behavior."

From behind the crack came a harsh whisper. "Go away."

"Susi...."

"*Go away!*"

Confused, he stood out from the wall. "Well, fuck," he said. But the whisper came again.

"Be careful."

"Careful of what?" he said. He walked slowly down the narrow alley. He wasn't much worried since he couldn't see who'd be avenging the honor of a middle-aged whore from Apia.

Thumps and curses erupted from the end crib. The thin door flapped open, and a young Samoan with a shoulder-length mane of curly hair and three gold necklaces propped himself in the doorway, shucking his dick behind the zipper of grubby white jeans. In the shadows behind him, the girl was mopping at her face with her lavalava and not caring much what went uncovered as a result.

"Eh," Welly said cheerfully, "Life's hard enough without that shit. You need money to pay her, I'll give you a couple of bucks."

He stepped closer. He'd been drunk in every city on the Pacific rim and he made his living by knowing how people's bodies work. He kicked the kid hard in the balls and was gratified to see a pistol drop from a half-hidden hand onto the gravel. The kid collapsed as a Samoan boy will when confronted by recognizable authority. While the boy writhed on the ground, Welly flipped a wad of bills to the girl, put the pistol in his pocket and walked out into the cobblestone street.

Like most surgeons, Welly was an adrenalin junkie: for a few minutes, the blood beating in his ears felt good. But if he'd been dry before, now he was a desert. Time for desperate measures.

He hiked up a short rise to a neat little house with deep verandas on three sides. A man sat alone on a low rattan chair on the porch on this side, his legs crooked out comfortably, drinking coffee and watching the sun rise over the bay. He wore only an old orange *lavalava* tied like a boy's.

"Eh," Welly called up to him, "Get beer?"

"I don't drink with dirty Tongans," the man said. "But you'd better get up here before the family starts throwing rocks at you."

Welly clambered straight up the stone foundation and onto the veranda. A girl appeared in the doorway behind them, beautiful and demure and not recognizably one of the immediate family. Before Welly could say anything, she disappeared back into the house.

Welly settled into the chair across from the other man. Sa'ili Tua'ua was his favorite among half a thousand cousins of one sort or another. Like most anyone else on the island who was employed, he worked for the government, though his was a cabinet-level post, kind of a minister of culture. He also sat on chairs when no one was looking, drank cold beer and had a carefully disguised sense of privacy that meant you could talk to him straight, like a mate.

From childhood, Saili had been the family's darling boy, the village Mr. Right, recognition that he was the nexus of several important village family lines as well as being tall, handsome, intelligent and not obviously a pervert. *Only a handsome man can do a thing well* went the proverb. What Welly also knew about him, and for years had thought the family didn't, was that Sa'ili had considered becoming a priest. Not one of the usual comfortable old hustlers, out to maximize their share of the village take, but one of those *least of these, my children* blokes. *The water in the bathing pool is sufficient only for the family* didn't really cut it with Sa'ili. Now, however, Welly guessed the family also knew this about Sa'ili and that was why, when the final decisions were made, a major title had never been settled on him. With their extended family, you could never tell, but it was a reasonable explanation for what was otherwise just stupid.

"Not my fault the bastard had a lousy heart," Welly said. "He wasn't my choice for Sapatu." The girl was back with a glass and a liter of Vailima, the beer from Western Samoa, misted with condensate. Welly grinned at her but she set the things on the table and slipped away, eyes averted. "Pretty girl. Western Samoa girl, eh?"

"Yes. A cousin of my sister-in-law. From Savai'i. And you leave her alone. About Sapatu: it's what the family's saying already."

"Bastard's barely cool. I don't want the Sapatu title. Never have. You know that."

"Yes. But they don't. How could they? Your claim was better in a lot of ways, at least through the women's side."

Welly shrugged, finishing the first bottle. "Got another? What the fuck would I do as a senior talking chief? I don't even know who my father was, much less all the family history and genealogy to the nth generation...." At Sa'ili's signal, the girl had brought Welly a second liter of Vailima, and he took a gulp. "...Including who paid who the most to re-invent whose bloodlines to justify their claim to what title. Not to mention having everybody pissed off at you all the time because you didn't redistribute all the ceremonial gifts right. What a pain. What about you? Your claim is a hell of a lot better than mine. Why don't you go for it? Lots of old ladies would put in a good word for you."

"I'd never make an orator. High chief's more my style, wouldn't you say? Sit back, gain weight, be the visible repository of family power and dignity."

Welly's grin, like the second liter of Vailima, lasted a little longer. "Your claim to the Nofonofo title's not that good. That's the trouble. Nobody's is. Old Nofonofo could have saved us a lot a trouble by willing it to somebody, but he thought diabetes was something the *palagi* doctors made up."

Sa'ili lifted his cup. *"I live in service.* If you didn't kill Sapatu for his title, who did?"

"Kill him? Bastard stepped in front of a bullet in the middle of a riot. Broke a bunch of heads before he went down too, from what I hear."

"It wouldn't be the first time someone was murdered over a title."

"Yeah, but you know how that is. The family finally makes up its mind and a sore loser shows up on the new chief's doorstep and blows him away in front of God and everybody. If you're lucky, it happens before the installation so you don't have to cough up all that bread for both the installation *and* all the payoff to smooth things over. Not to mention the funeral itself."

"You have a peculiar view of your native culture, my son. I need to talk to you from time to time to remind myself what I'm in the business of preserving."

"As Auntie Leoloa Palapala always said, it comes from being a Tongan bastard."

"Well, she should know. But you're right. It's not the way we usually do things. There's no need for ambush; we're so good at explaining away what's right in front of us. Speaking of which, I'd feel better if you'd explain away the gun you so obviously have in your pocket."

Welly grinned. "Oh, that." He had actually forgotten it. He pulled it out and set it on the glass top of the table. "I kicked someone in the balls and it fell out of his hand."

Sa'ili's broad gentle face remolded itself into a mix of relief and polite ignorance. Looking at Welly and not at the gun, he said, "I've been thinking about Auntie Leoloa a lot lately. Do you know what became of her boys?"

"Thought they all bought the farm for the *palagi* in Viet Nam." More Samoan boys had fought in Viet Nam proportional to the population than any other state or territorial unit in the U.S.

"Not all three of them as it turns out. Tanifa's turned up again. He's been over in the village for a week, holed up with Fa'atofi Jake and spreading a lot of money around."

"Take a hell of a lot of money for *him* to buy respectability...." Welly yawned. And yawned. For a moment he thought his jaw was stuck. "...But maybe he can make it up in service." The family said the same thing about Welly. So he had the right to say it.

Sa'ili looked at him critically. "Look. Why don't you go to bed. I need to talk to you about this stuff, but I need you sober and awake. You can stay here if you want, but leave this girl alone. She's a good child and she's not accustomed to the fast lane of Eastern Samoa."

Sa'ili was ushering him into the back in the direction of a thick pallet mattress under a mosquito net. After thirty hours on his feet and two liters of beer, Welly was suddenly semi-conscious. He crawled under the musty cloud of netting. Sa'ili sat down on the floor beside the pallet. "You need to go see the Tapuafanua sometime."

Welly muttered, "Old crook."

"No. You of all people shouldn't say that. He has become very traditional in his old age, but that's to be expected. It's very do-American-Samoa to call all the old chiefs crooks, but that's just part of being young and believing, because the *palagis* say so, that your opinion is worth shit. And most of the time, it's not. But something's going on over there. I'm too public now. I can't get close to the old man any more. You've got to go. And when you do, keep an eye on Fa'atofi Jake."

"Jake's nothing," Welly mumbled. He wished Sa'ili would go away.

"He's a second-rate title, but he's up to something."

"Bullshit," Welly said thickly. "Besides. He's dead."

"Who's dead? Jake?" Sa'ili's voice poked at him through the net.

"Nah. Tapu...fanu...last night...passed away.

"The *Tapuafanua?* How do you know? Why didn't somebody tell me?"

"Somebody just did," Welly said. And was asleep.

5

In the dream, Han was a child again. He stood on a dirt track leading into a village between two brown hills in the last light of day. The roofs of the village were brown thatch. He was cold and hungry and frightened. He was crying for his sister. She had gone to the nearest house to beg for food, leaving him hidden in a ditch. She was six years older than he was, only just big enough to carry him on her back, as all Korean children were carried, wrapped in a shawl, his legs tucked under her arms. They shouldn't have been alone, but they had gotten lost from the others in the flight south.

His sister screamed. She screamed again and he was standing there in the road, wailing in terror. And then she ran from the house, silhouetted by firelight from the door. She was no longer screaming but ghostly, her pale skin fluid through her torn clothes. She scooped him into to her arms and ran into the darkness. He could hear the men's coarse laughter: their shortest comrade had found a morsel fit for his size. He heard their voices even now in his sleep, their accents local, just ordinary men, *us* not *them*, but in this time of war, beyond family or village, lord or the rule of law.

"Lieutenant Han?"

Han opened his eyes. The *yo-u*, the fox sprite, the feminine Trickster that haunts the night thoughts of men, sat at the foot of the bed, regarding him with quizzical golden eyes.

"Lieutenant Han?"

The doctor, Ann Maglynn, with her spiky dark red hair and yellow-brown eyes, stood beside his bed, leaning on the bed rails as if she needed the support. "How are you doing?"

He was soaking wet, maybe from the nightmare, maybe from the plastic mattress under the bed sheet. He said *fine* and *When can I leave?* with a voice from some other reality than where he had spent the last hours.

"Show me you can feed yourself, and I'll consider it."

He lifted his hands, now mittened in gauze, in protest. The doctor's face relaxed into a smile. And suddenly, in a rush of winds between worlds, Han was *here*.

"I'd like a bath," he said. A cart loaded with little brown packets stood beside the bed. The doctor selected a pair of blunt-nosed scissors big enough to remove his fingers and began cutting the dressings off of his hands.

"You actually had a bath last night. Though you didn't participate very actively in it."

Not unkind, but wry and uninvolved, she was the quintessential physician. She had been much the same the night he had brought his wife to the hospital after the overdose. So, what did it take to involve her? The thought got him through the liberation of his hands with nothing more visible than a cold sweat.

He was sitting now at the edge of the bed. "I need to get out of here," he said again. She was packing up the cart, crumpling wrappings into a bag.

"I suppose you do," she said. "The classic face-off: I attend the living and you attend the dead. In this case, I can see that the dead have some precedence."

"Did you know Dr. Begley very well?"

She looked up from her little chores with the cart. "Not... personally."

"Any ideas who might want to kill him?"

"No. But whoever killed Ray Begley either didn't know him very well or needed him dead in a big hurry."

"What do you mean?"

"If Ray had stopped drinking, he might have lasted, if he were really lucky, maybe another couple of years. The way he was going, I wouldn't have given him six months."

"Liver?"

"That would have been enough. But he also had chronic pancreatitis–like digesting your body from the inside out. I don't think he'd have survived another acute attack."

"Did...a lot of people know this?"

"How sick he was? Well, his skin color wasn't a whole lot better when he was alive than what you saw last night. If you knew what to look for...." She was drawing the narrow shoulders and bloated gut with her hands in the air. "You could see his liver disease was pretty far advanced. Neil Hutchinson knew, certainly."

"Why didn't you say anything about this last night?"

She looked at him blankly. "Didn't we?" Han wondered if she had been to bed at all. "Maybe...because it...wasn't what killed him."

"Did his wife know?"

She snorted softly. "Well, it's always hard to know what Gloriana takes in. I've lived so many places. You have to learn to read people culturally, at least a little bit...." She shook her head. Han decided that she wasn't thinking about Gloriana but about him. Korean cop with Japanese wife. Who left him. Good cultural read. Gold standard. "...But I have no idea what makes Gloriana tick...." Her voice trailed off. "I can't even remember what I was going to say. Sorry."

"What about ambition? That's pretty cross-cultural."

She didn't answer for a long time. He wondered if she'd gone to sleep standing up.

Finally she said, "I would say that Gloriana is attracted to power. She practically has *I have connections to the governor* stenciled on the side of her car. But..." Her eyebrows went up and down. "She's not very bright. At least the way you have to be to survive that close to the political fire....maybe I mean astute....I don't know. But did she know Ray was sick? Yes." She rolled the cart into the doorway then came back to stand at the end of Han's bed. "Gloriana spilled it to me one day in great..."

Her hands fluttered and became long brown fingers, flipping wings of blond hair behind her ears. Han was seeing the Schutz-Begley rushing in to see the only doc on the island she had decided was worthy of her confidence.

"...great consternation. Well, justified enough. I'm no internist–I assume she came to me to score one off Neil–but this didn't need the Mayo Clinic. I told her to get him the hell to Honolulu for a work-up. My excuse..." She shrugged. "Which was legitimate enough, was that I was afraid he might have a cancer sitting in there as well. Or if he was on a short slide into fulminant pancreatitis....that's the most horrible thing I've ever been involved in caring for. Trying to care for that here would be...." She shook her head. "Unimaginable."

She smiled lopsidedly. "So then she decided she wanted the Nightingale called out, the military long-distance med-evac team, to take him to Los Angeles. Honolulu wasn't good enough. Had to be LAC/USC Med Cen, where he had trained. I tried to explain to her that there was no way in hell the Air Force was going to fly half way around the world for an aging *palagi* drunk with a belly ache–not in those terms of course but....much less take him to L.A. just because he wanted to go. She ignored me of course: I don't sit on the Off-Island Care Committee because technically I'm not a hospital doc, I'm public health. So she trotted off to the OIC committee, and they–of course–turned her down. So she called the Air Force herself. The legislature had a fit."

"Did they come? The Air Force?"

She grinned. "They weren't even polite. In fact, that's how the legislature got involved. Some very high level complaining."

"I heard they made Hutchinson Director because Gloriana was married to Begley. That true?"

She hesitated. Some kind of loyalty to the Schutz-Begley? Or just a disinclination to set some one up to be accused of murder? Or just his imagination, always a problem.

"That's....the excuse used in some circles, anyway. For people who couldn't base a decision on something else."

"There was some Army colonel involved, someone from Honolulu, who brokered the deal to get Hutchinson here. Where does he fit in?" Han knew the question wasn't strictly relevant. But he wasn't in a courtroom yet. And he was curious.

She was silent for a long time. Finally she said quietly, "Colonel Munro likes to think that he makes things happen. Which he certainly does. But rarely what he intended and essentially never what he promised. He's due down here this weekend–God, in the middle of everything else..." She sighed deeply. "...As some kind of mediator."

"Do *you* think Begley was the main reason his wife didn't get the Director job?"

The doctor's eyebrows went up and down, but she shook her head. "No. Not really. Though Ray had definitely pissed off a lot of people. What do you know about him?"

"Not a lot. Some kind of surgeon...?"

She shook her head. "Anesthesiologist. Puts people to sleep for surgery. The story I get from Welly Tuiasosopo is they turned up here, Gloriana and Begley, shortly after the present governor was elected on a 'Samoa for Samoans' ticket. Neil likes to say that her medical credentials would make better windows than doors, but she is certainly at least part Samoan. And around here, being from Western Samoa always has a little extra cachet. Like the culture is a little purer there. Like some Americans are about Brits. But Ray was trained in one of America's best trauma centers, Board certified. He must have looked like a god-send. Then stuff began to happen."

"Like?"

"Booze, certainly," she said. Carefully, Han would have said. "Big-time booze. And you know when Welly grouses about drunks in the OR we're not talking....over-delicate sensibilities. But there were a couple of patient-care incidents, infections–maybe just bad luck here where infections are almost unavoidable. But then the previously healthy young wife of a high chief died in childbirth–emergency C-section–where he was passing the gas. And clearly an anesthetic death, I'm told, nothing to do with the procedure itself. Baby died as well. There were threats to Ray's life. At least the Pago *Times* quoted him saying there were."

"Who made the threats?"

"Oh, family, one presumes. It would be almost a duty of the senior talking chief of the village of the high chief who's wife died. But was the threat actually made? Or does everybody just know he should have made it and therefore assumes that he did. Was it something personal? And how does that work in a society where the official *is* the personal? Who knows?"

"Do you know what village it was?"

"Actually, I do. Papasaa; Welly Tuiasosopo's village. Also the same village that your assistant police chief–late assistant police chief–Sapatu, came from. In fact, Sapatu is the orator title associated with the family that also holds the high chief title–Nofonofo–of the girl who died."

"You're saying *Sapatu* is the one who threatened Begley?"

"Well, might have. In the great Samoan logic of things. But not the policeman. The Sapatu before him. Your colleague only had the title for about...." She shrugged again and shook her head. "...Three months, maybe."

A Samoan nurse filled the doorway. Ann glanced at her, then back at Han. "Welly brought you some clothes. They're in the night stand. Your wallet and watch are in the drawer. There wasn't time last night for anything more secure." She lectured him on the care and follow-up of his wounds and then disappeared across the hall, her cart rattling ahead of her.

He fumbled in the night-stand for the clothes. Welly had left him a pale yellow shirt with a packet of matches from the hotel in the breast pocket, an old floral print *lavalava* in purple, orange, and olive green, and a pair of down-at-heel hot pink flip-flops. Tying the *lavalava* left him sweating again and wondering if this was one of Welly's little jokes.

Beyond the head-high partition of his cubicle, he began to be aware of a commotion. The sounds of leather-shod feet and a mumble of multilingual conversation were proceeding down the passageway. This materialized in Han's doorway as the Korean tuna fleet representative and the sub-consul, with Hutchinson looming behind.

Both Koreans were short, even by Korean standards: peasant stock. But they had evolved into opposite types. The fleet rep was a lower-level bureaucrat, pale and pudgy, as if a good pummeling could make him into any political shape. The sub-consul had retained his native belligerence, squat and tough.

The sub-consul would view himself as the senior rank. He spoke first.

"Good morning, Lieutenant Han. How are you feeling?" His choice of Korean verb forms addressed Han as an equal. Han was suddenly very alert. The cultural logic of this situation, Korean and Samoan alike, was that Han should be blamed for the riot. For the sub-consul and the fleet rep, this would be complicated by their recognition of Han's aristocratic family name but probably not enough to exonerate him so thoroughly. Was he supposed to get them out of some mess by acknowledging his guilty status? Han nodded but did not reply. The sub-consul could stew in his own inflections.

The sub-consul looked at the fleet representative and then back to Han. He scowled and said, "The fleet representative has something he wishes to discuss with you."

Normally, the fleet rep was due some respect, one scrambling toady to another, but the sub-consul's tones and inflections both were distancing. The fleet rep's face blanched, and Han was seeing the instinctive terror of the peasant for the military aristocrats who had run Korea for a thousand years. Han thought, if he calls me *father*, I'm going to shout at him.

Fortunately for both of them, the fleet rep pulled himself back to republican times. He swallowed. "Sir. Lieutenant Han. The Sub-Consul feels...I must tell you...you might not know, sir....All of our fleet captains have guns."

Delivered of his message, he was suddenly limp and sweaty. He mopped himself with a vast handkerchief pulled, like a circus clown's, from the inner pocket of his suit coat, equally absurd in this climate.

"Guns?" Han said. Even as he spoke, he could see the dungeon-like interiors of the metal ships and the whip-thin, sweating fishermen. So the captains had guns, did they? Probably not for shooting sharks.

"Yes. Yes," the fleet rep said again, suddenly voluble, the words tumbling over themselves as if in his haste to be quit of them and their association with him. "It's standard procedure. Each captain leaving Inchon for the first time is issued a pistol. We don't give them ammunition...." Han's face twisted incredulously. The little man's mouth trembled. "...But of course, they get it."

And I keep thinking Americans are crazy. Han said calmly, "What make of pistol?"

The fleet rep swallowed, clearly relieved that his neck still attached his head to his shoulders. He mopped himself again. "Well, it varies, has varied over the years. It depends on when a given captain takes over his first command...."

"Can you get me a list of the make and serial number of the pistol issued to each of the captains in port as of last night?"

"Oh, certainly, Lieutenant. It will take me most of the day, but I can talk to them all...."

"No," Han said. "I'll talk to the captains. You don't have that information?"

"Oh, no, Lieutenant. I would never have any need for that kind of information. The central office in Inchon perhaps, but..."

"But what?"

"Well." The little man's forehead beaded again. "They do get lost from time to time. The pistols, I mean. Well., I've heard at least. And guns are easy to get...in other places...you know."

"Like the ammunition."

"Yes. Exactly."

Han took a deep breath. Breathing hurt more than it had last night but at least he could still do it. "I need to talk to every captain who was in port last night. Also, a list of the ships, the captains, and the date each captain took command. Can you get me that from the information you have now?"

"Yes, of course, Lieutenant. Shall I bring it here? To the hospital?"

"No. I'll come to your office. Please contact your central office for the list of pistols."

"Yes, of course, Lieutenant. It will take a while of course."

"Not if you use the telephone. Something else. No ship is to leave port until I have interviewed its captain." The fleet rep's mouth worked again. But he recognized the issue: whatever cultural *wergild* you priced it in, a dead police official far outweighed a day's lost time in the fishing grounds. "But do *not* mention the guns. At all. Please."

"Yes, of course. We wish to offer every cooperation to the police. Of course."

The fleet rep looked at the sub-consul, who took over again. "And now, Lieutenant, we wish to visit the other wounded men. His honor, the consul in Honolulu, is awaiting my report. He expects to be here himself on the next flight from Honolulu."

Han snorted softly. Han's Oxford uncle, his guardian after his parents' death, had been the Korean consul himself in Honolulu once upon a time. Another life. With a short bow, the sub consul turned and strode off. The fleet rep bowed more deeply and trotted after him.

Hutchinson stood in the doorway. He smiled. "You walking out or is Ann springing you?"

"A compromise. She tells me Begley was not just a drunk but, like, terminally ill. That true?"

Hutchinson propped his rawboned figure against the doorframe as if, for anything more than a few words, he needed extra support. "I wouldn't say that. I mean, he had some serious chronic illnesses but...."

Han hadn't had a lot more sleep than Hutchinson. He tried to get his mind to clear. *Whoever killed Ray Begley either didn't know him very well or needed him dead in a big hurry.* "So," Han said slowly, "Patience wouldn't be enough if you wanted to get rid of him?"

Hutchinson shrugged. "Well, he was doing a pretty good job of drinking himself to death."

"Six months? Two years?"

"Maybe. If everything that could go wrong did. Or maybe longer. If he quit drinking." They weren't getting anywhere. But Han couldn't tell whether that was something purposive or just mutual exhaustion. "She also said he'd pissed off important people in a particular village, Assistant Chief Sapatu's village."

"I'm not sure how much you can make of that. Ray was a bad doc, but you'd have to be fairly sophisticated to know just how bad he'd fucked up."

"She said some patients died who shouldn't have, young people."

"One. Two, counting the baby. But a lotta people die here. This is the third world, in case you haven't noticed. In the six months I've been here, I've had two men in their twenties die of brain abscesses left over from childhood ear infections and there wasn't a damned thing I or Welly Tuiasosopo could do about it, though God knows we tried."

"What about threats made against Begley. About the young woman who died."

Hutchinson shrugged again. "Yeah, well *Ray* said there were threats. That was Ray's take on the world. He was always sure someone was out to get him. Maybe he lived in L.A. too long." He hauled himself upright away from the doorframe and motioned Han out into the hallway. "I'm actually here 'cause I think you've got a new problem."

He guided Han across the hospital through a series of quiet breezeways. "Of five dead fishermen we have now in the freezer, one was shot. Body was apparently among other fishermen brought in earlier who were unconscious but alive and taken inside for care. This guy was just laid out on the grass beside the parking lot."

Han was lost in the maze of screened passages, but the morgue was familiar enough. The only sign of official concern was Sarge in his neat black *lavalava* sitting cross-legged on a mat outside the door. He was leaning back against the wall, but he was awake.

The bodies were packed in the big cooler like sides of beef. Fortunately, the fisherman who had been shot and Sapatu were the top two.

Hutchinson grunted as he and Han and Sarge shifted bodies. "Village isn't going to like a dirty fisherman lying on top of Sapatu."

Not to mention Sapatu's ghost, Han thought, since the dead fisherman is the Tuna Pimp.

The dead Korean lay like a very small side of beef, or maybe a big fish, in his body bag, with two small purple bull's-eyes on his mid-left chest, maybe two and five inches down from the nipple. Three tiny black spots that might have been powder burns clustered near one of the wounds but the body had no shirt on. Hutchinson spoke first.

"Looks a lot like Sapatu, doesn't it?" Han nodded and Hutchinson went on. "But I'm guessing the post'll show Sapatu was a little luckier, at least initially." Han looked at him. "Welly's been in Sapatu's chest. So we know that neither his heart nor any of the great vessels were hit. He had a hole in his stomach and part of a lung torn up. They could probably have handled that if his coronaries hadn't failed him. This guy...."

Sarge lifted his chin slightly, questioning. Han nodded. The old non-com began pulling up the long zipper on the body bag.. For a moment, the sound dominated the room.

Hutchinson went on: "...Wasn't so lucky. Either the internal damage was similar and he just bled quietly to death while nobody noticed him. Or his heart or great vessels were hit."

"Neither of them have exit wounds. Him or Sapatu." Han said.

Hutchinson nodded. "So, almost certainly a pistol; maybe relatively small caliber, or it hung up on the spine. There are so few guns here...." Han kept his knowledge of the availability of guns to himself. "Somebody's gotta know about it."

"Did Welly retrieve any of the slugs from Sapatu?"

Hutchinson nodded and reached into the breast pocket of his aloha shirt, pulled out a pharmacy vial and handed it to Han. Han could hear the slug rattle inside: child proof. Also adult-proof if your hands feel like buffalo wings. Hutchinson took the vial back and opened it for him.

"As you say," Han said, looking at the splayed lump of lead. "Need a lab to be sure. But I've seen a lot of these in my time: nine millimeter soft nose. Standard police issue, among other things."

"Military too," Hutchinson said. "At least recently. Among the NATO countries at least."

Han nodded. "At least the nine millimeter part. Either of you see who brought him in?"

Hutchinson shook his head. "You saw what it was like here last night. I didn't know he was here until they brought him into the morgue. We were still there packing in bodies."

Sarge said, "Village boys. Everybody bringin bodies in."

"Do you know what village?"

"No, sir. New truck. Nissan. Maybe red, maybe blue. Colors no good at night...."

"You need a police guard on the morgue," Han said. For himself, he trusted Sarge's understanding of guarding better than most of his TPD colleagues' but the law said otherwise. "I'll send someone out."

As they walked back through the hospital breezeways, Han said to Hutchinson, "Just for the record, I need to check the inside of your car. What about the other docs? Most of them live here?"

"More or less," Hutchinson said. "The surgeon, the one I think Welly swiped that *lavalava* from, lives down on the beach in Utulei. Next door to Gloriana and Ray, as a matter of fact."

"Car?"

"Another jeep. Like mine. He's only been here two weeks, though. Can't imagine he'd get that pissed at Ray in that amount of time. That's the problem with most of 'em. Except for me and Ann and Welly, nobody'd known Ray that long."

They passed through the reception area and out a side door by Hutchinson's office. Hutchinson nodded to a taxi pulled up at the curb.

"Waiting for the fleet rep and the sub consul. I expect I can shame them into giving you a lift back to the police station."

Rain started, a sudden spilling of water from the sky, like an over-full pitcher. They stood together under the eaves, waiting for the downpour to ease.

Hutchinson said, "You guys armed?"

"Like the U.K.: only under special circumstances. Sapatu and the guys with him had shotguns last night. But I don't think they were used."

"I didn't see any buckshot wounds. That bother you, not having a gun?" Hutchinson was the amused liberal, tweaking a cop.

The corner of Han's mouth twitched. "No." He never minded a high-class pissing match. On the other hand, he did like to win. Which is possibly why he'd never made it past Sergeant in the SFPD. "Should it?'

"No. I mean, that's a rational response. In a place where there aren't any guns, I mean."

Han nodded and they looked out at the rain some more. But whatever was bugging Hutchinson, he couldn't leave it alone.

"So: how'd you end up a cop in San Francisco?"

Han couldn't say *My family's been in San Francisco since there was a San Francisco, so if I want to be a cop, I'll be a cop.* So he said, "Well, if there's one thing being a soldier taught me, it's I'd rather fight my wars one-on-one. At least I know what I'm fighting for."

Hutchinson grinned. *"The Tiger* or *The White Horse?"* He was showing off: not that many Americans knew Korea had troops with the U.S. in Viet Nam.

"Neither. Just one more draft-eligible American."

"Military police?"

"In the end."

Han almost said, so: how did *you* end up with a Japanese wife? But he let it go. The rain was easing. Without speaking, they stepped out of the shelter of the building. They crossed the road into a loose quadrangle of long, low, pavilions with mossy wood shingle roofs and glass-louvered sides.

"The old nursing school," Hutchinson said. "But they've been fitted into reasonable flats. For reasonable people." Across the quadrangle, Han thought he saw Ann Maglynn going into one of the end flats. "Housing is the only bribe I have," Hutchinson went on. "I've got six single-family houses at my disposal as perks for being here, and this clutch of one-bedroom duplexes. The pay is lousy and the adventure is mostly a pain in the butt, so all I can offer by way of amenity is housing. And only two of the houses are on the beach. A hard bargain for paradise. So the houses tend to go to the ones who bitch the loudest."

He led Han around behind one of the pavilions to where yet another hardtop Suzuki jeep was pulled tight up under the eaves in line with the building. "If you hold your breath," he said, "At least the person in the passenger seat can get out dry."

Han picked quickly through the vehicle. It wasn't very big and wasn't very clean. Han dutifully brushed up samples of the crud in the foot wells and tucked them into little packets folded out of clean paper from Hutchinson's pocket notebook. But nobody had been frantically trying to clean blood and bits of human flesh out of the vehicle any time recently.

"Thanks," Han said.

"Oh," said Hutchinson, "It was nothing."

They walked together around the end of the building.

And were almost run down by a baby-doll pretty *palagi* female with extravagantly sculptured boobs. Without being particularly attracted to the mammo-centric view of womanhood, he recognized her as a high-status item in European-American male culture and, given his recent involuntary celibacy, got the jolt she presumably intended.

"Neil!" she said sharply, not even glancing at Han. "Somebody told me one of the American doctors has been murdered! Why weren't we told? We're the most vulnerable family here, down on that beach. We should have had protection immediately. Instead of which, I have to hear it as gossip from my house girl. This is outrageous. The governor is going to hear about this. And our congressman."

Visibly, Hutchinson took a deep breath. "Ray Begley died last night. He may have been hit by a car. He may have been caught in the riot. Nobody knows for sure, but the police...."

"*Riot?* What riot?"

"There was a...disturbance. Between the Korean tuna fishermen and some Samoan kids in Pago village."

The woman barked a short, disgusted laugh. "I don't give a shit about some village squabble. I want to know what you're going to do to guarantee our safety until we can get the hell out of here. Which we are going to do tomorrow. I don't care what the fuck kind of contract my husband signed. We are out of here. I mean, I've had it. Up to here." She put a pretty little hand with a great big diamond on it up to her throat.

And then suddenly, as if the synapses were firing a little late, she said, "*Ray?* It was *Ray?* Oh, my God. Poor Gloriana."

Han said, "Did you know them?"

The woman looked at Han. "Who are you?"

Hutchinson said, "This is Detective Lieutenant Han of the Territorial Police."

The woman took in the yellow shirt and the purple *lavalava* and the hot pink flip-flops. "Show me your ID."

Han fished the laminated card out of his breast pocket with the two fingers that worked. The woman read it carefully, turned it over, read the other side, handed it back.

"They're my neighbors," she said. Her face said, *What's it to you?*

Like Leon Fischer, the attorney general, Han thought. They would be in one of the rickety duplexes along the beach in Utulei known as Penicillin Row, for the Navy physicians who had been the first residents in the 1940's.

"When was the last time you saw Dr. Begley?"

"*Me?*"

"Yes, ma'am."

The woman glanced at Hutchinson but apparently decided she had burnt that bridge. She looked back at Han. He could, his wife often told him, project a certain immobility, like a stone Bodhisattva. Not to be confused, she always added, with the Bodhisattva of Infinite Compassion.

"Were you home yesterday evening?"

"Until about seven. Gloriana invited us to a reception at the governor's..."

Hutchinson nodded fractionally.

"...We got home about ten. Later there were all the sirens and stuff. Was that about Ray?"

"No," Han said. "Before you went out, did you hear or see anything unusual on the beach or around the houses?"

She made a face like a teenager showing a last bit of resistance to authority. "What's unusual around here? Nobody seemed to be drinking on the beach, which was a relief. Nothing in particular going on at the club that I recall...."

The club would be the end building in the row with its collection of tatty Hobie Cats in front. Han was pretty sure the Begleys were the next building down.

"The Osgoods were playing one of their operas. They're such nice people, you hate to complain, but...." The woman's voice had grown more southern. Maybe that was her marker of neighborhood, community. Han knew the name Osgood. Osgood was head of the college. He thought the Osgoods were in the third building down, but he didn't know which side.

Han said, "Did you notice anything particular going on at the Begley's? You must be able to hear each other sneeze." The woman's pupils narrowed a little, focusing on his face. He thought she was surprised at the trace of humor. But she surprised him.

"Gloriana and Ray have both sides of their building." Han could hear the envy in the woman's voice. "We share with the Osgoods. But we are on the Begleys' side...." She was going to be delicate about overheard conversations. "Maria Theresa and Gloriana did get into it a bit. Maria Theresa is

Gloriana's daughter. She's sixteen. She was going to baby-sit for us. But there was some sort of to-do about homework. At least that's what we were told. Their house-girl actually took care of our little boy for us." Now she was the good citizen, helping with police inquiries.

"You heard both their voices, the girl and Dr. Schutz-Begley?"

"Yes." The woman's voice made a question.

"Was Dr. Begley part of the argument?"

"Ray? No. I mean, he wasn't there. He got home late. I mean, he didn't get home in time. We all, Gloriana and my husband and I, went up to the reception together."

"You and your husband and Gloriana–Doctor Schutz-Begley? Mr. Fischer wasn't with you?"

"No. I mean. He was there at the reception, but he didn't come up with us. He got there a few minutes later."

It's like a scent, Han thought, a thrill, a suddenly upping of the ante. He let his voice go routine, boring. "So Dr. Schutz-Begley picked you up about...seven?"

"No, actually, we drove Gloriana up in our car. Hers would have been better. It's that lovely old black Mercedes. But Leon drove her car up later when he came."

"Did you go to her house to get her or did she come to yours?"

"Well, my husband went over...." Suddenly, her face snapped shut like a very expensive purse. She knew she had said too much, probably about Fischer.

Han couldn't get anything more out of her. She denied having seen Begley at least since the day before, couldn't imagine who could have anything against him, thought he and Gloriana were such a charming, loving couple. Once or twice, Han thought she was about to say something about the clash with Hutchinson, but each time, she bounced a glance off Hutchinson's right shoulder and then repeated one or another of her prior platitudes.

"Thank you," he said at last. Dismissed, and knowing it, she shot one last frustrated look at Hutchinson and stomped away back to the parking area.

He looked at Hutchinson. "Should I search her car?"

"Jesus," the other man said. "If they killed him, maybe we could just give 'em a medal and get 'em out of here."

Across the road, the Korean delegation emerged through the screened front doors of the hospital and scurried for their taxi. Hutchinson was faster. Han got the back seat beside the sub-consul. The fleet rep rode beside the driver.

Sun pushed through the steamy air, and the prismatic brightness brought out Han's headache. Trees hung over the road as if the weight of the wet air was too much for them. The taxi's tires hissed on the wet pavement. The journey was otherwise silent.

As they passed through the village of Utulei, Han tried to work out the residences along Penicillin Row. There were four buildings. The sailing club was tight up against the outflow channel of one of the mountain valley streams, so no extra beach. Then the Begleys, with both sides of their duplex. Then two more buildings: the American doc and his shrewish little bimbo next door to the Osgoods. Fischer had to be the last building, sharing it with someone Han couldn't account for. Or was he important enough to have both sides of his too? Then a bit of open beach masqueraded as public access. Then the second stream outflow marked the end of the beach.

From there, past a last few buildings, the road began to rise gently and then more sharply toward the point where the hotel was built like its own village out on the headland. By the time they were nearing the entrance to the hotel, the road was running along a low cliff of huge lava boulders.

And Han had a good idea where Ray Begley had died.

As they let Han out at the police station, the fleet rep leaned out of the window.

"My office is across from the dry dock. It's my home as well."

Han nodded. *I know the feeling.* The taxi moved off slowly through the sandy puddles.

Office space had been found for him in one of the single story clapboard buildings attached by boardwalks to the back side of the main structure. The light was poor and the ventilation was worse. However there was some of each, and neither required electrical power. And when there was power, a spigot behind the building made a makeshift shower. From a file drawer, he retrieved a complete set of clean clothes, including a pair of black rubber thong sandals. Spare clothes were a habit learned early from the bizarre hours that are any policeman's lot. To which Samoa added several opportunities daily to get soaked to the skin. He didn't feel a whole lot better in the uniform shorts and shirt, but he did feel more like himself, and that was at least familiar.

He locked his office again and crossed the wooden catwalk into the main building. As soon as he was inside, the power went out, as it did most mornings about this time. He moved by feel down the windowless central hall that ran athwart the building. Task A + 1 was to go through the dispatcher's log to try to reconstruct some kind of frame for the discovery and subsequent handling of Begley's body. But Task A was talking to the chief.

As he reached the foot of the stairs to the second floor, the door to the chief's office upstairs opened. A single figure ejected itself through the bright oblong of exterior light, followed by the tense rumblings of the old man's voice. Han trudged up the long flight, rediscovering the scabs on his knees and wondering how much crap he was going to get about last night. Since avoiding problems with fishermen was, presumably, a big part of why he was here.

Han knocked on the chief's door and waited until he was sure he had heard the grunt of assent before he went in. He had never had any use for Assistant Chief—now the late—Sapatu. Arrogant, brutal, crafty rather than intelligent, Sapatu had been everything Han hated most about a lot of people attracted to his profession. The Chief was something entirely different. But Han was still working out exactly what that was.

The old man was standing looking out of the broad grimy window behind his desk, his back to Han, framed by The Rainmaker, the volcanic peak that dominates the entrance to Pago Bay. Like the mountain, he was tall and square-topped, his short hair white like the clouds that caught in the mountain's heights. Han carried a chair over and sat by the chief's desk. Even when the old man sat down, Han's head would be lower than his, the Samoan ceremonial position of subordination. In strictly cultural terms, Han should have sat on the floor to display his contrition. But, one, he wasn't about to do that to his knees and, two, he wasn't contrite.

About a minute passed. Then the old man turned and sat down behind the broad wooden desk. He looked steadily at Han. Finally, he said, "At least you are alive. This is good."

In his late sixties, he still charged around at a great pace on his long legs, the quintessential village bobby. Part of their relationship, Han suspected, was that Han could keep up with him.

"Now you must do your job. And I must go see that fool of a governor who will cry to me about the useless dead *palagi* husband of his girlfriend when I have a dead senior talking chief and his family to contend with. Not to mention inquiries from United States' Senators about civil unrest in the Territory of American Samoa."

He flipped across the desk toward Han a half-folded sheet of paper that had been routed from the governor's office. It was signed by the senior Senator from Hawaii, the Territory's most important voting advocate in the U.S. Congress.

"And I have to go to a funeral this afternoon in Papasaa. A great chief. An old friend." The lines in the old man's face shifted from the tight horizontals of command to the down-flowing angles of grief. He felt what he should feel and that was an end to it.

Han had never mastered the trick and wasn't likely to. "Is she his girlfriend, sir?"

"That's none of your damn business." The reply was quick and very Samoan even if the rough coat derived from a lifetime of dealing with the professional rudeness of *palagis*.

Han stifled a smile. "They going to bury Sapatu without his body?"

"Maybe you need to go back to the hospital. How can you bury a man without his body? The Tapuafanua of Papasaa passed away last night. A small village to have such a great man, to have a *tapuafanua*, but there you are. He just passed away. He was old."

"*Tapuafanua* is not a title, then?"

"Not a family title. It's for a man who has given up his title. It's very rare. As if the Queen of England gave up her title to the husband of Princess Di." His grin, for a high chief, was almost wicked. But she would still be the most special person in the country." His smile faded. "But these things have a cost...but you want to talk about a dead *palagi*, don't you?"

"And five dead Koreans and a dead cop. Four drowned and two shot."

"Two?" Han nodded. "You mean...other than Sapatu?"

"No, Sapatu and one Korean. No way to say for sure yet but possibly with the same gun."

"Why," said the old man slowly, voicing the first thing that had come into Han's head when Hutchinson had told him, "Kill one Samoan and one Korean? There must be two guns. Two killers. Pretty soon, we're going to be like L.A. Shooting people on the freeways."

Han forbore saying that first you needed freeways. He told the old man about the tuna fleet captains having guns. The old man shook his head and grunted in Samoan. Han recognized the proverb: *They bring night to the village.* It was the ultimate Samoan curse: evil arises under cover of darkness, when action is invisible to community attention. It was certainly a point of view a cop could appreciate. Of course, Samoans also took it to the logical conclusion that all privacy is evil.

"I need to search the tuna boats," Han said. "But I want a witness, a very senior Samoan that everyone trusts or it'll be too easy to accuse me of covering up."

"Nobody trusts anybody in Samoa. But I am too old to climb in and out of such places."

He meant too dignified. Like there are dukes in Britain who are dukes and there are dukes who are princes, there are high chiefs in Samoa and then there are the high chiefs of Manu'a. Several years ago, the old man's family had saddled him with one of the most prestigious titles in all Samoa. This was not, rumor had it, without some reluctance on the family's part but had been inevitable, given his lineage and the lack of anyone else with close to his qualifications. It hadn't slowed him down a lot. Its main manifestation appeared to be the red Suburban he had treated himself to that sat outside of the police station like a royal coach. But every so often, in Han's brief experience, the gates would clang shut on what the chief felt that he could and could not do.

"Sa'ili Tua'ua. Do you know him?" Han shook his head. "He will be at this funeral also. They should have made him Nofonofo long ago, for all that he is a bit young for such a title...."

"Nofonofo," Han said. He caught the glint in the old man's eye–interrupting was a serious no-no. He went on anyway. "One of the doctors in the hospital told me something about Nofonofo. Wife and baby died in childbirth. Something to do with Begley, the dead *palagi*."

"This is true," the old man said but didn't elaborate. "But Nofonofo was not young. And he was sick. Sugar, high blood pressure, all good *palagi* diseases. He died too. The title has been open since his death, for they are a foolish and greedy family run by three foolish and greedy old women who don't have enough sense to see the good men among them. Now that the Tapuafanua is gone, they will be sillier than ever. Sometimes I fear they will drive...but never mind. I will speak to Sa'ili so he will know who you are. What else do you want?"

"The kid, the young officer, who was assigned to wait for me on the beach, the one who brought Begley's body to the hospital. And I want my jeep pulled out of the ditch across from the guest *fale* in Pago." The old man gazed at him. Han wondered if he had reached the limits of cross-cultural impudence. But the chief finally snorted softly and picked up the telephone. Han didn't think he would see his jeep any time soon, but if the chief were involved, it might be by tomorrow and certainly before next week, which was the best Han could have done alone.

"If they find my equipment...."

"Do you know the difference between *fa'amoemoega* and *fa'atuatuaga*?"

"No, sir."

"The missionaries' dictionary defines both as *hope*. But the first means *expectation* or *anticipation*. And the second means, *revenge*."

6

Two hours later, Han had his jeep back, minus headlights, windshield, windows, muffler, and third gear. None of this was critical or out of keeping with the rest of the island's cars. What was critical was that, of course, his scene-of-crime bag was gone. But, then, he didn't have a scene-of-crime either. He put the jeep into whatever forward gears it had left and took off to pick up the young constable who had brought Begley's body to the hospital.

The kid lived another ten minutes along the coast road from Han's house. Han stopped at home and threw into a canvas carrier whatever might substitute on short notice for his gear—clean plastic bags of various sizes, a palm-sized Olympus 35 mm camera, a Swiss army knife. The house looked overgrown to him, as if he had been gone from it for weeks rather than hours. Maybe he had.

He found the kid more or less where he had been told to find him. And faced with the knowledge that the beach where Begley's body had been found had been uninvestigated already for at least twelve hours and that there was only one headlamp left on the island that would fit his jeep, Han made the logical choice. He went all the way back along the leeward shore and out to the airport to what passed as a dealership to get the headlight. As they went by, they waved to the cop Han had insisted be posted on the beach in Utulei.

An hour later, Han was still ahead by one headlamp. But not much else.

The constable, whose name in Samoan was John-son-of-John, showed Han where he had found the body, rolled against the low bulkhead that marked one end of Utulei beach. Assuming the kid had the place right, Begley's rest there had left no obvious signs. The sand was pocked evenly all over the beach with the uniform depressions made by the pressure of feet and the physics of dry sand. Maybe they could trace fragments of a shallow track about the width of a man's shoulders scored in the sand up from the water's edge.

"You found him here? You didn't pull him out of the water?"

"Yes, sir. No, sir." John-son-of-John grinned.

"Who pulled him out of the water?"

"I don't know, sir. Boys, maybe." Boys, maybe. Han looked up and down the beach.

"We have to find out who pulled him out of the water. We have to talk to them. Try to find out where he went into the water." He didn't say: *and not make up answers just to satisfy what you think is due my rank and the situation.* But he thought it.

The other young cop, the one Han had left posted there, whose name in Samoan was Jim-son-of-Jim, said, "He went into the water there."

He gestured along the sweep of the shore toward the headland and the hotel.

"How do you know that?"

"Tide, sir. Go out then. Very strong." He gestured toward the break in the reef. "Water path very strong, very fast."

Han thought about what he knew about the shape of Pago Bay, one of the great natural harbors of the world—being why, in that moment before World War I and having just secured Hawai'i, the U.S. had been so quick to snatch up the next coaling leg of the long haul across the Pacific. Here in Utulei, in the village's own little cove, they were still inside the shelter of the bay. He would have to check the tides, but it was a possibility. Even valuable if he could get some kind of bracket on the probable time of death. If Begley hadn't just been dumped off of a boat. Or bashed in the head and pushed into the water right here. He certainly hadn't been in the water all that long. Too many if's.

"Sir, we take boat out and look!" The TPD's patrol boat had spent a previous incarnation—one of many, Han suspected—as an inter-island ferry. It did have a new coat of paint.

"Maybe," he said. "But we won't see what we need to from the water. We'll finish here then move up the cove. Because," he nodded to Jim-son-of-Jim, "I think you're right." For this he was rewarded with another grin. "But we still need to go over this ground. Look carefully. Sift the sand a little." Friendly and cheerful, the two young policemen listened. Like puppies, Han thought. No wonder we eat them.

But they weren't bad retrievers. Because, he supposed, they had no preconceived ideas about what he wanted by searching the beach, they brought to him or called his attention to everything. Patient and methodical—it beat paying attention to how awful he felt—Han showed them how to seal, label and map their finds, photograph what needed to be photographed. There was little enough—just a few stained clumps of sand that at least supported the idea that Begley was indeed dragged up from the water's edge. But Han clung to that thin ledge of objective evidence like a climber.

Most of Utulei beach was the narrow strip of sand backed by the scrubby grass around the four duplexes of Penicillin Row. Han stood for a moment, leaving his two young hounds to sniff on without him. His hands throbbed horribly. He raised them to shoulder level like a man under arrest. Even if you could imagine one of the *palagis* flipping out and killing another over one of these roach-infested shacks, Begley would be an unlikely target. If anything, his death cemented Gloriana's hold on her house, not the other way around, if what he was hearing from the doctors, Hutchinson and Ann Maglynn, was true. Gloriana would have been the far more likely target.

Still holding his hands up and walking slowly down the beach after John and Jim, Han tried the idea of Gloriana as the intended victim. From what little he knew of Department of Health politics, that would certainly put either Hutchinson or his wife at the top of the list. But the victim hadn't been Gloriana. And it wasn't like it was hard to tell Gloriana and her husband apart, even in bad light. And killing Gloriana would have been stupid. And neither of the Hutchinsons was stupid.

Han walked up to the side of the duplex he thought was the Osgoods, the opera-loving neighbors of the bosomy doctor's wife who had tackled Hutchinson this morning. He considered the problem of knocking on a door with hands that felt as bad as his did. But there didn't seem to be anyone there. Nor was there a response at Fischer's door. There was no name on the rickety mailbox of the end duplex, the one next to Fischer, no car in the drive or other obvious signs of life. Street-side and bay-side doors were locked. But the bay-side door gave easily enough to the pressure of his shoulder against the jam and counter-pressure against the knob. His hands really didn't like doing that. He peeled off the plastic bags he had used as gloves, and a wave of nausea broke over him. He sat down on the chair by the door in a cold sweat and tried to think about where he was.

The space was simple enough, the basic layout presumably the same in all four buildings. The outboard half of the apartment was living room with a tiny kitchen in back. The half that shared a wall with the other side of the duplex had two small bedrooms with a bathroom between. The outer walls were glass louvers, good for air movement but not much by Western standards of privacy. Samoans viewed such houses as *palagi*-style: closed, hidden, a set-up for misbehavior. The furniture was the usual rickety rattan and mouldy bright print oilcloth; there was a small book-case of paperbacks. But there was none of the minor detritus that even an overnight visitor will leave, no smell of habitation. Han got up and paced around carefully. Bathroom clean. Bedrooms made up but empty. He grinned sourly to himself. The double bed in the bay-side bedroom was rumpled. Not much. It had been straightened up after it had served its purpose. He doubted that they had even bothered to pull the sheets down.

He opened the louvers on the window to the screened lanai and examined the pillows carefully. And for what it was worth, he got lucky. He had lent the Swiss Army knife to John for something, so he borrowed a fork from the kitchen. With it, he delicately lifted the hairs, one long—maybe red, maybe blond–and three short and pale, up from the pillowcase and into another plastic bag. He straightened up and thought about the two bedrooms, one on the land side of the building and one on the sea side. The lovers would have to be *palagis*. They would view the beach side of the house both as more desirable and more private. Their orientation was to the road. Samoans were oriented to the sea. The sea-side room might be higher status, but fornication and profanation of the more sacred sea-side space would be a double sin.

He went through the apartment again and found even less than he had the first time. Outside, he eased the stiffness in his back against the warm side of the jeep and looked out across the bay. The water glittered like abalone shell in the midday sun. So what about Fischer? Fischer as a lover for Gloriana? Solve all her problems: get rid of the undesirable husband, placate the legislature, have her to himself. Might fit. Just because the outsides of a pair of individuals were unappetizing didn't mean they didn't find solace in each other. Or have organs capable of producing orgasms.

Desire, like a cramp, passed over him. But he shut it down like all his other aches and pushed himself away from the support of the jeep. He walked slowly down the length of the bulkhead from the landward end at the drainage ditch beside the road to the beach end half a dozen yards from the water. They had been over it all more than once, he and John and Jim. And the chance of finding anything subtle in the dry sand and coarse grass was really small.

Besides...he thought about Begley's battered body...this was not subtle. Quick maybe. What had Ann Maglynn suggested? Hurried...impulsive perhaps...but it hadn't been subtle.

Han looked down the beach. Three *palagi* women stood at the water's edge now, one of them the doctor's wife he had met with Hutchinson. At this distance, her big boobs made her look fat. He smiled to himself. *Sour grapes.* Small children played together in the wet sand unheeded as the mothers talked intently, glancing occasionally up the beach toward Han. He looked landward. Cars passed one after another on the road, and people walked along the precarious sand strip between the narrow road and the drainage ditches. It was just all so damned public. He let his eyes ride up the rocky cliff toward the hotel. That's where they needed to be. His hands throbbed.

A Suzuki hardtop slowed and then pulled across the culvert into the rickety carport beyond Fischer's. A tall, gangling *palagi* with a mane of white hair unfolded out of the jeep and disappeared under an arching trellis of orange bougainvillea into the next duplex. Han waved John and Jim over and gave them directions to start working up the shore toward the hotel. Then he walked up and knocked gingerly on the door where the jeep had pulled up. The door jerked open as if it had stuck in the frame. The tall, white-haired man stood there with the door handle gripped in one big hand and a jar of American peanut butter in the other.

"Mr. Osgood?"

"Uh, doctor, if you're doing formal. But yes, I'm Hank Osgood. What can I do for you, officer? My God, I guess it's about Ray Begley, yes? I'm sorry. Please come in. Can I get you something to eat? Just spent the morning with the legislature arguing funds for the college. Thought I could at least get a decent lunch out of it." He waved Han in with the peanut butter jar, then set to carving thick slices of what had to be homemade whole wheat bread.

Han did accept a chair and a glass of water. He didn't think he'd ever feel like eating again.

But before he could ask the first question, Osgood peered at him. "I know who you are. You're the guy from San Francisco. Gonna come talk to me about criminology courses."

Since, as far as Han knew, this idea existed only in his own head, Osgood saying it was a bit of a surprise. But he also answered Han's questions readily enough.

"...excuse to get out of the reception, but neither of us could come up with anything good enough to make the political price worth it. We must have been out of here by about seven fifteen...."

Like a lot of *palagis*, Osgood said about twice as much as he needed to make his point. But he seemed decent enough. Good humored, anyway, with enough ego strength to cope with what most *palagis* experienced as the instability of the Samoan psyche without falling apart himself.

"...drives our new neighbors nuts of course, but we couldn't resist. It was a brand new CD my brother-in-law had sent down. He works for the St. Paul Chamber Orchestra. Picked it up on tour in Milan...."

Osgood was probably handsome by *palagi* standards, long past youth but ruggedly built, with long, strongly built limbs. If he had been an actor, they would have cast him as the President, his face mobile and weathered. Funny thing about *palagi* skin. They made such a thing about their white skin, and it was such an inferior product, as skin goes....

"You all right, Lieutenant?" Osgood's bright blue eyes speared Han to the chair. Han started to rub his face with one hand, then thought better of it.

"Yeah. Thanks. It was a rough night."

"So we heard. Funny all that going on in Pago and us all right around the corner here and not hearing a thing. Here, drink this." Osgood handed him a cup of Chinese tea. He didn't argue. "I did see Ray last night though. At least I think it was Ray. Remember thinking it was Ray at the time." Osgood poured his own tea and perched on a stool at the counter that divided the kitchen from the main room. "We left well before the shindig was over. We had walked up. It's not far and it's lovely to walk at night along that part of the shore road. Coming down the governor's driveway, there's a break in the trees and you can see out over the bay. See a little chunk of the road. I saw a man walking along there, then we were in the trees again and couldn't see any more...."

"Was he walking up...like toward the governor's house?"

"He was certainly walking up, not down."

"When was this?"

"A little after nine, maybe?"

"Before or after the power went out?"

Osgood laughed. "After. That's how my wife and I made our getaway."

"But you thought the man was Begley."

"Yes. Which is strange, isn't it? Let me think about that. Of course, when you're out in the real dark–starlight or moonlight–you can see, once your eyes adjust. It's the artificial light makes you blind. But even against the bay, he'd have just been a silhouette. A car must have come by, lit him as it passed, big guy, tall, bulky, wearing long pants and shirt. Not shorts, not a *lavalava*. But also, *palagis* walk differently than Samoans. They kind of stomp, with their arms swinging, like they've always got shoes on. Samoans kind of roll, like they're being careful where they put their feet...."

Han really was trying to pay attention. Particularly now that he had one person who was willing to admit to seeing Begley around the time he must have died. But he couldn't help wondering about a man and a woman who enjoyed each other's company. Who would rather walk home and watch the Southern Cross rise over the bay than climb the ladders of local status. And the rest, the dark house, the sound of the water, the welcome of each other's arms. He could imagine it. But he certainly had no personal experience to relate it to.

"...Anyway, I thought it was a *palagi* at the time and I think I thought it was Ray. Knowing that he hadn't gotten up to the reception yet."

"And he was alone? You didn't see anyone with him? Any one else at all?" The tea was strong enough to pave the street with, but it was probably the only thing that could have pulled Han together. That and the possibility that he had just learned something useful. "How about Dr. Hutchinson? Head of the hospital?"

"No, it definitely wasn't Neil. For one thing, he and his wife were at the reception when we left. And Neil looks tall because he's skinny, but he's not really all that big. Ray was bigger in every dimension than Neil." Osgood grinned suddenly, wolfishly. "Except character."

"What about Leon Fischer?"

Osgood's mouth moved in a *maybe* gesture. "Shape, maybe. But Leon was still at the party, too. And Leon wouldn't walk to the bathroom if he could drive."

"Did your wife see the man on the road?"

"I don't think so. She was to the outside, seaward, of me, but she was watching her footing or glancing toward me as we talked, so, away from the road."

Han nodded. He had emptied his mug. Osgood poured him another and he drank half of that down as well. "You suggest Dr. Begley's character left something to be desired."

Osgood smiled and put his napkin down on the counter and looked at Han. "Shouldn't have said that, should I? As if we *palagis* don't have enough trouble here pretending our moral superiority without badmouthing each other every chance we get. Poor old Gloriana. She's not nearly as bad as Neil and Adele think she is. But she's also not nearly as bright as either she or the governor thinks she is. You know, I don't pretend to know anything about medicine, but I do know how to run a program that delivers services. In my case, it's education. Gloriana can't balance a checkbook. She can't drive a car. Literally or metaphorically. And marrying Ray was a real disaster. He was a bad man, Lieutenant. She's going to be a hell of a lot better off without him."

"Would she kill him?"

Osgood shook his head. "No. She wouldn't know how. And if she tried to hire somebody to do it, she'd do it so clumsily, everybody from Auckland to Honolulu would know about it before she'd written the check."

"You say Begley was bad. How?"

"Can't get away with that either, huh? Okay, well, fair enough. He was a drunk, certainly. But then a lot of people around here are drunks, and those that aren't are on their way to being. I hear he was incompetent medically. Though I don't know anything about that myself. But my wife thinks—and she's volunteered in big city women's shelters—that he physically abused Gloriana. One too many bruises with funny explanations. Of course, there's her little fainting number that she does. But that wouldn't account for bruises on her neck. Though Gloriana denies it all of course."

"What about somebody trying to do her a favor? Knight errant?"

"Can't imagine who. You mean Leon? Can't imagine him risking himself."
"The governor?"
Osgood looked at Han for a long time and then grunted. "I couldn't say."
Han put his cup on the counter.
"Thanks for the tea."
"Oh," said Osgood. "Consider it nothing."

Han stood for a moment among the bougainvillaea at the edge of Osgood's carport. He actually didn't feel any worse than he had an hour ago. He chose to view this as a good sign and crossed to Begley's street-side door. He couldn't see how his two assistants were doing. He just hoped they remembered what they were doing.

His first knock got nothing. His second got an angry female voice calling for someone. He knocked a third time. The angry female voice was answered this time by another voice, also female and irritated, and the door snapped open.

Han thought: Maria Theresa. She could have been any Californian teenager, pudgy and paler than you'd expect of someone who lived in a place so pretty. Her hair was a Medusa-like tangle of red-gold waves.

"Yeah?" she said. "What is it?"

Han introduced himself and showed his ID.

"My mom's sick," the girl said shortly. "She can't talk to you."

"I understand that she is distressed," Han said. If he'd been a cat, he'd have been purring. "But I am investigating what she and I both believe is a murder. I do need to ask her some questions about your stepfather's movements yesterday."

He also knew that somewhere on the other side of the paper-thin walls, he was talking to Gloriana. The girl sniffed derisively at the word *stepfather* and thrust her mane behind her ears with her mother's gesture. Han thought about the long red-gold hair in the plastic bag in his pocket and reminded himself that his job was to find out who killed Ray Begley. He didn't have to like the diagnosis once he made it.

"She won't talk to you," the girl said.

"If you would please ask her." He stood, obviously not going anywhere.

The girl sighed and turned away. Then she stopped. "I guess you might as well come in."

That was as far as hospitality took her. She left Han standing in the small space by the door and disappeared into the area of the bedrooms.

Han looked around. They did have both sides of the duplex, but it seemed to have confused rather than liberated them. The kitchen had been closed off into a tiny cubicle to the right of the door. The remains of the room had been jammed with heavy wooden furniture that would have crowded a formal dining room three times its size. But the pieces looked strong enough to prop up the roof if it collapsed. Which, Han thought, did appear likely.

He could hear querulous female voices in the back. The girl returned. "She won't see you."

Han nodded. He held out his hands like stigmata. "Could I get a glass of water from you?"

He watched the girl's face. She wanted to say *no*, but all of her various cultures–probably even Catholic schooling–required that humblest kindness. She shrugged and moved her mouth in a last silent protest but passed into the kitchen. Han occupied the doorway.

"What did you think of your step-father?" Maria Theresa handed him the glass of tepid water. Like most adolescents, she seemed dumbfounded by being asked for a genuine opinion by an adult. She shrugged again and, as if she couldn't think of anything else to do, ran herself a glass of water. But she sat down at the tiny table in the kitchen, not really avoiding him. He didn't believe the old saw that you could always tell when a girl was no longer a virgin by the way she behaved around men–rape comes in too many forms and a cop sees all of them. But he didn't think this girl was a virgin, even without the hair on the pillow. "Did you like him?"

She shrugged again. Her gaze flickered briefly as far as Han's chin. "He was okay, I guess. Except when he was drunk. Which was most of the time." She got up suddenly and put her glass in the sink. "I mean, like he like lived at the hotel bar."

"Did he go there last night?"

The girl moved one shoulder. Her face was about to say *Sure*, but she looked past Han's shoulder and her eyes widened. Han heard a silky rustle behind him and Gloriana's sharp voice.

"You can't be in here asking my daughter questions. It's against the law. It's against the law to ask a child questions without a parent present."

"Ah, but madam," Han said, turning. "You were here."

Gloriana stood framed in the inner doorway, dressed in a long red kimono. She stared at him for a moment. And then she collapsed onto the floor. Neither Han nor Maria Theresa moved to cushion the fall. And once again, she landed with her cheek pillowed on one forearm.

"She's got to stop doing that," Han said.

"I know," said Maria Theresa.

Dealing with Gloriana was definitely women's work, and Han left Maria Theresa to it. But he did get from the girl that Begley had left home about quarter to eight. If he had walked straight up to the hotel—not stopped in at someone else's house, not gotten a ride—it would have taken him about ten or fifteen minutes. Far too early to be the figure Osgood had seen on the road. So: had he gone back? Or was there someone else?

Han went looking for John and Jim. They weren't on the last little stretch of beach before the shore curved out toward the point where the hotel stood. And he couldn't see them farther along on the tumbled lava boulders. Irritated, he drove through the north end of Utulei and out toward the hotel. *Damn*. The two young Samoan policemen were well up the slope, almost at the hotel drive. They couldn't have gotten up there being careful. Not in the way they would have to be to find anything subtle after fourteen hours and a rainstorm.

But as the jeep wheezed up the slope, he saw that he had misjudged them. He parked the jeep and got out, walking, by habit, carefully on the asphalt to avoid stepping where he might leave prints, though all that could be seen in the muddy, asphalt-stained sand were the streaks of coursing water. The two young men were working down the boulders now. They stood up and waved to him like children on a picnic.

What they had seen and gone straight to was the one place along that roadside cliff where an unconscious person could fall or be pushed and tumble all the way down into the water. Anywhere else, the body would have caught in the boulders. He looked up the road. And saw something else. From here to up where the driveway went off to the right toward the cluster of hotel buildings, the shoulder of the road was littered with pieces of cinder block.

There was no point in asking why. Had someone tried to build something here that failed? Had they just fallen out of the back of somebody's truck and nobody bothered to stop and pick them up? It didn't matter. They were here, a few here, a few there, a few feet to a few yards apart.

He stood, suppressing excitement. It didn't prove anything. But it did make it possible, specifically rather than theoretically possible. He looked back down the road. No. From here up, there was this litter of broken blocks, like the spoor of a cement-shitting dinosaur. From here down, certainly other forms of typical Samoan trash—cans, plastic containers, used Pampers—but not such handy, head-smashing weapons.

One of the young officers hailed him. Cautious with his sore hands and rubber thong sandals, he worked his way down to where they stood just above high-tide level. Here, a particularly large boulder had created a tiny sheltered spot, a few yards where sand and vegetable detritus had collected landward, away from the water. In places, the rough shape of the boulder overhung this minute beach. Lying there in the lea of the boulder was a shard of cement block, a grey triangle about a foot long, roughly half of one of the hollow sides of a block, twin to any of a couple of dozen of such pieces Han had just seen up on the roadside. Probably twin to other dozens hurled off the cliff top by casual walkers. What made this one different and why these two boys, not yet much in the way of cops but astute to the natural world, stop and look, was that one edge of this piece was very clean, as cement blocks go. And it hadn't been lying on that bit of sand and mud for long.

Han pulled the tiny Olympus out of his pocket. The lens wasn't suited to this kind of work, but it was all he had. John and Jim watched, greatly entertained, as Han stretched out on one boulder, trying to get enough angle on the light to pick out detail. He knew it was bad luck to hope that the clumps of brown muck on the dirty side and edge of the shard were bits of Ray Begley. Or that this piece of roadside refuse would fit the dent in the dead man's head. Han covered his hands with plastic bags in lieu of gloves, lifted the shard delicately off of the sand and reversed one of the bags over and around it. He took another couple of shots of the impression in the sand where the shard had lain. People live in hope. Die in hope, too, much of the time.

He nodded to John and Jim to keep looking and climbed back up to the jeep. Now, at least, they had a place, a method, and possibly a piece of the murder weapon. And Han had that feeling an early guru in his forensic training had called *I'm-gonna-get-this-son-of-a-bitch*.

A big old black Mercedes came around the corner of trees and low buildings from this end of Utulei village and started the climb up the slope. There was only one car like that in all of American Samoa. But why, Han thought, feeling a smile creep across his face, was it not in Gloriana Shutz-Begley's driveway just half an hour ago and why was the attorney general, Leon Fischer, driving it now? It swept passed him, and Han saw not just Fischer but the passengers, Gloriana and Maria Theresa. Han walked slowly up the roadside along the scattering of convenient cinder blocks and thought about Maria Theresa as the murderer. The big car disappeared above him around the sharp turn to the left along another curve of shore to the village of Fagatogo.

Suddenly, on the hillside above Han, the big old black car came and went through a break in the trees like a nightmare vision of a giant cockroach.

Han knew he was looking at the opening along the driveway to the governor's house through which Hank Osgood had seen his man on the road.

Han stopped walking. He was maybe a dozen yards above where the scattering of cider blocks started, where his jeep was parked now and where John and Jim were still patiently picking around among the boulders. So if Osgood was right and he saw a big man dressed like a *palagi* walking up here after the power went out, the question was...the question was, when did Begley get to the hotel bar? If he got there at all.

"Usual time," said the bartender. "Maybe quarter to eight, eight o'clock." Since the clock on the wall of the bar proclaimed the usual random time, Han wasn't sure how the big man came to that conclusion, but he seemed certain. The bartender moved one shoulder. "Always comes, same time about." The bouncer, perched on a barstool at the far end of the bar like a very large bird on a very small twig, nodded.

"Anybody with him?"

The bartender shook his head. "Nevah. Likes to drink alone, Dr. Ray." The bouncer nodded in chorus.

"Who else was here? Guests? Locals?"

The bartender nodded. "Bunch a guys from California. Somet'ing 'bout computers." He pointed with his head to a low round table back in a corner beyond the far end of the L-shaped bar. The bouncer said, "Guys from New Zealand." The bartender looked uncomfortable.

Han said, "California or New Zealand?"

The bartender looked even more uncomfortable and the bouncer looked smug. "Both," said the bartender. "Kiwis ovah there." He pointed with his chin this time to a group of chairs and low tables under the windows.

"Did Dr. Begley join either group?"

The bartender shook his head. "Oh, no. Like I say, he like to drink alone. I try get him go talk story wi' the California guys, him being from there. But he no went go."

Han had an inspiration. "You say the guys at this end were New Zealanders. Was Welly Tuiasosopo with them?" What was the likelihood that anyone from New Zealand could be on the island and Welly not know about it? The bartender looked uncomfortable again, and the bouncer looked even more smug. Bingo.

The bartender shrugged, his face unhappy. "Yeah."

"Did something happen between Dr. Begley and Dr. Tuiasosopo?"

"Not in here." The bartender said it as if he meant that to be all.

The bouncer snorted. "That's right. Happened out in the hall by the Gents."

Han looked at the bouncer. "What happened?"

"A little shoving," the bartender put in. Han looked at the bouncer, who shrugged as if he wasn't really disagreeing.

"They say anything? Threats?"

"Nah. Just...you know. Talking dirty."

"Anybody else involved?" Both men shook their heads.

"What time did this happen?" He really didn't need to ask.

"Just before the power went out."

"Then what happened?" Both men shrugged.

The bartender said, "Everybody go back to drinking."

"Dr. Begley and Dr. Tuiasosopo too?"

"Oh, no. Dr. Ray, we accompany him to t'e driveway."

"How far?" They looked at Han. "How far did you walk him? Out to the road?"

The bouncer shook his head. "Across the courtyard maybe. He know t'e drill. Sometime, we drive him home, but last night too many people, no can go."

"You said 'we'. You and who else."

The bouncer's broad brown face was blank for a moment. Han didn't think he was hiding anything, just checking a memory, then rejecting it. "Only me 'n him." Han looked at the bartender, who nodded.

"And Dr. Tuiasosopo?"

Both men shrugged. The bartender said, "Don't know where he get to. T'en lights go out. But Dr. Ray cause t' trouble, no lie. Always get big mouth, Dr. Ray, when he's drinking."

"But you say he didn't threaten Dr. Tuiasospo."

The bartender shook his head. "No. Just...talking dirty. Insults, like."

"Enough to start a fight."

The bartender's face crimped unhappily. "Nah. Just a little shoving. Like I say. Like boys. You just separate 'em. Let 'em sober up a little."

"Anybody else see it?"

The bouncer said, "One guy...." He nodded toward the table tucked in the back corner, the computer party from California. "W' t' runs. In and out the bat'room coupla times. Him, maybe."

"Where are all these guys now?" Granted, it had to be only about noon, but Han had never known that to slow up enthusiastic drinkers. And trips to American Samoa by mainland *palagis* usually encouraged enthusiastic drinking. But they couldn't get off island until tomorrow.

"Gone to Apia." *Shit,* Han thought. He'd forgotten about Apia. You could always get a hop flight to Western Samoa and from there to God knows where.

"*All* of them?"

Both men nodded. "All together. Go to New Zealand for conference."

One step forward, two steps back: the damned detective waltz. The two barmen really couldn't tell Han any more, so he hunted out the hotel's manager. The manager confirmed the origins of the two big parties and gave Han names and addresses. Han noticed there was none of the privacy bullshit he would have gotten at home. Samoans had very clear ideas about commitment to social order–possibly why they destroyed it so spectacularly when they did blow.

He tucked the manager's list in his breast pocket. His nose considered the option of a hotel hamburger: vintage grease-on-Styrofoam. His stomach vetoed the idea, though not as violently as previous offers. What he needed more than food right now was a telephone. And ways to avoid thinking about Welly Tuiasosopo.

He drove back down to the police station working out time zones. Samoa is almost as far south of the equator as Honolulu is north of it, but the time is only one hour behind. California is two hours on beyond that in the winter and three in the summer, but, whatever, still day-time. Han wasn't sure about New Zealand but it would at least be mid-morning there. But first, Apia.

Back in his office, he called the airport, confirming, one, that the telephone was working and that, two, all his quarry had indeed boarded a puddle-jumper for Apia this morning. Even as he negotiated with the operator (given his experiences with the telephone system, she probably was *the* operator) and placed his call to the airport police in Apia, he knew what the answer would be: the Samoan equivalent of *who* are you? He'd been through this before: if American Samoa is Samoan, Western Samoa is even more so and proud of it. Just to prove it to himself, he spent the usual ten minutes arguing with various officials about who he was and why he needed to know about eight *palagi* males off of the morning flight from Tutuila. And got the usual nowhere. He rang off in disgust. For this, he needed Sasa: most sacred chief of police, high chief of Manu'a.

He sat thinking about New Zealand. He didn't know anyone in New Zealand. One side of his mouth twisted. But he did know someone in L.A. He reached for the telephone again.

Sometime after the usual electronic protests of disbelief, a phone rang somewhere. Han hoped, in the bowels of a south L.A. police precinct office.

Han had met Derrick Lee at an inept conference on race relations in California law enforcement. Derrick's father was presumably a black American G.I. and his mother, an enterprising girl from night-time Seoul. He had been adopted from an orphanage and raised by a childless multiracial couple from wealthy Pacific Palisades and, like Han himself, had a very peculiar view of the world. He was also of an age where *Star Wars* had been the chief refuge of his late childhood.

The familiar voice said, "Hey, you pirate! How y'doin?"

Han outlined his problems.

"Lot of that stuff, you can get off the Internet," Derrick said cheerfully. Han could hear the tick of computer keys in the background.

Han said, *"You* can get it off the Internet. I'm lucky the telephone works today." His friend laughed absently, the way people do who are looking at computer screens with telephone receivers tucked between shoulder and jaw.

"Well, for what it's worth, your dead man can't practice medicine in California any more."

"You mean, other than because he's dead?"

"Was on probation for inappropriate prescribing of controlled substances until about a year ago. Then revoked altogether for non-response to Board queries."

"Anything else on him?"

There was another brief silence accompanied by key stroke sounds and Derrick's slightly off key humming. Finally: "Nope. But I'll keep looking. How's it otherwise down there?"

"About what you'd expect."

Derrick laughed. His specialty was the Samoan immigrant community of south central LA. His inside knowledge had been a useful edge for Han as their respective bad guy communities recycled through the two great cities.

"That bad, eh?"

7

Welly Tuiasosopo stood across the road from Fagatogo's grubby village green in a clean white shirt borrowed from his cousin Sa'ili, black cotton trousers and his best black flipflops. He had a decent quality ceremonial fine mat rolled into a bundle clamped under his left arm and an envelope with two hundred dollars tucked into the breast pocket of Sa'ili's shirt. The fine mat and the money were also borrowed from his cousin. Sa'ili, having done his bit for family solidarity, had told Welly, at that point still staggering groggily around Sa'ili's house looking for cigarettes and a bath, that he could find his own way over to the Tapuafanua's funeral. Welly stood now lighting his third cigarette in consideration of this problem when a Public Health jeep came around the corner from Utulei. Even better, a Public Health jeep driven by Ann Maglynn. She slowed in response to his wave.

He called, "Get ride?"

"Sure. But I'm going over to Papasaa."

"Where else?" he said, climbing in. "Tapuafanua's funeral." Like him, she was wearing white, the color of mourning and formality. Or at least, her shirt had only a tiny pale blue print–sort of a cross between mourning and the blue seersucker of the public health nurses' uniform, he decided. He tossed his fine mat in the back seat with Ann's collection of funerary gifts: another fine mat rolled in tapa cloth, a case of corned beef and a manila envelope which, like Welly's, probably contained more money than she could afford. He couldn't resist twitching the wrappings on Ann's fine mat to get a look at it. Then he flopped back into his seat.

"That looks like a good fine mat. Old."

Ann headed through Fagatogo toward Pago and the dirt road that would take them almost two thousand feet up the mountain ridge. And then two thousand feet down the other side.

She nodded. "I found it in my flat at the hospital. Gar Munro used to stay in that flat. I assume the fine mat was given to Gar after the governor's surgery. Gar wouldn't be tuned in enough to know he should acknowledge the honor gracefully but give anything that valuable back. And, being Gar, having scored, he left it behind. It would just be a big, old, folded up grass mat to him, however finely woven. Probably made his allergies worse." She glanced at Welly, and he recognized that the subject was about to be changed. "You...family to the Tapuafanua?"

"Sure. Who isn't?" He nodded. "Me closer than most, actually." She smiled and nodded, as if that were something she should have known.

He had written her off sexually long ago. She was not unattractive, if you kinda like boys—not that he did, much—nor was she oblivious. She just didn't engage. His advances just beaded up and rolled off like water off a sea bird's wings. Of course, that did make being up to your elbows in somebody's belly with her on surgical assist a little less distracting. And at some level, he knew that was why she did it. So he patted himself mentally on the back for wishing her well.

"Good to see the Public Health honoring the Tapuafanua with the presence of their jeep."

Ann laughed. "That's very graceful. Very Samoan. *Palagis* would say I was misusing government property for private ends."

For the next three hours, she drove and he hung on, one foot on the dashboard and one arm wrapped around the doorpost, fingers laced into the car's rain gutter. He even managed to smoke.

Halfway down the windward side, in deep South Pacific rain forest, they ran into a traffic jam. A pickup had rolled part way over and hung between the banks of a road cut. A dozen young men in their best white shirts and black *lavalavas* stood around laughing and making desultory efforts to right it. The truck bed was empty and nobody seemed to be hurt. Without seeming to give the action much thought, Ann drove the jeep up onto the lower of the two banks, worked it past the wreck and back down onto the track.

Welly looked at her. *"Malo fa'auli."* *Good steering,* the boat-passengers' thanks to the helmsman who gets them over the reef.

Ann smiled. *"Malo tapua'i."* The helmsman's thanks: *good praying*. "You know, a couple of nurses and I were here yesterday morning doing a clinic. The Tapuafanua looked fine."

"He was an old man." Palagis were always getting wrapped around the axle about the inevitable. One reason he liked Ann was that she didn't usually do that. "Like you say, he was in good shape. But he was still eighty-three. Or whatever. He'd had a long life." Welly was suddenly irritated and depressed about the mess the Tapuafanua's death was going to make of family politics.

Ann said, "And a good one. He's one of my heroes, you know. You wonder if you could ever do anything that brave and good when you meet someone like him."

"You mean the leprosy thing, bringing the lepers home from exile?" Welly shrugged. "He was the right fella in the right place at the right time."

"There are a lot of right times. Not so many right people."

"Well, most recently, he's just made a mess of village politics. Aw, shit. I don't want to talk about it." He dragged on his cigarette. And he meant it too. For about ten seconds. "He's about the only important person left in our family that supports Sa'ili for Nofonofo. You know, the high chief title."

Ann nodded. "In his day, he held both a high chief and an orator title."

"Lineage and brains."

"And being a medical officer all those years. He, like, knew everybody. Like, everybody."

"So whatever genealogic or service or any other argument anyone could offer on title discussions, he could go them one better."

"Yeah. And. He really *knew* people. Like who they really are." He said it uncomfortably, remembering the old man's diagnosis of himself as a boy. *You are too palagi to be any use to the family and too Samoan to be any use to yourself. Fortunately, you are intelligent. Though it will not content you.* He grunted disgustedly. "So Nofonofo stays open because the aunties go for anybody with half a chance, long as it's not Sa'ili, and the Tapuafanua just holds out for Sa'ili."

"What have they got against Sa'ili? I'd have thought he'd be perfect: lineage, brains, service. He's even tall, good looking, and a nice guy."

"Yeah, but he's also all *tala lua Tuna ma Fata.*"

Ann's forehead wrinkled as she worked out the proverb. *"Pray for both Tuna and Fata.* Consider everybody. So...the family can't trust him to put their interests first."

Welly nodded unhappily.

"Well," Ann said, smiling. "At least they keep talking. Like Quakers trying to reach consensus. Probably a better way to keep a community together, in the long run, than winner take all. But you do have to wait for the opposition to die off, sometimes."

It was the wrong thing to say. It made them both unhappy. Just to say something, he said, "So who d' you think killed ol' Ray?"

"Well, if you or Neil or Adele didn't kill him, I'm not sure I care."

He guffawed, then stopped when he saw she was serious. "Me? Hell, no. Besides, Samoans never kill anybody unless the other person has something they want, usually a title."

"Well, certainly Ray didn't have anything that I'm aware of that anyone else could want." Welly thought suddenly of Gloriana, silly old cow. They grinned conspiratorially at each other. "Are you titled? I never think of you as a chief. But I expect that's my problem, not yours."

"Oh yeah. One very minor title. The most minor in the village. Probably the only title in the whole history of either Samoa conveyed on account of doing fifty circumcisions in one weekend."

"Circumcisions?"

"Yeah, you know." He gestured with one hand, stretching a foreskin, clipping....

She laughed. "I know what a circumcision is. Done 'em too. At least, on newborns. Why fifty at a go? Group rates? Economies of scale?"

"Nah. *Palagis* causing trouble, as usual. At least the well-meaning ones. Bad ones easier to deal with–you just knock em off....no: the *palagi* pediatricians that came down here in the seventies all said circumcisions bad for the kids. Didn't understand that it's a big part of *fa'a Samoa*."

Ann grunted. "Probably not the worst thing for personal hygiene either, given the heat and the skin infections. So you had a whole cohort of boys and young men in need of a sympathetic surgeon....with a good hand." She grinned at him. "No wonder the villages were grateful."

"Hey. *I live in service.* How I got to know your buddy, Munro, being he's a urologist." The jeep was jouncing too much for him to be watching her expression closely. "Munro, though, he's something. Sailed up here a couple of times from New Zealand. Met his team here. Now there's a life." He grinned over at her. But her smile was strained and she was keeping her eyes on the road.

Welly knew she was prickly about Munro. Knew in fact that she had sailed with him on one of those trips from New Zealand. But Welly's life was so littered with defunct affairs that as long as they didn't pose a danger of physical reprisal...no, as long as they hadn't actually *resulted* in physical reprisal, he didn't worry about them. He knew that women did see things differently than men, but he didn't understand it. She was a fine woman, though she didn't seem to notice that. She could do better than Munro. They bounced down through the gnarled gray trees of the dense, lower-slope forest, and Welly thought about who that might be. Since it clearly wasn't going to be him.

And suddenly they were out of the forest and into the stately calm of coconut groves on the banks of the little river that emptied here into the sea. As they climbed out of the jeep and assembled their gifts, Welly noticed that Ann's shirt was actually a dress. He had never seen her in a dress. Walking a little behind, he watched happily as she hitched it up to wade into the ford.

But walking up the sandy bank on the village side of the stream, he figured he had probably had his last pleasurable experience of the day. He had hoped to get here late enough maybe just for one or two of the multiple sermons and the interment, avoiding the main social jockeying and the most formal part of the redistribution of funeral gifts. Always a tense moment in Samoan social life, his family had a talent for doing the giveaways so as to piss off just about everybody, legacy of a long history of second-class talking chiefs. But now he guessed he'd blown it again.

The village was paved with people. Some stood in small groups. But most sat on mats in widening circles of expectation around the great guest *fale* at the edge of the beach and back landward across the village green, waiting for the speeches to begin and to get their cut of the take. The scents of wood smoke and scorched pork drifted through the trees and over the crowd.

Welly threaded Ann through the islands of seated people. Behind him, he could hear people saying *Wonderful! Just beautiful!* as they caught sight of the fine mat Ann had brought. Finally, he got them to the main cache of mourning gifts.

The outpouring was unbelievable: stacks and stacks of fine mats and tapa cloth and ornaments made of shell and beads and cases and cases of canned fish, corned beef and biscuits, barrels of salt beef, flour, and sugar. There was plenty of cash too, but it was disappearing quickly into the safekeeping of the orators running the show. Fa'atofi Jake, the village's most senior junior orator was hovering nearby like a blowfly, barking orders to two underlings who were frantically trying to list the gifts as they came in. What the family was doing about the fact that their senior orator was lying in a body bag in a freezer in Fagaalu wasn't clear.

Welly saw Jake catch sight of Ann's fine mat and make a dart toward it. Welly considered meeting the little man's face with his foot. But before he could ruin himself in the family's eyes permanently and forever, a soft deep voice rumbled. Welly looked up. A few yards away, a spare, regal figure stood watching them. He was decked out in tapacloth kilt and carried a long staff, the sennit fly whisk of a presiding senior orator draped over one shoulder.

Jake glared briefly at Welly, lifted Ann's fine mat so that the senior orator could see it and acknowledge its beauty with a nod, then marched off with it toward the neighboring chief's *fale*. The Tapuafanua would be lying in state there, awaiting the interment. The pandanus shutters on the landward side of the chief's *fale* had been let down, shading the body and forming a backdrop where the most beautiful fine mats would be displayed.

As they backed away from the loot, making all the appropriate greetings to all the appropriate people, Ann said, "Who's the senior orator? I was wondering how they were going to manage. Under the circumstances."

Welly grunted. "Impossible proves the rule: an honest talking chief. Senior orator next village over. Knows the family trees of all of Samoa back to God. Famous for basically giving everybody back what they brought, keeping things fair. It's the same district, so I guess he can make it work."

"Bend the ceremonial genealogy sufficiently to include himself? But a good solution. To invite him."

"Don't know if they got that much sense. He may have just invited himself, knowing how they are." Welly guided Ann out again through the throngs of seated family, stepping over children and dogs as necessary and scattering birdlife at the periphery.

Glancing back toward the guest *fale*, he said, "Holy shit." Sa'ili was there, introducing a man in *palagi* clothes to the old talking chief. Tall, handsome, graceful, the two younger men could have been twins. "Damn, I thought he was dead."

"I would guess. Being a funeral."

"No. He's a cousin of mine." He started toward the others, all but dragging Ann with him.

"Everybody's a cousin of yours."

"Yeah. Except a lot of 'em are dead. Sa'ili said he was back. But I didn't believe it."

Coming up to the group with Sa'ili, Welly saluted the old orator as politely as he knew how and looked around for Ann. She had disappeared off somewhere. Well, the hell with her. He turned to the stranger.

"Tanifa?" Welly stuck his hand out, *palagi-* style, and the man grasped it. "Welly?"

They embraced. Under the white shirt, Tanifa's body was startlingly fit. Welly could tell that Tanifa's shirt, like his own, was borrowed. It pulled a bit across the big man's shoulders, unlike the perfect Dockers trousers and Teva sandals. Hadn't been planning on funerals, Welly thought. Or had forgotten that element of village formality.

"Hey, man. What the hell are you doing here? I thought you were dead."

For a few minutes, the three younger men stood around grinning at each other and saying stupid things about being kids together. Welly thought Sa'ili was a little less enthusiastic than he might have been. But the hell with him, too. So Sa'ili had a little competition for once. In his own white shirt and white with-pockets *lavalava*, he looked more like a courtier than a prince. And maybe that was a problem. Typical Sa'ili, though, he was shifting them away from the ceremonial center of things so their chatter was a little more seemly.

"Not quite sure what I'm doing here," Tanifa laughed. "First chance I've had for vacation since I got out of the Army, and that was ten years ago. Actually, ran into Jake in Vegas about three months ago. 'Hey, man, just come and check it out. Best of both worlds. Come stay in the hotel—just like Vegas—for a couple of days, get your feet wet, so to speak...'" He shook his head. "But then I guess Jake got the aunties started. 'Cause here I am in the village again, the Once and Future Bad Boy bein' treated like nobility." He rolled his eyes. They all laughed. The aunties were the Tapuafanua's three daughters, great-grandmothers themselves at this point and definitely the village power brokers. Kind of like if King Lear had gotten onto Prozac and the three girls had made it up.

"It's okay," Welly said, pulling his face into mock seriousness. "We get Sa'ili to protect you. He's got a gun now."

It was worth it: both other men's faces drooped in surprise, and Welly giggled.

Before either of them could say anything, a murmur went through the crowd. A red Chevrolet Suburban had pulled in across the river. Old Sasa, chief of police and high chief of Manu'a, got out of the passenger's seat of the Suburban and strode into the ford as if he expected the water to part before him. The young officer who had been driving trotted after him carrying three fine mats wrapped in tapa cloth. The old bear was coming right for them. The senior orator moved to meet him, and Sa'ili stepped away from his cousins to join them.

"Who's that?"

"Chief of police, among other things." Welly also named his title.

"Oh. Yeah. Wow. Okay. I been away a long time."

Welly looked up at his long-lost cousin. He would have said Tanifa was the least likely of his closer cousins to have survived childhood, much less Viet Nam and whatever else he had been doing for the last twenty years. He could count on the fingers of both hands the number of times he would have liked to kill Tanifa himself. But you can't tell about people.

"So. You staying with Fa'atofi Jake?" Tanifa hesitated, then sorted out the name and laughed.

"I'm certainly stuck here for the time being. If I'd had any sense I'd'a rented a car while I was on the other side. But I can't say I thought I'd be there for long. " He looked around. "And I never thought I'd ever come back here." He grinned at Welly. "Palapala not being exactly the favorite family flavor. But it seems like things really have changed. " He chuckled. "Best of both worlds."

Through his fatigue and hangover, Welly's thoughts were suddenly complex. For one thing, Tanifa was talking *palagi: me* was where he was coming from. *Me* was a different kind of person to reckon with. Not bad–any more than something like that was bad in Sa'ili–but not the same as a village man. Welly had known men who were still village boys after years of living in L.A.–Faatofi Jake was one, title or no title–indeed, most Samoans were. But there was a line there somewhere and Tanifa had crossed it. Maybe he had years ago and that's why he'd been incomprehensible as a child and left the village so easily and for so long.

But also, *Palapala* was a play on words. It was Tanifa's father's name and so used as Tanifa's second name, but it was also meant *rotten*. So, could Tanifa buy his way out of that? Buy his way to a title and, therefore, a good name? Officially, no. You had to have at least some genealogic basis for a claim to a title. Welly's knowledge of the multilayered webs of his family was not perfect, but he didn't think Tanifa had a serious claim. But why the hell would he even want to? Either you're in or you're out.

That's the palagi in you talking, said the Tapuafanua. Welly started and jerked around. He shivered. But, ghost or hallucination, the old man was right. Being Samoan meant being what you were supposed to be when you were supposed to be it. *Keep it together,* the palagis said. Samoans said, *Teo le va*, keep the betweens, keep it apart. Being mentally healthy meant knowing how to do that. Palagis called it being a sociopath. Or was that the final blow of European culture to Samoans, to foster sufficient individuality that a man might resent his inferior status *and* come to believe–almost certainly incorrectly in traditional Samoa–that he could do something about it.

Welly shifted his shoulders in a kind of cosmic shrug and wished desperately for about a gallon of beer. His mind only worked this way when he was sober, which is why he stayed drunk as much as he could. For himself, he had made whatever peace with his childhood had to be made and all he wanted was to get the hell out. Sa'ili, maybe because the cultural cards he held were so good, had made his peace from the inside. Welly couldn't imagine that third position, of wanting to get back in. But he guessed it might exist.

Welly and Tanifa stood together for a moment, a quiet island with the village eddying around them: hoards of expectant relatives and the endless tangles of family relationships hanging all but visibly in the air above them like ghosts. *Aitu,* Welly thought, ghosts. Like the boys who commit suicide on the mountain-sides, hanging themselves in their *lavalavas* because the family has nothing to offer them but a life-time of servitude and no reward.

Across the clipped grass of the village green, the tall palms lifted languidly to the sky, shading the old-style chief's *fale* with its polished wooden pillars and thatched roof at the edge of the glimmering white beach. Beyond, the grey-green mountains stepped down to the silver-gilt sea. They could hear the sounds of the ocean, breaking on the reef.

"Like I said," Tanifa said, as if to himself, "The aunties are real busy."

Across the intervening crowd, Welly saw Fa'atofi Jake standing momentarily alone, looking around as if hunting for someone. *That's who's busy,* he thought.

"Yeah," Welly said, lighting a cigarette and wondering what the likelihood was of finding anything usefully alcoholic anywhere in the village. "Maybe they see you as the answer to some heavy family politics." He grinned up at his cousin. *"O faiva 'aulelei."*

Tanifa looked puzzled. "Something *good.* Haven't spoken the language regularly in years. Find I miss a lot."

"Only a handsome man can do a thing well." They saw Sa'ili emerge from the chief's fale.

Tanifa said, "What about him?"

"Sa'ili? Well, you know. He always was the village good-boy."

Tanifa laughed again, "Yeah. He seems to have gotten over my beating the shit out of him when we were six. So I guess that's a good thing."

Welly said, "You beat the shit out of *me* when we were six, too."

Tanifa looked at him, his face remorseful. "Oh. Yeah? I don't remember that."

"Not to worry." He offered his cousin a cigarette. "You beat up everybody when we were six." They grinned companionably at each other. People were getting up now and moving into their ceremonial positions in the guest *fale* for the more formal parts of a great chief's funeral. Sorrier than ever that he hadn't gotten here later, Welly allowed Sa'ili to marshal Tanifa away to a prime spot and himself to drift back through the crowd toward the trees. Back among the less important *fales* and less important people–like kids and dogs–there might be a little peace.

He made use of Jake's outhouse and then wandered along the inland edge of the village, smoking and thinking. Or avoiding thinking. Without words, he knew what it was now, the panic. The forever being trapped here *on the landward side of things*. Except that the fucking land went straight up for two thousand feet and then came down two thousand feet and there was another goddamned strip of coconut groves and beach and then the ocean. At this particular point, it was exactly a mile and a half wide. If you started at a third of a mile up in the air.

He glanced back across the village. Tanifa and Sa'ili had disappeared into the crowd. Whether Tanifa was truly *keeping the betweens* or just doing the *palagi* thing of romanticizing a Stone Age culture once it poses no threat to you, he did look prosperous. Rich enough to buy the childhood he had never had. On the other hand, maybe rich enough to buy Welly the hell out of here.

Guiltily, Welly thought of Hutchinson. But he couldn't help Neil now. Ray Begley's death had cooked that goose. Welly would have done–had done–anything he could to save Neil. And Neil would have done the same for him, done anything he could to get Welly back to New Zealand. But now.... Around the end of a palagi-style house, he stumbled into a whispered conference between two young men. One of them looked vaguely familiar, but then, everyone in American Samoa *was* vaguely familiar to him. They ducked away quickly into the trees. *Shit*, he thought. You want to screw each other? Go ahead. You want to screw somebody else? Fine.

Ahead, he could here the steady rumble of the ocean on the reef. He was coming out of the trees at the upper end of the village, at the far end of the chief's *fale* where the Tapuafanua was laid out. Ann Maglynn was standing outside of the *fale* on the sand, gazing in at the old man's bier. She wasn't alone–you're never alone in Samoa–but the old ladies sitting around the laid-out corpse, them in their old white lace dresses and him with the white lace draped over him doubling as a fly-sheet, were one of a silent piece. Ann stepped up onto the stone foundation and knelt beside the body.

Welly was surprised. He didn't think of her as devout or as a hypocrite. A little disgusted, he walked over to stand beside her.

"I suppose it wouldn't do to touch the sheet," she said in a tiny voice.

"Do what the hell you want," he said. He caught the flash of one of the old ladies' eyes as she glared at him. She would tolerate any manner of foolishness from an ignorant *palagi*, particularly this Samoan-speaking *palagi* doctor who had come all the way over to Papasaa to honor the family and the Tapuafanua on multiple occasions. But even though the old lady didn't understand the English, she understood rudeness from a young man—from her point of view—who should know better.

In the same small voice, Ann said, "Do you see a bruise on his neck?"

"Bruise?"

"Maybe a hand's breadth above the clavicle. At the carotid."

"Maybe they tried to do CPR. Who knows? Besides, blood extravasates after death. You know that." One of the old dragons growled at him. He put his hand on Ann's shoulder. "Come on."

She looked up at him. "I want to look. Please."

"Worth your life," he said mockingly. But he flipped up the near corner of the lace. And for an instant, they both saw the livid mark. Ann had a lei of deep red plumeria blossoms around her neck that someone had given her. She took it off and laid it beside the old man's shoulder as if that had been the purpose of lifting the lace. Welly replaced the filmy shroud and smirked at the old toads. They smiled and nodded back. Ann rose to her feet and bowed to the old ladies. She and Welly backed off of the plinth and drifted back down the beach.

"Actually, it doesn't extravasate," she said. "Not unless there's been injury to the tissue. And only within a narrow range of time." The crowd around the guest *fale* had dispersed some. There was still the religious service to go and the interment, but there was more milling around now.

Some of the cars on the far side of the ford were gone for the long haul back to the leeward side.

"I've seen it," Welly said. "Dependent livido." Sa'ili and Tanifa were coming towards them across the green. Sa'ili had a fine mat tucked under one arm. Both men carried stacks of cartons. The cartons were about a foot square, and the men carried them as if they were heavy.

"Also known as hypostasis," Ann said.

Sa'ili stopped in front of them. "These are for you."

Ann smiled politely at him, as if he might have been addressing Welly, but went on intently: "But it's a different process. Besides, his neck couldn't have been lowest. It'd be his back or legs."

Sa'ili said, "May I present our cousin, Tanifa. He's been living in California, but he's staying in the village just now. This is Dr. Maglynn. She works at the hospital in Fagaalu."

"Yes," Ann said, smiling. "We met. When I was here yesterday." Tanifa set his boxes down and they shook hands. "We talked about windward village medical services."

Tanifa looked shyly at his cousins, as if he had been caught out in more misbehavior. "Just worried me there's no telephones. I mean, like, Jake's got a cell phone but it doesn't work 'cause he can't recharge it. What do you do if there's an emergency?"

"People pray a lot," Welly said. "Besides, even if you could call the hospital, neither of those ambulances could make it over here. And they sure as hell couldn't make it back loaded."

Tanifa's forehead creased. "Yeah, but there are other vehicles." He jerked his head toward the police chief's Suburban. "You could fit one of those as an ambulance."

Welly grunted. "If you've got the money. Not to mention the will to do it."

"Yeah. Well. I do as a matter of fact."

The four of them were silent for a moment. Finally, Sa'ili said to Ann, "These are for you." He was still holding his armful of boxes and the fine mat. "The senior orator wanted me to give you these. He thought you'd gone. The fine mat is not nearly so wonderful as the one you brought. But he wanted you to have something."

"Good thing he was here," Welly put in around the end of a fresh cigarette. "Even I'd'a'been embarrassed if the family hadn't acknowledged that fine mat."

Ann smiled. "I'm pleased to have it back where it belongs. Not to mention bagging eight cases of wahoo. I did physicals on twenty cannery employees and only scored two."

Welly snorted. "Tuna Pimp must have made a killing, all this wahoo."

Sa'ili looked pained.

Tanifa said, "Tuna Pimp?"

"Scruffy little Korean chap. You want wahoo gift like for a big wedding or something, he can always find it for you, even when there's been no run in a while."

Welly saw Ann's face had gone flat. "You know he died too last night?"

Welly didn't know that. "No shit? In the riot? Now that's too bad."

Before anyone could say anything else, Fa'atofi Jake appeared at Tanifa's elbow and cut him away again from their little group as smartly as a good sheep dog. He herded his prize off toward the chief's fale and the next stage of the funeral services.

"Little bastard's found himself a ringer to make the running for him," Welly said sourly.

Sa'ili looked at him. "You think that's it? I wouldn't have said he had the family to pull that off." He meant Tanifa's genealogy. Jake's was exceptionally good for the title he had ended up with. Which was the only reason he had it. "But then," Sa'ili went on, "I'm no orator." They watched the squat figure of Fa'atofi Jake and Tanifa's tall, graceful one stepping up into the chief's *fale*.

"Between the two of them," Welly said, "They just about make one good man."

"I wonder," Sa'ili said thoughtfully. Then he laughed as if a cloud had lifted. He said, "Are you headed back to Pago now? And could I get a ride? Sasa tells me he's promised my services to his pet Korean–something about searching the tuna boats for guns. Sounds dreadful but I do feel obliged to get back there. The aunties are going to get their knickers in a twist, but I'd be hard put to say who I'm more afraid of."

They laughed together, redistributed the boxes of wahoo and started across the ford. Suddenly, Tanifa was wading along with them, scooping Ann's boxes out of her arms, his face in a droll grimace. "I have *got* to get out of here. Even if it's just for the afternoon. Fifth sermon of the day and suddenly I'm remembering why I left all those years ago. Can you guys give me a lift over to the other side?"

"You're welcome to come," Ann said. "But I can't get you back...."

"Hell, you can walk back in less time than it takes to drive. If you're not too dignified."

8

On the advice of his stomach, Han put the investigation into the death of Dr. Begley on hold and took up the investigation into the death of the Tuna Pimp. Suddenly, he was hungry. He headed the jeep toward Pago. Before the road dropped into the main village, on the narrow strip of rock between the mountain and the bay, an assemblage of rickety structures hung out over the water. Collectively, these were Nozaki's, the dockside general store and snack stand run by the island's only Samoan-Japanese family. It was also the only source of anything like a noodle lunch.

Han watched the middle Nozaki daughter open a package of ramen, drop the noodles into a Styrofoam cup of water and stick the cup in a microwave which appeared to work. The power must be on. The glide of the girl's buttocks under her lavalava and the promise of the coppery skin where her neck rose from her tee-shirt made Han sweat. Or maybe it was just the climate. He looked through the open back door of the shop across the water to the tuna fleet and thought about guns. The girl handed him the cup of soup and a packet of throw-away chopsticks and smiled. He gripped the chopsticks, peeled off the paper, split apart the pair of little wooden sticks and rubbed them together, smoothing out the splinters, using the pain in his hands to focus. Somewhere in there, he thought, there was probably a metaphor about his marriage.

He looked over at the girl and said, "Beka, you know the guy they call the Tuna Pimp?"

"Sure. Everyone knows the Tuna Pimp."

A sharp voice called through the back door. "Whaddyou want, Mr. Policeman?" Old Mrs. Nozaki waddled through the back door wearing a muumuu a lot like the lavalava Welly had left him. She wasn't very tall, and she was just about as wide as she was tall. "You, girl, go unpack those boxes." With her russet skin and full cheeks, the old woman made Han think of an angry pumpkin.

"The Tuna Pimp died last night," Han said around his noodles. "I'm trying to find out what happened." Behind the old woman, he saw the girl's face spark with interest. The old lady turned. Her head jerked pointedly toward the back door. Suddenly demure, the girl left. The old woman turned back to Han.

"So? Tuna Pimp get himself killed, eh? Lotta people get beat-up last night. Some die. Happens. Stupid boys. Stupid fishermen. Stupid police. You want to know about Tuna Pimp, you go ask up t'e cannery. *Mauka*." *Toward the mountains*. In Samoan, it was part direction, part curse.

Han put money on the counter and got himself a soda from the cooler. "At least there aren't any guns around here," he said. "Big mess like last night not as bad as it could be."

The old lady grunted and looked him up and down. "Looks like you went get hit in t'head, same as everywhere else. People say Sapatu killed wit' a gun."

"He was shot. Died of a heart attack."

The old lady grunted again. "Same same."

"So who's got guns around here?"

"Who knows? Damned fishermen maybe. Stupid kids come back from L.A. like t'ey got no family. Or ones here too stupid to know t'e difference." She jerked her dumpy chin toward the bay. "You go ask over t'ere, to the cannery. *Mauka*." She turned and stomped out the back door. The boards of the dock creaked under her weight.

Starting up the jeep, he wondered how specific the old lady's *damned fishermen* was. The two Korean officials had come to Han as if they had a great secret. Or maybe they figured the smell of the shit was going to get to him eventually, so better they get there first.

Driving through Pago, the village was its usual self, a row of low buildings like Wild West main street. Pago had hit the skids a hundred years ago when the U.S. Navy blew in. Not much more could happen to it short of a typhoon. Today the same windows were broken—no more, no less—the same trash was in the street; the same people, standing around. There were, however, no stray Korean fishermen walking around. Even the Korean Cultural Center building at the other end of the village looked deserted. Han pulled up in front of the fleet office across from the cannery. Time to harass the fleet rep about the list of pistols. Han saw the activity as just that, harassment. He had no real hope that the fleet rep would actually be able to produce the list now or maybe ever.

But the man surprised him. For one thing, the fleet office air-conditioning worked. The fleet rep bounced up from behind his desk and bowed. The sweat patches under his arm pits did suggest that the AC hadn't been on that long.

"Ah, Lieutenant! Good to see you! I don't have the whole list yet, but I have been able to get some. The City of Pusan Police tried to register the fleet's pistols a couple of years ago....left-wing foolishness of course. But I was able to get a partial list for you." He was still trying for collegiality, in the brother-brother inflection.

Han's fraternal feelings were strictly for the City of Pusan PD. He held out his hand for the paper. It was a list in *han-gul*, the Korean alphabet, of the eight ships now in port in Pago with the names of the captains and executive officers. Four of the entries had *Makarov* written in the margin—a make of Russian pistol also made by the Chinese to the original specs—and a serial number. The Makarov 9mm would be Han's vote for the most popular pistol in the non-industrial world. But no way these were the originally issued pistols. They would have been picked up on the cheap in Hong Kong and Gaoshung and even the black market in Pusan itself.

Han folded the list and stuck it in his pocket. "Like they say in English, half a loaf is better than none. Thank-you. Please keep working on it." Han had spoken more Korean since coming to Samoa than he had in thirty years. The slip into uncle-to-nephew, advise and command form, had been automatic. He went on. "The chief of police suggested I take a man named Sa'ili Tua'ua with me to talk to the captains, as an observer. But I can't collect him until after he gets back from a funeral." Upside down, the watch on the fleet rep's wrist read five after three. "I'll check in with you again in about two hours. I want you to go with us." The fleet rep's head dipped subserviently. Han could tell he wasn't happy about going but also that he knew he didn't have much choice.

Han said, "What can you tell me about the man the locals call the Tuna Pimp?"

The fleet rep's face tightened. "You've seen him, sir. An agitator. He should be arrested."

"Fisherman?"

"Was once. Not for long. Too much like work. Grew up a street kid in Itaewon...." Itaewon was the commercial and red-light district near the U.S. Army base in central Seoul. "Learned a little American from the soldiers. Thought it made him a scholar." The word hung between them, ironic and derisive. A Brit, Han thought, would have said *a gentleman*. Han thought about the fleet rep's attainments, far beyond his grandparents' expectations.

"Any idea why he's called the Tuna Pimp?"

The fleet rep snorted. "I can guess. But I have other concerns than one worthless renegade."

And just to rub it in, Han said, "Is the Consul actually showing up from Honolulu tomorrow?"

"We are deeply honored by the Consul's attention to our plight."

Right Han thought. But he let the poor man off the hook and stepped back out into the warm, damp afternoon.

Leaving the jeep in front of the cannery office, he found a foot path behind the building that tracked up to the settlement on the mountain side. The fleet rep had confirmed Old Lady Nozaki's general directions to the Tuna Pimp's place but hadn't known any more. The clouds were thick now, catching in the high ridges and tumbling down the leeward sides of the mountains. The afternoon light had gone gray-green. Like mold, Han thought wryly, pushing through a screen of wet leaves like a gate at the top of the path.

In the opening beyond, a scattering of rough *fales* clung to the slope, half hidden in the trees and undergrowth and patches of giant taro. Han couldn't see any people. A scruffy brindle dog, thin as sticks, trotted through the clearing. The dog saw Han and shied off into the bushes.

The clearing was actually sort of a road with the little buildings oriented along it. The damp ground in front of the nearest one, a shack with closed sides, showed vehicle tracks, so it was accessible from somewhere to the left, in the direction of Pago. There were deep ruts, still partly filled with the morning rain, in the greasy red earth where the tires had nearly stuck.

The shack itself was a thin skin of rotting boards set vertically on a concrete foundation about ten feet square and roofed by a sheet of rusting, corrugated metal. A long shuttered opening like a shop-window made up most of the front wall. A door on the near side was shut. Han walked around to the other side. The door on this side was a few inches open.

He called out in Samoan. *"Talofa?"* The only answer was a sudden buzzing, like flies lifting off of something. He pulled another pair of plastic bags out of his hip pocket as makeshift gloves and pushed the door open. It scraped across the bare concrete floor. The flies lifted again.

The room was empty. Well, close enough. Han stepped up into the space and walked across the floor, his thong sandals slapping uncannily loudly against his feet. He opened the door on the other side for more light. Then he turned and hunkered down to one side, just looking, at the level that a Korean or a Samoan would have known that room.

A dirty, torn, Korean-style sleeping mat lay askew in a back corner, pushed partly up the wall and flopped over itself. The flies settled back aggressively around the mat, swarming onto broad pools of stain on its surface. The room didn't smell like shit or rotten fruit. There was only one other thing flies would be that interested in. But he waited, still looking.

A makeshift oil lamp lay on its side in the far front corner, a tiny juice can with a piece of a shoelace for a wick. A counter ran the length of the shuttered front window. On the floor under the counter lay a pair of long, narrow books like ledgers. And nothing else.

Han stood up. Other than the mat and the lamp, there was no sign that anyone lived here. It didn't look like a room you lived in. The only openings were the store-front window and the two doors. He walked over and looked at the frame of the door he had come through. The jamb was splintered. The lock had been forced. He pulled out the little camera and did what he could to document the scene.

Suddenly, a face was looking up through the doorway at him from outside. A little boy stood there, maybe four or five, a skinny kid with the dark skin and kinky hair of a Tongan or Fijian. A ragged tee-shirt made a shift that fell crookedly to the child's knees. Han hunkered down in the doorway, moving slowly, as if a wild thing had come out of the forest.

In Samoan, he said gently, "Tuna Pimp live here?"

The child scampered off down the track and disappeared.

Han turned back to the room. Still wearing his makeshift gloves, he picked up the two books lying on the floor and set them on the counter. The top one was a simple ledger, written in Korean, in *han-gul*, long lists of purchases and sales. There was no real description of items, just the Korean word for *cases* and the syllables *oo ah oo*, which didn't make any sense. The second book was more like a journal. On the inside cover, a name was written in *han-gul* and in Chinese characters: Kim Pil-whoon. Han smiled sourly, remembering the fleet rep's words: he thought it made him a scholar.

He heard the soft step outside and looked up. The torso of another child, a girl this time, was framed in the doorway. A couple of years older than the other kid, maybe seven or eight, she could have been his sister. Like him, most of what she was wearing was a tee shirt.

In Engish, she said, "Where Kim-pili?"

"Kim-pili?"

The girl nodded. "Everybody know Kim-pili. He help my sisters."

Kim-pili. So, at least in this community, the Tuna Pimp had his own name. "Yes?"

She nodded and then turned and nodded again, indicating the three *fales* farther down the track. "Fishermen come. Kim-pili see they not sick, not bad men."

"Is this...." Han wasn't quite sure how to ask this knowing child if her sisters turned their tricks here. The girl gazed around the empty room.

"Where Kim-pili boxes? Men with truck take boxes?"

"When," Han said, exquisitely gently, like putting a brush-stroke on paper, "Did the men come with the truck?" But she looked at Han incomprehendingly, as children will when asked about time. "Are your sisters home? Could I talk to them? How about your mother?"

She shook her head. "Go laundry." The island's only laundromat was at Nozaki's.

"Did you see the men with the truck?"

The girl shook her head again. "My sisters say, men come with truck to Kim-pili house, so they must be got lots of money." She looked around the room again, uneasily this time, as if she had remembered something that frightened her. But before Han could say anything more, she too ran off down the track and disappeared into the forest.

Standing up, he saw one more thing. Tucked up in a corner, in the space made by a corner post and one of the two-by-fours holding up the sheet-metal roof, was a tiny package of black plastic. Reaching up, he eased it out of its hiding place.

The plastic was a shred of garbage bag. In it were a matchbox containing three live jacketed hollow-point 9 millimeter cartridges.

He heard the hiss of tropical rain marching down the mountainside. *Damn!*

Setting the box carefully on the floor, he ran outside. But too late. Even if there had been something he could have pulled over the tracks in the dirt, they were gone already. Whatever trace of the truck that had nearly gotten stuck there had been erased by the pounding of water from the sky. Han stood looking at the blank red gash in the earth. He thought: get out of the rain, stupid.

Back in the shack, he went through it like a vacuum-cleaner, even sweeping the dirt on the floor into one plastic bag and picking little bits of crud off the walls into others. And was rewarded for his diligence with a single spent shell that had fallen between the foot of a loosened wall board and the edge of the foundation.

Han pried it out of its hiding place, bagged, sealed, and labeled it as if it were a twenty-carat diamond. Smiling to himself, he thought: the diamond would be less fragile. He slid the Tuna Pimp's ledgers into one of the plastic bags and the tin can lamp into the other, sealing and labeling each one in its turn, taking notes in the tiny notebook he kept in another pocket. He liked this work, though technicians did most of it now in the real world. This was the real investigation. Of course, he had no witnesses. But also no radios, no sirens, no city sounds, no noisy colleagues covering up their fear and their ignorance with bad jokes and expletives, none of his own increasing irritation as they blundered around disturbing his concentration and causing more damage to the scene than they illuminated. So what was better, the legal letter of probity or the best possible exploration of the scene? He smiled to himself. Depends on how well his did his job.

He disturbed the flies again and folded up the mat. No maggots had hatched yet. What did that mean about timing: eight hours? twelve hours? How much could you pin on a fly's life cycle?

A thin stream of clear, pinky-yellow fluid trickled out of one corner of the mat and spattered onto the floor. He whipped out another small plastic bag and was able to catch maybe a couple of tablespoons of the dribble. With great care, he sealed the first bag, slid another bag over it and sealed that, then carried the whole thing like an eggshell down to the jeep and nested it in the jeep's mug holder.

Back up at Kim's shack, he slid the blood-stained sleeping mat—the only thing that smells like blood is blood—into a big black garbage bag and sealed and labeled it like the others. Then he went outside and worked around the outside of the building. He got soaking wet and he didn't find anything. And you could, he thought, stand in either of those doorways and heave something—like a gun or a handful of spent shells—off into the jungle and lose it for eternity.

He had to get going. But he left the last of his specimen bags in the doorway to the shack and followed the track along into the forest in the direction the two kids had run off.

The first of the small *fales* was empty. But beyond the second one, he saw of flash of alien color in the universal green.

"*Talofa?*" A rustle came from the patch of giant taro behind the second *fale*. The head of the little girl Han had talked to poked up among the broad leaves like a flower. She grinned at him, pushed out through the leaves, and ran off toward the third *fale*. Han followed.

Beside the track, a thin pipe had been run up from somewhere in the village below. The last few feet of it rose up like a cobra to a spigot. An older woman stood there, filling a bucket with water. The girl called to her. She finished with her bucket and carried it back to the *fale*, smiling broadly. Han guessed this little enclave at least saw Koreans as a positive part of their economy.

He introduced himself in Samoan. The woman smiled and nodded again. Han thought, she doesn't understand a word I said. But his Samoan wasn't going to take him much farther. About the best he could manage was "What do Kim-pili?"

The little girl touched the woman's arm. The woman looked down, and the little girl spoke quickly to her. The woman nodded.

"I say," the little girl said shyly, "You come about Kim-pili boxes all gone." Han nodded.

The woman's face shifted openly from bland welcome to interest, surprise, concern. She began describing something, gesturing with one hand along the track through the forest. Han caught what was probably the word for *men*, but the woman's mix of Samoan and Tongan was beyond him. She stopped talking and looked expectantly at Han. Han looked at the little girl.

The little girl had half hidden herself now behind the woman, shifting into the expected role of an island child: seen but not heard and maybe not even seen, certainly not at the center of adult conversations. But her bright black eyes sparkled.

"She say: men in truck take all Kim-pili boxes."

Han had fallen into this linguistic trap before.

"Did she *see* the boxes in the truck?" He gestured, first to his eyes and then drawing out an imaginary box, putting it down on an imaginary tailgate.

The little girl nodded enthusiastically. "She say 'men in truck take Kim-pili boxes'."

Right Han thought. But he had to admit that the problem might not just be his own ignorance of Samoan. It was possible that the language itself didn't distinguish *must have done* from *did*.

He tried another tack.

"Did she know the men?"

The little girl stared at him for a moment, and he wondered if he had gone beyond her English. But she spoke to the woman, and the woman shook her head.

"No."

He thought about trying to ask her if she would know them if she saw them again, but he couldn't come up with how to even begin. Much less ask about timing. *Never try this without a translator. Never.* He thought of

Welly Tuiasosopo but that was not a comfort at the moment. He wondered what time it was. Time to get off of this wet mountain and find Sa'ili Tua'ua, the Chief of Police's designated stand-in for searching tuna boats.

He thanked the woman, got a grin from the little girl as some kind of reward for something, collected the last of the bags from the Tuna Pimp's shack, and slid down the muddy track to the jeep. On the edges of Pago, he found what he thought might be the road up to the Tongan settlement he had just left, a narrow track headed slant-wise up the mountainside. Two young women walking side by side, with equivalent globes of curly black hair, their buttocks shifting under tightly wrapped lavalavas in identical rhythm, were just disappearing into the foliage. Each carried a soft bundle balanced on one shoulder. Han hailed them.

They turned with identical grins of welcome. They were the same Tongan mix as the family on the mountainside. They were also identical twins.

Han set his brain down very carefully on one side of his being and his body down on the other. Then he said, "What happened to the Tuna Pimp's...." He remembered their name for him. "...Kim-pili's boxes?"

The two young women looked at each other and giggled just like their little sister. "Men in truck," said one. "Take Kim-pili boxes," said the other.

A few minutes later, climbing back into the jeep and heading for the station, Han was fairly sure that, about the time of the riot, the girls had seen two men in a pickup truck of unknown make and color drive up the track toward the Tuna Pimp's shack. They had heard shots. But they weren't sure—or he hadn't gotten the question right—the direction the shots had come from. Han thought about the twin whores. Throw-away people in more than one culture. But to those men off of the tuna boats, with the Tuna Pimp's mediation, they must have been the most toasty brown warm and soft, delicious and exotic flavors any of those used and exhausted men ever could have dreamed of.

Normally, he hated wet clammy clothes.

And he still didn't know what was in those damned boxes.

9

Back in his office, Han pulled his last set of dry clothes out of the filing cabinet. There wasn't a shirt; he couldn't remember why. He hadn't solved all of the housekeeping problems his wife's departure had left, but laundry he could usually deal with. Or at least Old Lady Nozaki dealt with it if he dropped it off with her a couple of times a week. He hefted the shirt Welly had loaned him at the hospital. It wasn't part of the uniform but it was clean and dry and at least it wasn't purple. He pulled it on, fishing in the breast pocked for whatever detritus Welly had left there.

The matchbook from the hotel.

It lay in his hand like a tiny, bright bird. Or an egg, he thought, that he should have hatched hours ago. But Welly Tuiasosopo, like every other damned body he needed right now, was at some old man's funeral on the other side of the island. So he put the matchbook back in the pocket and one more set of feelings on hold and went back to work.

He couldn't store the Tuna Pimp's bloody sleeping mat in his office. For one thing, he didn't have room for it. For another, it had to be in a cooler if he could find one big enough and dependable enough. Which let out anything at the police station. He climbed back in the jeep and headed for the hospital. Having your only pathology support also a potential suspect was a stupid damned situation. At least Hutchinson was a suspect–if he was a suspect–for a different murder. And he had said he might be getting a pathologist on Sunday's plane from Honolulu. Of course, like a new windshield for the jeep, you believed it when you opened the box.

He thought about Hutchinson. To what extent *was* Hutchinson a suspect any more? Less and less. His position taken front and center by Welly Tuiasosopo. Han turned right off the shore road up the dirt lane toward the hospital, the jeep's rear wheels skittering on the sand.

He found Hutchinson in the Emergency Room. Inspecting Han's wounds and grunting non-committally, the doctor said, "Ann usually does this shift. But she wanted to go to the old man's funeral, so we switched. Whaddya need?" Han told him about the sleeping mat and the fluid. "Sure," Hutchinson said. "Just pop it in the cooler with the stiffs you're sending to Honolulu."

Another of the things that was supposed to have happened in the last few hours was the police guard on the hospital morgue. That didn't altogether solve the problem of the Samoan tendency to accept the order of any person of superior rank over a theoretical concept like *guarding*. Han fetched his fluid sample and the bagged mat from the jeep. He was rewarded by finding John-son-of-John, one of his assistants from this morning, sitting outside the morgue door snacking on a large place of taro and bananas. John greeted them cheerfully, stowed the mat as instructed, and gave every sign of the best in alert young police officers. Han hoped, anyway. He followed Hutchinson off through the hospital.

Hutchinson was saying, "As for your sample there, any pathologist should be able to do that. Actually, so should I. If I can remember what I'm doing. Want to give it a try?"

It isn't for nothing that the Lord's Prayer mentions temptation. In normal forensic procedure, what Han was doing was crazy. But this wasn't normal forensic procedure. This was Samoa.

"Just give me something to go on. I'll be shipping the mat off to Honolulu tomorrow all right and proper. But I'm in a whole different ball game if this is pigs or chickens."

Hutchinson pushed through a door marked *Laboratory*. A Samoan youth in the usual brightly printed shirt and dark lavalava and the less usual latex gloves, grinned at them but kept on with what he was doing on a far counter amid a clutter of notebooks and racks and tiny containers.

"Glove up," Hutchinson said. "Double glove, even. You're extra vulnerable to anything blood borne with your hands like that." Han thought about the Tuna Pimp's shack. "Here, use Loa's, they're triple X's." The Samoan youth smiled again and passed over a box of latex gloves.

Hutchinson took the bagged fluid and held it up to the light. "You think this might be the guy in the tank? The Korean who was shot?"

Han nodded. "Possibly."

"Well, if it's human blood, I may be able to do you one better. We could try to type and cross-match it with the blood of the guy in the tank. I can't prove it's the *same* blood for you, but it gets you one step closer."

"Go for it." Han broke the seal on each bag and wrote the time and initialed each cut seal. He was out on another legal tightrope. But like most people doing something stupid, he told himself he didn't have a choice. He did note each action in his book as if careful documentation might balance out tampering with evidence in the company of a suspect. They did compromise on Hutchinson's peculiar legal status by getting the Samoan kid to initial as witness. Hutchinson decanted the fluid carefully into a graduated cylinder. Han dutifully noted the exact amount of fluid.

"All right if I dilute it a little?"

"Do what you have to. Honolulu'll get more than they need out of the mat itself."

Hutchinson went through the lab pulling out tiny beakers and a test tube rack, a handful of clean, empty test tubes, pipettes, a jug of sterile normal saline, laying them all out neatly on the lab bench in front of him. Han thought of the *cha-no-yu*, the Japanese tea ceremony.

First, Hutchinson diluted the thick fluid with saline until there was enough to half fill five of the test tubes. He dropped one of the test tubes into a small centrifuge and spun the dial. Pulling over lab stools for himself and Han, he said, "Probably enough to manage without diluting but gives us a little more to play with."

When the spin time was done, or maybe just when he got impatient with it, Hutchinson stopped the centrifuge and pulled out their tube. The fluid was clearer now, and a tiny red pellet had formed in the bottom of the tube.

"Red blood cells." He poured out most of the fluid, flicked the tube briefly to resuspend the cells in the remaining few drops of saline, then tapped this out onto a clean slide and slipped it under a microscope.

"Well," Hutchinson said, eyes still applied to the scope, "It isn't chickens. Or any other bird." He sat back and motioned Han in to look. As Han struggled to orient his brain to an image which seemed across the room and was in fact only a few inches from his nose, Hutchinson said, "As you probably know from your forensic training, birds have nucleated red cells, mammals don't."

Gazing at the array of minute pink shapes on the slide, Han said slowly, "So these are a mammal's red blood cells? But we could still be talking pigs?"

"Ah," said Hutchinson as Han looked up. "But. We have other tricks." From the refrigerator, he took four small rubber-stoppered bottles. "Sera for typing and cross-matching human blood." He pulled over the rack with the test tubes of diluted blood fluid. "If we get a response, the blood is human." He put a few drops of one of the test sera in the first tube. Nothing happened. Same with the second test tube and the second serum. Hutchinson shrugged and picked up the third test serum. "No response, we don't know what we've got."

In the third test tube, with the addition of the serum, tiny specks appeared. "Bingo," Hutchinson said. "Type A." He added a few drops of the last test serum to one of the tubes that hadn't reacted. The tiny specks appeared. "Rhesus positive. Not the Word of God, but close enough: human blood, A positive."

Han said, "The most common blood type in north Asians is A positive."

"'S what I've heard," Hutchinson said, nodding. "Want to try your man in the cooler?"

"You bet."

Han hadn't thought about how they would get the Tuna Pimp's blood, so watching Hutchinson jam a hollow four inch spike on the end of a twenty cc syringe up under the dead man's ribs toward his heart was a little startling. But the maneuver produced another tablespoon or so of red fluid. And, back in the lab, the test sera produced the same pattern as with the fluid from the sleeping mat from the dead man's shack.

"Like I said," Hutchinson said when they were done. "I can't tell you the blood's the same." He grinned again. "But if they were two different people, I could use either of their blood to transfuse the other."

At the end of the hospital drive, in the tiny village of Fagaalu, Han turned the jeep left, back toward Utulei. He thought, what were the chances, even with the unexpected potential excess of hand guns from the tuna fleet, that the death of the Tuna Pimp and the death of Police Lieutenant Sapatu were not connected? But why kill one Korean and one Samoan? Where, for instance, in both of those deeply traditional societies, did who the individual was leave off and who he was in his culture take up? Where did the balance tip when the fulcrum was murder? For Sapatu, the answer seemed straightforward enough. On the night of the riot, he had done exactly what his profession and his culture expected of him and had, in the end, died for it. Being personally a sonofabitch was probably irrelevant. Though, like about cops in the States, most Samoans seemed to assume a talking chief was a sonofabitch by definition. As for the Tuna Pimp....Han thought about the journals now locked in his filing cabinet. One more thing that was just going to have to wait.

Driving sedately through Utulei, as if a switch had turned in his head, he began thinking about Begley. Of the three men who had died that night...no, he told himself, seven, counting the four drowned Koreans...Begley's death seemed the most likely to be connected with who he was as an individual. Something more specific than being the victim of a violent robbery (of *what?* What was taken from the Tuna Pimp's shack?) or a line-of-duty casualty of a riot. But that meant a white man's murder on white men's terms and a politically connected white man at that. Was that why he, Han, had so fucking little interest in solving it?

The thought startled him so that he pulled sharply off onto the shoulder of the road overlooking the bay and turned off the jeep's engine. The sound of the waves rattling through the lava boulders came up to him. No, he thought, if he had one over-riding belief it was that all assholes are created equal and all dead people are dead. And if somebody made them dead on purpose, you figure that out on a sufficiently objective basis that even a moderately dim prosecutor can't fail to make a case. Beyond that, justice may well be something else, but that's God's business, not yours.

I attend the living the doctor had said to him. *And you attend the dead.* He turned and walked slowly up the shoulder of the road toward the hotel. *I don't have time for this.* He snorted softly. There's a palagi thought for you. There's always time in Samoa. No time like the present. Time or money. He yawned and, stepping, fell off the edge of the broken pavement.

The raw edge was only a couple of inches, but it sandpapered the inside of his foot. Standing stork-like and cursing, he thought, *damn*, practically the only good skin I've got left. He looked up the road. At intervals down the slope, the sandy soil had been washed away from the asphalt, leaving these stony edges. He couldn't imagine doing this in the dark. Much less drunk. Was that it? Had Begley just stumbled off one of these edges and toppled himself down the slope? Maybe. But.

It just wasn't that far. Not that you couldn't do a lot of damage to yourself. The state of Begley's body certainly suggested that he had made that tumble. But unless he had the kind of paper-thin skull that defense attorneys and mystery writers mostly imagine possible, Han couldn't see how Begley could have achieved that squashed melon look to the back of his skull by just rolling down the slope. Even without the suggestive evidence of the cinder blocks by the road and the piece of block his constables, Jim and John, had found.

What about bleeding? One thing Han did know about bad liver disease was that it could turn you into a bleeder. Would that have been enough to turn an unpleasant but survivable fall into a fatal one? But that still didn't explain the skull.

And so, he couldn't have just been pushed either. Not and be sure that your victim wouldn't survive. No, someone had come up behind him and hit him hard. And if it wasn't with that piece of cinder block they had found, it was with something a lot like it. Which, he thought, at a number of levels probably lets out Gloriana or Maria Theresa.

Watching both where he put his feet and the shoulder of the road, he continued up toward the hotel. Like a lot of things in Samoa, logic said that he should be doing something else. Like finding Welly Tuiasosopo and asking him where the hell he went after roughing up Ray Begley and why the hell he hadn't told Han about any of it. He glanced down at his breast pocket. Or was that what the matchbook was supposed to be? Some kind of reminder? Or just the fatal giveaway?

Damn. He needed time. He needed time and investigators. He needed all that and a forensics lab and a night's sleep and a body that didn't feel like hamburger left out of the refrigerator too long. Damned palangi murder, damned palagis: like babies, they demanded attention.

Baby. The thought broadsided him. His daughter. Gone now with her mother to grow up to be a Japanese. To despise her father as a Korean and herself as a female. Or to grow up to be a new age American, despising her father as inadequate, *absent* was the buzz-word. As if he'd had any choice in it. Not to mention despising him as a cop.

Furious, he stomped back down to the jeep and drove off to Fagatogo to find the police chief's pet official Samoan.

10

Half an hour later, when he finally found Sa'ili Tua'ua's house, Han was still irritated. He pulled up behind the blue Public Health jeep, wondering if it marked some kind of health care crisis late on a Saturday afternoon or just misuse of American Samoa Government property.

The house sat up on a little hill, in but somehow above and separate from the village, under tall trees. It was a mix of palagi and Samoan, closed private rooms in back but with a deep, fale-like porch that wrapped the three sides toward the sea. Four figures sat Samoan-style on mats on the far side. Two of them rose to meet him. Even in silhouette, he recognized Welly Tuiasosopo.

Welly grinned at him. "Y'here to arrest me, mate?"

"Maybe," Han said. The man who had come out with Welly wore a crisp white shirt and tailored white with-pockets lavalava and introduced himself as Sa'ili Tua'ua.

Welly's voice pushed in. "You got to the hotel, yeah? Talked to the fellas in the bar? Bout my little dust-up with Ray?" Anybody else, Han thought, would have groveled, knowing they'd been caught. Welly was quizzing him, making sure he'd done his job right. Sa'ili listened, perhaps guarding the dignity of his house, perhaps just curious.

Violating polite norms in every culture he could think of–not to mention police interrogation procedure–Han said, "So where'd you go afterward? Follow him out into the dark? Follow him down the road?"

"No. Went and played poker with the mates from New Zealand. In their room."

"What time?"

"I don't know. Bartender didn't want me back. I knew that. Fellas came out, invited me to play. Bout that time, the lights went out. We stood around in the lobby for a few minutes 'til the generator came on. Then went out to their fale."

"How long did you play?"

Welly shrugged. "Coupla hours." He grinned. "Went through a bottle of real good scotch. I was walkin down the road to Fagatogo when the ambulance went by. When it came back, they musta recognized me, cause they pulled over and picked me up. Musta thought they were gonna need me." His grin got wider. "That was the one you were in. But I don't think you remember."

"You're right. I don't. In the bar: did Begley threaten you?"

Welly's eyebrows drew together. "Threaten me? Nah. Just mouthin off. He does that. He didn't care about me. It was Neil pissed him off." He stopped abruptly, as if even he knew he shouldn't have said that. "Besides, I didn't even really hit him. Just, stumbled into him, like. Though, all that belly hanging out, it was a real temptation."

"Who saw you and Begley? Anybody besides the bartender and the bouncer?"

The eyebrows shot up. "Everybody. The mates I was with, three fellas. Then a whole bunch of 'em back in the corner. Not all white skin whites but palagis by the look of their clothes. Musta been five or six of them back there."

"Bartender said this happened out in the hall by the restrooms."

"*That* did. Thought you meant the whole thing. Look, you just need to talk to the kiwis. They'll verify it. Or d'you already do that and you're just havin' me on?" He grinned up at Han.

Han shook his head. "They all hopped to Apia this morning."

Welly grunted. "That's right. They're all on their way to some big computer conference in Auckland. Saving the third world for computers. Or computers for the third world. Or something." He turned to grin at the other two people, a man and a woman, who had been sitting on the porch and who had risen now and were coming out to join them.

The man was introduced to Han as yet another cousin. Dressed in western clothes, he looked like one more American Samoa Government employee, except with maybe a little less gut. The woman was the doctor, Ann Maglynn. Except that she was wearing an ankle-length dress of pale blue that slid over her body like water. She was smiling at him. "How are you doing, Lieutenant? I probably should never have let you out of the hospital."

"I'm okay," he said shortly. Because now he had a problem. Being horny was not, in itself, a problem. You deal with it like any rambunctious animal—a big dog or a young horse. But unlike the diamond studded bimbo on Penicillin Row or the cheerful Tongan whores or even pretty little Beka Nozaki, Ann Maglynn had a mind that met you square on as well as a body you wanted for itself. But like everything else today, it was all just going to have to take a number and wait in line.

More abruptly than was probably necessary, he turned to Sa'ili Tua'ua. "Did the chief explain what this was about?" Of course, in Samoa, *chief* might be damn near anybody. On the other hand, there was only one *the* chief.

"Something about searching the tuna boats for guns?" the big man said serenely.

Welly put in, "Becoming quite an expert on guns, our Sa'ili."

Sa'ili looked pained. The doctor touched his arm lightly and said something in Samoan. In good Samoan fashion, the tall man's face switched from distress at the socially inappropriate behavior of a family member to bidding ceremonial farewell to a guest. The doctor shook hands with him and with the other cousin.

"Please," she said to them, as if concluding a conversation that had been going on for some time. "If you think you can get your aunts to release the Tapuafanua's leprosy papers to me, I'd...." She shook her head as if trying to find words. "...I'd mortgage my soul for a chance to try to get them into print. At least to be able to review them." They went another round of cordialities, and then she climbed in the blue jeep and drove away.

"What about guns?" Han said sharply.

"Got one of his own now," Welly said cheerfully.

"From *you*," Sa'ili said, as if his good breeding had finally reached its limits. "And I wish you'd stop telling everybody about it as if it *were* mine." Han noticed that they squabbled in English. Was that to include the third man or keep him out?

"Show me," Han said. The three Samoans looked at him, their faces suddenly blank. He wasn't in uniform. He and Welly knew each other, and, beyond being friends, respected each other as technocrats. But the other two had no intrinsic reason to do a damned thing he asked them to.

"Of course," Sa'ili said, and led them into the back of the house. From a drawer in a cabinet, he pulled a compact pistol with the unmistakable swoop-throated barrel-tip of a Makarov 9mm.

Han pulled the last of his plastic bags out of his hip pocket. A pistol isn't a particularly useful source of fingerprints, but there was no point in going out of his way to make things worse. Locating the serial number, he unfolded the fleet rep's list of the fleet captains and their pistols.

According to the fleet rep's notes, the pistol in Han's hand was registered to Captain Hong Jong-wook of the *Pusan Morning*.

Han looked at Welly and Sa'ili. "Where did you get this?" The extra cousin stood by, polite and slightly bored, like a friend of the family at a children's play.

Sa'ili looked sternly at Welly. Welly shrugged. "Took it off a kid this morning."

"At the hospital? One of the fishermen?"

"Nah. Kid was beating up a whore behind the Gooney Bird." The Frigate Bird was the sleaziest of the four saloons in Fagatogo. Which was saying something.

"Samoan?"

"The kid or the whore?" Welly grinned. Han didn't say anything. He needn't have asked. The race of the whore didn't matter, and no Asian with a will to live went near the Frigate.

"What time this morning?"

Welly looked at Sa'ili. "Just before I came up here. About dawn."

Sa'ili said, "About six-fifteen."

"Did you recognize the kid? Would you know him if you saw him again?"

Welly was shaking his head. "Just a kid. You know." He shrugged. "Untitled men." Then he grinned again. "But he will have bruised testicles."

Han snorted. "I expect. And in case you didn't notice, he's got yours in his untitled teeth."

Welly's eyes glittered up at Han. "You think this's the gun shot Sapatu?"

"Maybe. Or killed the Tuna Pimp. Or both."

Welly shook his head. "Damn. Ann told us about that. You know: I can see shooting Sapatu, but I sure wouldn't kill the Tuna Pimp."

Han snorted again. "And just for the record, you want to tell me again that you were walking alone down a dark road toward Pago when Sapatu was shot?"

"No," Welly said, instructing a favorite but slightly slow child. "I was playing poker probably. 'Cause Sapatu was in that ambulance with you when they picked me up by the governor's driveway. That's not even Fagatogo yet, much less Pago.

"The Chief of Police told me," Sa'ili put in. "That Sapatu was shot during the riot." Han noticed that unlike Leon Fischer, the attorney general, Sa'ili chose to emphasize the Chief's status by using his title–or at least the title that Han would know him by–rather than his own status by calling the chief by his nickname, Sasa.

Han nodded. "Just before midnight."

"The Governor's reception was breaking up about then," Sa'ili said.

Han thought about his other murder. "Did you know Ray Begley?"

"Gloriana's husband? Yes, of course. Socially, anyway. One had to."

"Was he at the reception?"

"No. Though expected, I would have said." The big man smiled gently. "Gloriana has her 'with Ray' persona and her 'not with Ray' persona. 'With Ray' is very California mafioso–lots of hair do, lots of make-up, lots of slinky dress. 'Without Ray' is dignified Samoan matron–white linen, often a hat. Last night was definitely 'with Ray'. Though I never saw him." Han remembered the electric blue dress: spaghetti straps, skirt slit to the thighs. But he wondered about this man whose exterior was so smoothly upper class Samoan and who had just shown Han a laser eye for telling behavior.

"Did she leave before you or after?"

"After."

"How about the attorney general, Leon Fischer?"

"He was still there. Both Gloriana and Leon were there when I left just after twelve."

The questions were just routine, just trying to stay awake.

"What happened when the lights went out? You notice anybody leave?"

Sa'ili laughed. "The lights never really went out. One suspects the governor of being prepared: lots of romantic hurricane lanterns on the lanai. I did see Professor Osgood and his wife slip out–they haven't much patience with that sort of thing and they'd done their bit for the College."

"What did you mean by 'California mafioso'?"

Sa'ili hesitated. Not Welly. The little surgeon snorted.

"That's Ray. They always said he had some nasty connections back there in L.A."

"Who? Who said?"

Welly shrugged. "Call your police brah's in L.A. They'll find out for you."

I already have, Han thought. He looked at Welly carefully and then at Sa'ili. "I apologize for taking up your time, sir." He noticed that the formality didn't surprise the tall Samoan. Han liked that about Samoans, though he knew it drove palagis crazy. At least the ones who couldn't tell the difference between inconsistency and subtlety. He got out his roll of tape, sealed and labeled the bag with the pistol. "You've already given me most of what I'm looking for."

"A gun," Sa'ili said, "That would not be there when the man was asked to produce it. But you must...be sure that's the only one...."

"Uh," said Welly. "Maybe we should go find that whore.

11

Han had a very strong will to live, but he was also well enough known in his professional capacity at the Frigate not to need a baby-sitter. But in the way of titled Samoans, who can't believe that anything to do with the welfare of the community might not be any of their business, Sa'ili swung himself regally into the passenger seat of Han's jeep. Han did need Welly to ID the girl if they could find her. He did not need the extra cousin.

"What the hell," said Welly. He opened the back of the jeep, and he and the extra cousin clambered into the back. "This is Samoa. You can always use a couple of extra hands in a fight."

"Jesus," Han said. It sure as hell wasn't s.o.p., but it was probably the local equivalent of a couple of back-up units. He eased the clutch, and the jeep limped down the rough stone track.

Han pulled up in front of the Frigate. Three bar girls sitting on the curb scattered like pigeons.

"There she goes!" Welly burst out of the back of the jeep like an excited hound. He ran up across the narrow front veranda, slipped on something and disappeared off the far end. The others followed more cautiously. The little surgeon was righting himself slowly on the cobblestones, blood trickling from a scrape on his forehead. He grinned at Han and held up his unscathed hands.

"S'okay," he said. "Surgeon's hands are his most important part...."

"Not," said Sa'ili as he and Han hauled Welly to his feet. "To be confused with his head."

Mopping that organ with his cousin's clean white handkerchief, Welly nodded to a side entrance of the Frigate, one long step up into an open doorway. "She's in there."

And what's the chance, Han thought as they heaved themselves through the doorway, that she's also not just right out the other side.

But he hadn't allowed for the power of Sa'ili's presense—or even, perhaps, his own. The inside of the Frigate stank of rotting fruit, spilled beer, and women. The only light came from a Coleman lantern hanging over the bar. The power must be out. Or maybe they just didn't pay their bills. The lantern hissed in the sudden silence. The four of them pretty much filled the place.

The bartender was a woman today, his two-piece post-missionary gown a clean bright hibiscus flower print. Like a beaten dog, one of the girls crouched at his feet. Welly reached familiarly behind the bar and fished what was perhaps the only ice-cube in the place—possibly on the island—out of the refrigerator and dabbed his forehead with it. The bartender said something to Sa'ili who looked at Welly.

Welly nodded. "S her. They call her Pualeai."

You could translate that, Han knew, as *no flower*. But it also might just be a name. In the tiny human silence that followed under the hissing lantern, Han felt another linguistic black hole coming on, like they say people feel seizures before they start. But at least four of the six people present spoke workable English.

To the bartender, Han said, "Welly says this girl was being beaten up by one of her tricks this morning. He says he took a gun off the kid and ran him off. Can she verify that?"

The bartender's voice rumbled at the girl at his feet in the strict tones of a pastor's wife scolding the Sunday school. There was another hissing silence. Then the girl spoke in a small voice.

"*Ioe.*" Yes. Not only *yes* but polite yes, as to a chief.

Sa'ili began speaking to the girl. His voice was like nothing Han had ever heard in Samoan: kindly, comforting. He saw the girl's face flick in surprise, though she still couldn't quite bring herself to look all the way up at the tall man's face. There was another small silence. Then she answered him in the same tiny voice.

"She says," Sa'ili said to Han, "That she didn't know his name or his village, though she has seen him here before a few times."

"Western Samoa girl," said the bartender. "Not been here long."

Sa'ili went on. "He told her his village was the Army."

Welly snorted. "Not with that hair. Not recently anyway."

The bartender spoke down sharply to the girl, one hand making a gesture like wavy hair to the shoulders. The girl said *yes* again, though less politely.

The bartender nodded. "Useless shit name Uli. Family from Matagituai. But t' mother moved to Matagi-fou long time ago, took t' kids. None of 'em any good." The bartender had, Han knew, some of the gifts of a low-life talking chief. He was also able to tell them that the kid had turned up about sunset with more money and more attitude than usual. But he hadn't caused any particular trouble and had come and gone several time through the evening, though with whom and at what times, in the ebb and flow of people, the bartender couldn't say.

"What about during the riot?"

The bartender looked at Han and shrugged. "When begins, we don't know not'ing was happenin'. Later...." He grinned. "Every body go pick up bodies."

"OK. The fishermen had their meeting starting about eleven. Do you think he was here then?"

"Maybe." The bartender's head was nodding. So maybe a little more yes than maybe. "Eleven-thirty?"

"Maybe." This time, the man's shoulder moved. So maybe a little more no than maybe. From the floor, the girl murmured something. The bartender said, "She says, he leave befo'. He's angry because she go wit' another customer." He nodded. "Is true. I have to warn him."

"And he didn't come back again?"

"Oh, yes. Mebbe...after midnight. One o'clock, maybe, not too long before closing. Everybody come back and drink a little bit for being so good, rescue fishermen, takin' to hospital."

"So Uli was here between one and two this morning? Any idea where he went after that?"

The bartender shrugged and shook his head, presumably a definite no. With a little more coaxing from Sa'ili and scolding from the bartender, the girl told them that she had not seen Uli again until he had tackled her in the alley just before dawn. He had shoved the gun into her mouth, offering her a choice of what she wanted shoved where. What Welly had come in on was her just managing to convince him to move into the crib instead of taking her on the cobblestones.

Han said, "Did Uli have a gun when he was here in the bar? Any time he was here. Before or after the riot. Anything about him—the way he looked, anything he said? I mean," he looked at Sa'ili. "It's not like people have enough clothes on to hide things."

As if for emphasis, Sa'ili translated the question into Samoan.

The bartender glanced down at the girl but his shrug seemed to be the answer for both of them. "Not before. After: too busy to notice."

With nightfall and curiosity, people were drifting into the bar. Han and Sa'ili talked to all of them. Most of them had been there the night before. The ones who knew Uli agreed that he was a bad lot, a young man outside of the control of a chief. *Acts like he has no family* was the verdict. And coming from the patrons of the Frigate, that was an indictment. The ones who had noticed, confirmed the bartender's impression of Uli's comings and goings and that he had been by himself. One older man with a mass of woolly hair who looked like he might be some connection to the Tongan family up behind the fleet office said, "He have boy wit' him. Stay behind in truck."

Han said, "Truck."

The man nodded. "Yeah, get fancy pick-up. Parked up t' street wit' a kid in it."

"A kid? A child?"

"Oh, no." This from someone else whose memory was returning. "A boy." Sa'ili said something to the men in Samoan. They answered, laughing, and he turned to Han.

"Probably a teenager or early twenties."

Welly said, "An untitled male anywhere from eight to sixty years of age. A boy."

Sa'ili glared fleetingly at him. "About twenty."

None of The Frigate's first round of patrons could remember seeing Uli today. And neither of the men who said they'd seen the boy in Uli's truck had known who he was or had any idea when or how Uli or his truck left the place where it had been parked.

Outside, Sa'ili said to Han, "Matagi-tuai—Matagi means 'windy' so 'Windy old village'—is two hours by boat from our village, Papasaa. There's no road." Han had never been to Papasaa, but he knew that it was a half-day trek there and back by unpaved mountain roads from the leeward side. "Matagi-fou—Windy new village—isn't much better. Ever been there?"

Han shook his head.

"You approach it from a totally different direction. About half-way down island, there's a road that cuts up through one of the valleys and then over the crest. The mountains are much lower there and the new village is up on like a..." He waved his hand back and forth, making a flat place. "...But it's a good three hours from here and I wouldn't do it at night." Not to mention the fact that no one would talk to Han anyway because it was after dark and he might be *aitu*, a ghost. He certainly felt like one. On the other hand, it might be an improvement. He didn't think that ghosts felt pain. Or was that the point about being a ghost?

Opening the door to the jeep, Han said over his shoulder to Welly, "I'll leave you and your cousin...." He nodded to the third man. "...At Sa'ili's."

"Hell, no," the surgeon said, grinning at his cousins. "This man needs a little night life. Tani'n me gonna do the Gooney Bird some more. See you fellas later."

"Don't you ever check on your patients?"

"Ann'll do it for me. She likes playing surgeon. I'll see 'em later."

Han and Sa'ili got back into the jeep and headed around the village green for the shore road. It was almost dark now. There was still no power. Like the cannery, the tuna boats had generators to run their refrigerated fish holds. In the silvery dimness across the water, the boats were a ghostly, floating landscape netted with hanging light bulbs.

The fleet rep's station in life did not seem to involve a connection to the cannery generator. Behind the plate glass window of his office, the glow of a kerosene lantern wavered as people moved around it. The light from the jeep, swinging across the front of the building, spotlighted more men standing outside the door. White shirts with shoulder tabs: the fleet captains, their faces lean and grim.

The problem, Han thought, is authority. Gotta think Korean: the stability of society is relationship and all relationships boil down to the Confucian triad: father-son, uncle-nephew, brother-brother. It was what was driving the fleet rep crazy this morning, not being able to fit Han into one of those slots. Han snorted to himself: so how did the poor sod deal with these guys?

Han left the jeep running and the light on them. He got out slowly, deliberately. Maybe it had been a mistake to leave the other two men. They were civilians, but, like Welly said, this was Samoa. Sa'ili unfolded slowly from the jeep to tower over every man there. Eight to two, Han and Sa'ili would be mobbed. But they were the biggest men there, and they could cause a hell of a lot of grief on the way down. The opening round in the universal pissing match was just about even.

"The captains are waiting," the fleet rep said unnecessarily. "They are very anxious to be at sea. A big storm is coming and it's safer to be in open water." Not to mention, Han thought, the storm of Taiwanese fishing boats out there getting the fish instead of them. But he had to give the man credit. He had dumped all his Confucian cards on the table at once, speaking in the most formal inflection Korean has, marker of an exchange of the greatest importance.

"All of you," Han said without preamble and in the working conjugation of exchange among equals, "Were issued pistols when you assumed command of your boats." A grunt of surprise rippled through the group. Whatever they had thought this meeting was about–most likely being blamed for the riot–this wasn't it. "I don't care whether you still have your original pistol or not. But two people who died last night, a Samoan police officer and a Korean resident here, died of gunshot wounds."

He let them think about that for a moment. He had to get these guys to show him everything they had, not to think there was anything to be saved by showing one and hiding others.

"I believe that I have now the gun that killed both of these men. But since the Samoan authorities know that you have guns, I need to be able to account for them. That's why I've brought Mr. Tua'ua, one of the governor's cabinet officers, as a witness to this interview." With a wordless prayer to the diplomatic spirit of his Oxford-trained uncle–clear communication and evidence that you are not defenseless–Han shut up and let the silence work.

The silence was human only. Across the road, through the open door of the fleet rep's office, the cannery generator roared. The captains' dark eyes glittered in the lantern light. Koreans, Han thought, have never been afraid of a fight. Maybe that's why authority has always been such an issue. On the other hand, the fleet rep looked like he wanted to hide under his desk. Maybe, Han thought, he knows something I don't.

The group shifted slightly, almost like a single body. Suddenly, Han was looking at five pistols. They weren't really pointed at him. If you chose to interpret their positioning liberally. But they could have been. Beside him, Sa'ili took a long breath. Slowly, very obviously with thumb and forefinger only, Han fished the list the fleet rep had given him out of his breast pocket. He unfolded the paper with great deliberation, stepped forward and spread it on the desk.

"Thank you," he said. At least one of the ugly little metal mouths not quite facing him was a Makarov. He bent intently over his list like a good bureaucrat and said , "Ah...." He picked one of the Makarov captains from the list, anybody but the one he already had. He looked at the narrow hard face above the gun and said, "Captain Pak Byong-gie?"

The man's eyebrows jerked. He grunted in assent.

"Could you check the number for me, please? It should be on the left side, just above the trigger." If it's Chinese made, Han thought. But he didn't say that.

Finally, slowly, as if he was having to push the gun through some heavy substance, the captain turned the gun in his hand and looked at the number.

The room was too dark to read the tiny numerals. The captain had to step closer to the lantern, turn up the flame. He growled out the number and Han checked it off. Han really didn't give a damn if the number matched. He just needed to get as close as he could to knowing that the gun Welly and Sa'ili had given him was the only one in play. Or at least the only one off the tuna fleet. He held out one hand.

"May I examine it, please?"

There was another silent moment. But the man handed it over. Han turned the pistol over in his hands. It was dirty and probably as much a danger to the man firing it as its intended target. And it didn't show any obvious signs of being fired recently. *One down.*

The rest came slowly. But they came. All but the last. The man held back, arguing and cursing. The face of one of the captains without guns finally twisted in disgust.

"Idiot. Let him see it." He wrenched the gun from his colleague and handed it to Han. "Like a damned kid," the man said. He didn't flinch as the disarmed captain leapt at him but was restrained by two of the others. "Stop," the first man said. He had an extra star on the tab on his shoulder. The disarmed man quieted down, pulling himself away from the others.

Han checked the man's name off. The gun was an old N-frame Smith and Wesson .357 with a barrel big as a cannon. But, like the others, he didn't take very good care of it. It didn't look like it had been fired recently either. Han looked expectantly at the remaining three men.

The man with the extra star on his shoulder, the one who had disarmed Dirty Harry Wannabe, said, "Mine was stolen a couple of years ago. Never bothered to replace it." His face said, *A gun doesn't make a man a captain: I take care of my crew and catch fish.*

"Stolen?"

The captain nodded. "One of my men jumped ship here about the time it went missing. Always figured he took it. He was a clever bastard, but he wasn't much interested in work."

"Was his name Kim Pil-whoon? Locals call him the Tuna Pimp?"

The captain grunted, his eyes narrowing. "Yeah. Know him?"

"Not well," Han said. He looked at his list, still playing the good bureaucrat. But he remembered the name. "You're Captain Hong Jong-wook? Of the *Pusan Morning*?"

The man nodded curtly. "Should I have shot him while I had the chance?"

"Possibly. Why didn't you go after him? If you knew he was here."

The man laughed shortly and moved one shoulder. "If he was going to try to live in this godforsaken hole, I figured he probably needed it more than I did."

The other two captains claimed their guns were aboard their boats. Han invited himself and his witness to accompany the captains to demonstrate that. They all crunched across the gravel together to the main gangplank and out to the loose platform of boat decks. *U-keo-e*, Han thought parenthetically: the floating world of old Tokyo, whores and musicians and actors. *Godforsaken holes are in the eye of the beholder.*

The decks shifted like the sides of a sleeping dragon as they trooped aboard, one after another down the narrow web of bridging gangplanks, Han and the captains, Sa'ili and the fleet rep. The heat was appalling. It radiated from the metal decks up through the soles of their sandals, one with the stink of men and diesel, metal and fish.

Han never quite knew how he got himself down into the dragon's guts. He was afraid of water like some people are afraid of flying, of being trapped down in it with nothing but a leaky metal wall between you and suffocation. He was glad of Sa'ili's company.

Sa'ili followed Han down each narrow ladder into the captains' cabins, each narrow metal coffin hardly big enough to hold the man and his few possessions, much less Han and the towering Samoan. Across a narrow gangway, less than the width of Sa'ili's shoulders, was a single junior officer and a small amount of storage. And these were the privileged ones. The boats had crews of eight men each, layered, Han knew, into fore-mast cabins with bunks eighteen inches apart, four on either side. With four men dead and another dozen in hospital, even if the toll of the riot had fallen equally, Han couldn't see how they were going to put out to sea.

But that wasn't his business. His business was guns. As promised, the last two captains each produced a pistol. One was the fourth Makarov on Han's list, grubby as all the others. The last captain unlocked a tiny wall safe and pulled out a wooden case. Inside, nested in clean, oiled cloths, was a small pistol with the distinctive markings of a pre-1941 CZ 27 made in Czechoslovakia for the Nazis. Han didn't even want to imagine how this guy had gotten hold of such a firearm: it sure as hell had never been issued to him. There was no way without technical help to know if the gun had been fired recently. But it was also only a .32. Which meant it didn't matter. Probably.

Han followed Sa'ili and the fleet rep up the ladder onto the deck. The boat shuddered under their feet, like a horse trying to get rid of a fly. All three of them were soaked with sweat. On deck, at least, the air moved a little. They trooped across the decks to the main gangplank. They had hardly seen any of the crew, only flitting shadows from time to time. Like rats. They left the fleet rep at his office. Silent, Han drove himself and Sa'ili back through Pago and around toward Fagatogo. Out across the bay, the Southern Cross was rising. Han felt its blessing, having returned from Hell.

12

What Han wanted most in the world, even more than sleep and maybe even more than sex, was a bath. But he settled for tea. Welly offered him Sa'ili's beer, but Han had to be feeling really sorry for himself to drink alcohol.

Welly peered at him. "You get Asian flush?"

"You know about that?"

"Sure. Plenty Chinee in Christchurch." Sa'ili looked back and forth between them. Welly went on, "Lotta Asians missing an enzyme liver detoxifies alcohol with. Slows down clearing one of the breakdown products. Gives 'em hot flashes."

The extra cousin seemed to have disappeared.

Welly shrugged. "No stamina, that guy. One drink and he was ready to go back to the village. Got him a ride to Mata's, in their *aiga* bus."

"But that's only half way," Sa'ili said.

Welly shrugged again. "Oh, well. He can stay with Mata overnight. Or he can walk from there." He grinned. "Since he's not afraid of ghosts anymore." Sa'ili shifted, his face flat, as if he disapproved of people who weren't afraid of ghosts.

They sat together companionably, like survivors, cross-legged on thick soft pandanas mats on the wide front lanai overlooking the harbor. The power was back on—the outage had probably just been the usual knockout by the whole island turning on the six-o'clock news. They watched the lights come on across the water. Odds and ends of brothers-in-law and another cousin joined them, and the wives and a couple of pretty children brought them supper.

Emerging from a brief bliss of cold yam, young taro leaves slow-baked in coconut cream and a canned fish that tasted like beatified tuna, Han said, "What's *oo ah oo*?"

Sa'ili frowned. "*U'a'u?* That's not Samoan...."

"Wahoo," Welly said. "You're eating it. The contraband the Tuna Pimp flogged. S'why they call him the Tuna Pimp."

There are other reasons, Han thought. "Contraband?"

Sa'ili laughed. "Not exactly. But it's a game fish. So, it can't be sold commercially. But, as you see, it's quite wonderful. So when a wahoo gets caught in the nets by accident, the canneries freeze the individual fish until there're enough to do a special canning run. Makes wahoo an even more prized item as a ceremonial gift. The man they called the Tuna Pimp was a kind of banker. Even when no one else had any, you always knew you could pick up a few cases from him. Nobody knows how he got hold of it, but it didn't matter. He...supplied a need in the community."

"The ultimate entrepreneur."

Sa'ili nodded and frowned. "As Welly says, it doesn't make any sense to kill him. At least from the Samoan point of view, it would be like...what is the palagi fairy tale?"

Welly said, "Killing the goose that laid the golden eggs."

Sa'ili nodded. "You're sure it wasn't an accident?"

"I'm not sure of anything. Except that people get killed for lots of reasons, most of them involving stupidity or greed. Doesn't have to make sense. I just have to be able to prove it. May have been an accident. Probably during a robbery."

Sa'ili shook his head and muttered in Samoan the same proverb the police chief had used: *They bring night to the village.*

"Probably a good thing," Welly put in meditatively. "...That the Tapuafanua passed when he did. Gonna be a long time before anybody can get that much wahoo together again. Maybe never."

Sa'ili went on, "So. You think the boy, Uli, may be the killer? That *would* make sense. In a twisted way: a stupid killing by a stupid boy as part of a robbery. Somebody who had lost touch with the normal flow of *fa'a Samoa.*" Han wasn't inclined to look for culturally correct explanations. For one thing, there were too many cultures involved. But Sa'ili was into it. "Of course, that doesn't explain what he was doing with a gun belonging to a tuna captain."

"What you really need," said Welly, "Is to know whether that's the same gun put a hole in Sapatu." He grinned over at Han. "Or maybe that's me needs to know that."

Han grunted, suddenly irritated with himself. Like with Hutchinson, he had gotten too comfortable with these men. A good police officer doesn't do that. Doesn't make friends with civilians. In case they turn out to be suspects. "Well, I don't have a forensic firing range and I don't have a ballistic scanner. So, like a lot of things, I'm just going to have to wait for Honolulu."

"Can you wait that long?" Sa'ili's voice was almost apologetic.

"What do you mean?"

The big Samoan looked even more uncomfortable. "This afternoon. When Sasa spoke to me about going with you. I thought...well...he did rather sound like he expected Sapatu's killer from us on a platter. Like...tonight."

"Funny he didn't tell me that." Han hadn't missed the *from us* either.

"Well, he wouldn't. Would he."

Han looked at him. "Meaning what?"

Welly grinned. "Meaning there's a chain of command and there's *fa'a Samoa,* the Samoan way of doing things."

Silent, Han gazed at both of them. Finally, he said, "You mean: because, of all the people killed last night, Sapatu was the most important. And because his killer is mostly likely to be Korean and I'm Korean." Sa'ili poured out more tea. Welly played with his beer bottle.

"Actually," Welly said, with the air of a cheerful anarchist, lobbing a bomb into a party, "Sapatu may not have been the most important person killed, even by Samoan standards. Ann was thinking she saw strangulation marks on the Tapuafanua's neck."

Sa'ili's voice was harsh. "You're out of your mind! No one would harm the Tapuafanua!" He spoke again in Samoan. Han didn't understand it all, but it sounded like the same thing. Sa'ili switched back into English and said it again. "You're out of your mind. You drink too much!" He sat back and motioned one of the children in to clear the plates.

Welly lifted one eyebrow. "Just passing on the observation. Didn't look like that to me."

Han said, "You saw this mark?"

Welly shrugged. "I saw something. Looked like post-mortem changes to me." He grinned, nodding at his cousin. "Just wanted to see if I could get a rise out of him. But look, you know, if you really need to find out if that's the gun that killed Sapatu, you can probably do it. Even here."

In the process that leads a person to do something colossally stupid, the kind of thing he would never do under normal circumstances, the point of no return is farther along for a well trained and experienced person than for a beginner. For Han, that point was somewhere along after being isolated, frustrated, injured, exhausted, out on a half-sawed limb legally all day anyway and now, suddenly, pressured to produce results about important people for important people. Not that he gave a special shit about Sapatu—he didn't think of Sapatu as a policeman, more a political burden. But he did care about Sasa. So maybe it was something deeply Korean in him, responding to a revered master's wish. So he did something stupid.

He said: "How?"

Welly shrugged. "Dissecting scope at the hospital lab. Good enough for preliminary. Otherwise, just need to shoot into something kinda soft, so you don't squish the slug up too much."

"But," Sa'ili said, "Someplace that isn't going to terrify folks there's a gun battle going on."

Han grunted. He did recognize that he had just been presented with a career-ending move, if what they were proposing were ever disclosed in a real courtroom. On the other hand, what were the chances of anything he did here ending up in a real courtroom?

Whatever was going on behind Han's eyes, the two Samoans were in high gear. Welly was saying, "....Reservoir up above Pago. Closest houses are at least a quarter mile down the slope. You could fire into that cut bank there and...."

"...You'd need lights. At least a couple of lanterns..."

"...Some kind of a target, so you'd know where to dig in the bank...."

"...Should work."

"...The ghost stories alone you'd start up would be worth it."

Normally, Han had a tiger-like grip on reality. But half an hour later, winding up the road to the high pass above Pago Pago, he guessed he was losing it. The jeep was losing its grip on second gear. So they ground along slowly, following the wobbly light of the single headlamp. It was late enough now that even when the sharp barking of a dog or the shine of a tin roof in the starlight marked a homestead, the lights were out. And there were certainly no lights on the road.

"Almost there," Sa'ili said, peering out of his side of the jeep. Welly was just the gleam of a cigarette in the back seat.

At Sa'ili's direction, Han pulled into a clearing that opened on their right. Han had the pistol, still in its plastic bag. Welly lit a pair of lanterns. Sa'ili pulled out an old seat cushion that Han had persuaded his two self-styled ballistics techs was more useful to fire into than a mud bank. A brief rain fell, spattering noisily through the forest canopy. The three of them stumped up the trail to the clearing around the reservoir tank.

The rain turned the trail into a mud slide. And while that might have been okay in bare feet or hiking boots, in their rubber thong sandals, the three men slid and tangled feet and ankles in mud and springy rubber and roots, grabbing at whatever they could to stay upright. Around the end of a sodden cigarette, Welly cursed his way steadily up the slope but kept his lantern lit. All Han kept hold of was his temper and the pistol.

Once there, though, he saw their point. The reservoir tank had been set onto a natural shelf on the mountain side, but the area behind it had been widened, leaving a raw dirt bank that rose sheer into the darkness. Wiping his hands, now muddy as well as scabbed, on the seat of his shorts, Han took one of the lanterns while Sa'ili and Welly scouted for a place that would suit their purposes.

He pulled out the little pistol. *I can't believe I'm doing this.* What were the chances they could pull this off to any purpose? What were the chances they could pull this off without destroying whatever forensic evidence might still be clinging to the pistol? The one certain thing that was about to happen was that when he was asked by the prosecutor if this was the pistol that he had sealed and labeled in evidence, he would no longer be able to say *yes* in the sense that it was meant, that he had maintained it, inviolate, since coming into possession of it. The imaginary defense lawyer who haunted Han's dreams screamed at him: *What the hell did you think you were playing at, Lieutenant?* Actually, probably back to Sergeant by then. If he was lucky.

Lifting the masking tape seal with great gentleness—he thought of trying to give a whore an orgasm—he peeled the plastic bag back only enough to free the barrel. *On the other hand,* Han thought, not for the first time today, *this is Samoa.* But that was a damp and clammy comfort.

Sa'ili and Welly had set up their little firing range, the funky old cushion set against the bank's talus of fallen dirt. Han motioned the two Samoans away from their target. "Makarovs are pretty accurate, but I may not be. No: leave the lantern there, please." They grinned at him like little boys, their formal white mourning clothes smeared with red clay mud, and moved off a few steps. "Why don't you come over here and stand by me."

The other problem was that it was not Makarov ammo. The Russians had made their pistol so that its ammo wouldn't fit anyone else's 9 millimeter, but they could use anyone else's, with some sacrifice in accuracy. But if all you need is to blow away a couple of your rioting crew at point blank distance, that's not a big issue.

In his hand, it was a solid little weapon, for all its almost feminine lines. Four of its possible eight rounds—the same kind of Remingtons he had found in the Tuna Pimp's cache—were still in it. And he had the Tuna Pimp's cache, though he didn't want to use them if he didn't have to. He raised the little pistol and recognized his last moment of being a conventional, well-trained, first-world police officer. He fired. The cushion bounced out away from the bank and flopped over.

The slug had gone through the cushion into the bank. Welly and Sa'ili darted forward.

"Wait! Just set it up again." He got them out of the way and then fired twice more. What the hell. Once you've lost that cherry, everything else is just business. "Okay. But go gently. They're not going to be as easy to find as you think."

They scrabbled at the dirt bank like excited puppies. Han sealed the little pistol up again and left them to it. Whatever he still had in him tonight didn't involve digging in the dirt with his hands. He noticed that the surgeon's hands were getting no more respect than his white clothes.

Sa'ili exclaimed sharply in Samoan. Welly grinned at him and shook his head. *"Ma'ama'a:* little stones." But his grin went out a notch and he opened his hand. In his palm lay a dark lump of something splayed into a ragged mushroom. "This is what you're looking for."

They never found the third one. But they did get two. Rain started again, almost cool up here. Han held the two slugs out in the palm of his hand and let the sky-water pour over them.

Welly grunted. "Come on. Let's get out of here."

They scrambled and slid down to where the jeep was parked. And discovered that they had more problems than a dearth of forward gears.

Above and below them, the darkness opened out as a world of jewels. Stars fired the tropical sky beyond the rolling clouds. The great dog-leg bay stretched out below them, its outline studded with the lights of the shore road and the villages. At the foot of the mountain, even the village of Pago was an earthly Pleiades. The problem was, right below them, the closest lights were in fact moving up the road toward them. Close enough, in fact, that they could see the young men carrying lanterns in one hand and bush knives in the other.

"Oh, shit," said Welly. "This looks like serious *fa'alavelave*." *Trouble*, Han thought. It was the first Samoan Han had ever learned. In fact, this looked a lot like last night. He felt the weight of the Makarov in his pocket. One shot left. Three rounds in his other pocket. And the little sucker hard to load even in broad daylight with fingers that worked. Not that a gun would do anything but make whatever was going to happen a hell of a lot worse. He slipped the pistol and the live and spent rounds out of his pockets, folded them up quickly in his shirt and stuffed the packet tightly under the driver's seat of the jeep.

"Get in," Sa'ili commanded. Welly opened his mouth. Sa'ili said, "Shut up. Leave your lantern on." To Han, he said, "Drive down toward them. Very slowly. Stop enough short that you don't threaten them but close enough that they can see us." To Welly he said again, "Shut up."

Han did what he was told. In Viet Nam, Han had learned that whatever you believe about your own courage is probably wrong. He did not think of himself as brave or not brave. You just do what you have to do. But driving slowly down that dark road by the light of a single headlight, highlighted by the two lanterns, one behind him held by Welly and one beside him held by Sa'ili, was seriously unpleasant. A sign of middle age, maybe.

"Stop," Sa'ili said softly. "Let them pick their ground." Han eased the jeep to a halt. Not even a fucking windshield. Downhill in neutral, he could probably bowl through them. But he couldn't afford to do that much damage. Human or otherwise.

The crowd of young men gathered on the edges of the light from the jeep. Three stepped forward, chiefs by their demeanor, and one spoke sharply. But, Han thought, just a little uncertain. He would recognize Sa'ili, and not be quite sure of himself. Potentially more dangerous than a man who is totally sure of himself. Sa'ili looked at Han and said softly,

"Keep him quiet." He wasn't talking about the young man standing in front of the jeep. Behind Han, Welly grunted but kept silent.

Sa'ili climbed out of the jeep. He spoke slowly, evenly, the phrases sonorous and courtly. After about three words, Han was lost. He recognized that as the archaic syntax and pronunciation of chiefly interactions, a recognition of the importance of the occasion and a compliment to these men from one very much their ceremonial senior. He was even taller than they were.

After Sa'ili's opener, there was a short speech by the first chief. Then Sa'ili replied in what Han did recognize as a five minute way of saying *yes*. Sa'ili turned to Han. "I'm going to walk down the hill with them. This guy and the one right behind him are going to ride with you. We're going to that guest fale at the second turn down. Go at walking pace—we're all going together."

And if I lose first gear? Han thought. But down they went. The jeep's engine temperature gauge didn't work, probably a good thing. The whisper of footfalls rose around them over the grind of the engine. Bush knives gleamed like the men's skin in the light from the lanterns.

Somehow, they got down to the road-side guest fale, built long ago for the old ladies trudging over the high passes to Fagasa and Papasaa on the endless rounds of ceremonial visits. There was another palaver beside the road. Sa'ili bent to Han's window. "It's going to be okay, but it's going to take at least another hour or so. I appear to have convinced them that you two are heroes of last night's shameful episode in the history of Pago and ought to be allowed to go home to bed. Particularly," he glared briefly at his cousin, "As you have nothing to add to the talk."

And so they got away, Han and Welly. Han put the clutch in and let the jeep roll as fast as he could and still make the turns. Neither of them spoke until they were out on the flat at the back of Old Pago and he put the jeep in gear again.

"Your cousin certainly seemed intent on keeping you quiet."

"He thinks I'm irreverent."

"I can't imagine why."

"That was probably even stickier than it looked. Those guys take all that stuff real serious."

"*Stones rot, but words last forever.*"

"You bet."

They wound along the shore road toward Fagatogo. "You staying at Sa'ili's or...where?"

"Home's okay." Home would be one of the new doctors' residences built behind the hospital in which Welly had installed his wife. This was possibly the only recompense for having to put up with Welly as a husband. "Besides," Welly went on, "Gotta find us a microscope."

Han glanced at the surgeon. "You must really not have shot Sapatu. Either that or you've got colder blood than a Samurai."

Welly had a new cigarette going, one elbow cocked out of the window. "Well," he said, "What the hell. You don't kill one person, you probably did kill someone else." Before Han could ask him what the hell he meant by *that*, Welly went on. "You know, you oughta take Ann Maglynn out."

"Right. Where? The hotel bar?"

"You know what I mean."

Han did know what he meant. And it was the first time in five years that his automatic response, spoken or unspoken, to a proposition like that wasn't *I'm married*. He thought about that. It was a funny, empty place inside of him, a room someone had moved out of. But for the first time since his wife had left, he couldn't remember who had moved out of that space, her or him.

They drove around the point past Nozaki's. Han thought fleetingly about his dirty laundry. A good reason not to be going out with anybody. Surely he had a clean tee-shirt around somewhere.

When the silence went on, Welly looked at him carefully and said, "There's nothing wrong with her. I mean, because she doesn't have any family."

"That makes two of us," Han said.

If Welly had heard, he wasn't listening. He went on philosophically. "She's all right. Got some rough edges, but.... Somewhere between thirty-five and forty-five, human beings either close down or they open up. She's an opener. She'll be all right." He grinned over at Han, his teeth blazing white in the sudden light from the village center. "And I don't mean open that way."

Right about there, as the jeep grumbled slowly past the police station and on around past the docks and up the rise toward the hotel, Han understood that Welly had never gotten Ann Maglynn to bed. The thought took him all the way up the hill and around toward Utulei.

But where ever Welly's head was, it was still there. "She ended up down here because of this Army urologist, dick-doctor, she knew in Honolulu. Now he's a serious jerk." The cigarette end blazed like a torch. "And he's gonna be on that 'plane tomorrow 'long with your Korean Consul."

"Not mine," Han said. "What the hell for? That's pretty fast action for the Feds."

"This's been brewing. 'Cause of Hutchinson's problems with Gloriana n' Ray. N' keeping doctors here n' all that. This guy reamed the gov's plumbing n' didn't foul up the wiring so he couldn't get it up, so he thinks he's God on earth."

Han guessed that he had just heard a brief description of an intimate surgical procedure the governor had undergone without the untoward effect of losing sexual function. Who exactly thought who was God on earth still wasn't clear but probably didn't matter.

Welly went on: "Y'know, palagis get all wrapped around the axle about Samoans explaining everything away, y'know: *does Samoan culture permit the confrontation of true evil?* But they're pretty damn' good at explaining stuff away themselves...."

They were just passing the far end of Penicillin Row in Utulei. There was a party going on at the Yacht Club, and lights blazed at Gloriana's as well.

Han said, "It's called the legal system. But at the rate I'm going, it's probably going to be fairly easy for someone to explain away Ray Begley's death."

"Ray. Shit." Welly snorted. "He was dead anyway. Just confused people 'cause he was still walkin' around. Whether somebody killed him on purpose or whether he just passed out in the road and somebody ran over him, don't matter a damn in the great river of time." They wound along the coast to the tiny village of Fagaalu in its deep protected cove–the name meant *Gone-away Bay*, the exit, the last sheltered spot short of the harbor's mouth. They turned up toward the hospital.

Cautiously, Han said, "That's basically what Ann told me. That he was terminally ill." He pulled up in front of the hospital. *Just don't let it be Welly.* He fought the thought, like wrestling with a demon. *Just don't let it be Welly.*

He said drily, "You need somebody to walk you up to your house?"

"Hell, mate. I ain't even had a beer in almost two hours. And you're the one with no shirt on. Come on, maybe we can find you a scrub top along with that microscope."

Abashed, Han pulled the balled-up shirt with its cargo out from under his seat. He was also barefooted, since one of his thong sandals had dislocated itself in the slide down the mountainside.

"Oh, forget it," Welly went on. "Nobody gives a shit. Lucky when people bother with pants 'stead of just a tatoo, much less a shirt. Come on." He bounded through a side door into the hospital.

And all but careened into Ann Maglynn walking down the back hallway. She was back in her unisex uniform of aloha shirt and loose white trousers. But Han remembered the other just fine.

"Hey," Welly said cheerfully. "Done my rounds for me?"

Ann laughed. "I'm considering doing a scholarly paper on the combined effects of sand and booze in wounds." Her head cocked to one side. "You gentlemen been mud wrestling?"

"Nah," Welly said. "Pursuing objective data. Get dissecting microscope?"

"Not personally. But I suppose we could look in the lab."

Han walked beside her feeling really stupid wearing nothing but a pair of muddy shorts. He said, "Is that sand taken internally and booze on the wounds or the other way around?"

Ann laughed. "You're right. I will have to estimate the amount of sand taken internally. Quite a lot, I should think, from the external evidence."

After twenty minutes of opening every cabinet in the lab—including the refrigerators—at least twice, they had to admit that the laboratory probably did not have a dissecting microscope.

"I have an idea," Ann said. They followed her loping walk through the breezeways to the emergency room. The ER was very quiet for not much past twelve on a Saturday night, but perhaps communal bad behavior had exhausted itself the night before. "What my old dermatology professor used to call the dermatologist's stethoscope." She pulled out a free-standing flourescent lamp shaped in a circle around a six-inch magnifying glass. "That'll give you about four power. Put these on...." She handed Han a headset of magnifying glasses. "...Gets you maybe another four power."

To the entertainment of the Samoan medical officer on duty and the two nurses, Han and Welly laid out their lumps of deformed metal on the white paper covering of an ER bed, the two mud-smeared men bending over them intently. Han had the slugs taken from Sapatu's chest. Like the ones they had retrieved on the mountainside, these were sealed in a clear plastic bag, so, technically, he wasn't breaking chain-of-custody. He wasn't sure whether that made his original sin better or worse. But, like talking to his Catholic Samurai wife about original sin, he also wasn't sure he cared.

The makeshift scanner took a moment to get used to, but the scorings in the slugs were so distinctive, you could almost see them without the magnification. Yes, it would have to be confirmed. But as far as Han was concerned, Honolulu would have to work to prove they weren't all from the same gun. He stood back and handed the magnifying headset to Ann.

"The cartridges are just a bit too small for the gun. So before they really set into the rifling, they slew a bit. Bungs 'em up in that distinctive way."

Ann lowered the lens visor and bent over the lighted lens. He could see the bones of her back and shoulders through her thin cotton shirt. He looked at his hands: filthy, scabbed. Not something a woman was likely to invite to touch her. He turned to a nearby sink and let cool water run over his hands while he watched Ann and Welly chatter over the slugs. (*Yes, sir, I did permit Drs. Tuiasosopo and Maglynn to examine the slugs. But they did so under my direct observation and the bags remained sealed. Yes, sir, there are other witnesses who can attest to this.*) He hit the wall. Not really. But in that way that you know you have squeezed every last bit of adrenalin out of your physical capacity. He looked around for something to sit on.

Ann had turned on her stool and was pulling off the magnifying glasses. She looked at him. "I should probably be doing formal wound checks on you, Lieutenant. It being about twenty-four hours out. But it looks like I should be offering you a bath instead." Over her shoulder, Welly flashed him an impish grin and waved good-bye.

13

Whatever Welly's expectations, Han's bath turned out to be a shower in the surgery suite locker room with Sarge sitting guard outside. But the towels and the set of surgical scrubs they got out for him were clean and dry and didn't smell of mildew, so he guessed he was ahead. Ann was gone when he got out. Sarge tried to herd him to the main exit, but Han stopped.

"I want to talk to the fishermen." The old guard shrugged and led him back to the surgical wards. It was just after change of shift, and the nurses were out taking temperatures and blood pressures. They wouldn't let him talk to anyone who had managed to stay asleep, but two men were awake in one ward and three in another. All five remembered the Tuna Pimp's speech. None of them remembered seeing him after that. But Han did find out one interesting thing. The pair of fishermen from one ward were from the *Cheju Star*.

"No," they told him. "No one was robbed. At least not Friday night. Just somebody got drunk and ran out of money and got pissed off. You know how it is."

And the jeep died halfway down the slope into Fagotogo.

Han rolled it the rest of the way down the hill and into the only service station on this half of the island. He walked from there to the police station. The dispatch officer was asleep curled up on the floor behind the desk when Han walked in. But apparently not as soundly as he looked.

"Sir! Old Lady Nozaki left this for you." The young man fished a soft, clean-smelling bundle out of a file drawer and tossed it across the room to him.

Han nodded his thanks and tucked the bundle under him arm. Part of him, all that old soldier and cop and aristocrat–kick butt and keep order–told him that he should have raised hell about the kid being asleep. But, unrolling his old futon on the floor of his office, the part of him that had survived all that knew, if a call came in, the kid would wake up and deal with it and, if Han had disturbed him, he wouldn't have remembered to give Han his laundry. Han slept soundly.

Church bells woke him. He looked at his watch. He didn't have a watch. He lay looking at the ceiling. Grey light through the screens up under the eaves suggested it was still early. Other than a lot of tea, he needed two things: a jeep that worked and someone who spoke Samoan, preferably with roughly the same view of objective reality that he had. And he knew where he could get both of them. And maybe even the tea.

An hour later, with the aide of a wide awake hospital telephone operator and an early morning truck headed down island, Han was walking up through the loose quadrangle of the doctors' flats. Ann opened her door as he approached.

"Thanks for the extra time," she said, "I got my rounds done. So I'm free basically for the rest of the day. At least until this evening. And I can give you some breakfast."

They sat outside her door on the edge of the narrow lanai that ran around the building under the eaves. Han recognized the Samoan gesture of making their interactions entirely public, observable by anyone who cared to. And, considering how horny he was, probably not a bad move. She was wearing the dress again.

Catching his look, she said, "Since it's Sunday. And this is a formal journey."

Formal journeys were a big thing in Samoa, Han knew, visitations from one village to another with many obligations of gift-giving and social score-keeping. Well, that wasn't what was on his mind, but he got the point. And she hadn't just been doing rounds and putting on a dress. The biscuits she laid out for him were fresh and warm. With them, she set out a jar of purple stuff and a spoon. The label on the jar was a miniature landscape with green mountains and a flower meadow in one corner, the lettering an elegant European calligraphy.

"I've heard of blueberries," he said. "But I've never eaten them. Is that because I'm from Korea or from California?"

She smiled. "Where ever I've lived in the world, my sisters send me blueberry jam. They can't imagine why anybody would leave Connecticut. But at least they can send the blessings of a enlightened lifestyle to the less fortunate."

"Beats war and religion."

"Religion comes in many forms. War, too, I guess." She laughed gently and rose to clear away their plates. "In my sisters' case, it's the practice of....superior domesticity. With or without nannies, administrative assistants, and the company of men."

"No brothers?"

"No." He could heard the water run, the clink of the dishes on the edge of the sink. "My father had three wives and extremely bad luck. Or at least, the wives did. All three of them died of breast cancer. The first two after producing two daughters each. And the third after producing me. I was supposed to be a boy and that's kind of how I turned out, I guess. But it beats sitting around listening to your DNA tick and wondering when it's going to explode. Maybe that's why the great epidemics always fascinated me: plague, leprosy, tuberculosis. Breakers of empires. Not just hearts. Though that too, I guess."

Han's mind went blank. But she was standing in the doorway, talking. "In reality, my oldest sisters' mother was probably from a 'cancer' family–breast and ovarian cancer in the women, prostate cancer in the men. My dad shopped more carefully after that. But life still faked him out. You should probably use the bathroom before we leave. It's going to be a long ride."

Traffic was already heavy. Four thousand cars, Han thought, and forty miles of road.

"If you have a car," Ann said. "It's especially important to be seen driving it to church."

Han said nothing. Somebody once said a cop is someone who wants to speed legally. Fair enough. Creeping along in traffic made him crazy.

He gazed out the open windows at tiny villages, the entrance to the airport, the island's newest attempt at a shopping mall being hacked out of the forest, the garbage dump. Beyond the airport, the leeward skirt of the island spread out from the mountain ridge in broad meadows and coconut groves. The villages here seemed more prosperous, less claustrophobic.

Ann turned the jeep to the right onto a narrow road that ran up into one of the mountain valleys, changed to dirt, and started up the leeward escarpment. It was a damned long climb. The road was the usual series of hair-pin turns gouged out of the red dirt and scored into a washboard by the constant run-off. At the top, the forest cleared suddenly as if mown by the wind, opening a view to windward and the sea.

Ann pulled over, and they both got out. The sun was bright and the wind laid her dress tight against her like a second skin. Her spiky short hair lifted in the wind, fired bright red by the sun. If he'd been a different man, he'd have taken her right there by the roadside. He thought again of the feminine Trickster, the fox-sprite. Would she disappear and leave him there with his aching groin, laughing at him?

"Storm coming," she said.

"How do you know?" The fleet rep had said that last night. Han didn't have the country man's feel for weather.

She smiled. "Mainly because Neil Hutchinson was rushing around this morning trying to organize shutters for the hospital. That's most of why you found us all so active that early on a Sunday. But the sky gets a kind of glaze to it; the leaves of the trees turn in the wind, showing their silver underbellies." She laughed. "That's a direct quote. My father made his living as a professor of landscape architecture, but he's really a painter. His whole life is light and color." Her eyebrows went up and down, and her smile was crooked. "People do rather get in the way."

She gazed out down the mountainside and out to sea. "I grew up on the north Atlantic," she went on quietly. "And I've been 'round the Cape of Good Hope, in the south Atlantic. Atlantic light is very blue and cold. It's so different here. In the middle of the greatest ocean in the world, as far from the Arctic as you can get."

She could have, Han thought, had anything she wanted from him right then. But maybe she didn't want it. She looked at her watch. "We'd better get going. Even if we get lucky, it's going to be a push to get you back out to the airport by two to get all...your stuff onto the plane."

The road across the highland was not quite as bad. The jeep settled into a steady rattle. Ann flashed him a smile. "Sorry for being a bit morose." And then she laughed. "It comes from trying to accomplish things in Samoa. Or at least palagi things."

Feeling like he'd lost something in the conversation somewhere, all Han could think of to say was, "What were you trying to accomplish?"

He was just fishing, a policeman's habit. But there was enough of a pause before she answered that he was suddenly very alert. But she still surprised him.

"Do you know about the Tapuafanua, the old man whose funeral we went to yesterday?"

"No. A great chief." Han remembered Sasa's description. "A retired chief." And then he thought of Welly and Sa'ili. He thought, *a murdered chief?* But he didn't say it. He had enough murders to deal with right now. He didn't need imaginary ones.

"He was also one of the first fully trained Samoan medical officers, way back when. Rather a scandal, as he was from a very important family. Titles aren't strictly hereditary in Samoa like they were in Europe, but they do stay *in* the family. He was bright and energetic: a clear set up for the family's major title. In fact, he ended up with two of them." Her face grew thoughtful. "Rather like Sa'ili, in a way, but...what do you know about leprosy?"

He had a hard time getting the words out. "Not a lot. Skin disease. Kills people."

"Not exactly. It actually a disease of peripheral nerves, that is...." She sketched her arms and legs with one hand. "Nerves once they get out away from the brain and spinal cord. Untreated, leprosy can be very disfiguring; on the face, horrifyingly so. In the past, people with leprosy were ostracized, killed outright. But the disease process is slow. Transmission occurs from close contact with an infectious person who may not yet be showing signs of disease. Kids are especially vulnerable because in most societies, they're the people who are touched the most. But you usually don't know that the disease was transmitted until much later."

Han was still having a hard time thinking. He said, "On our honeymoon, in Hawai'i, my wife and I hiked down to the old leper colony at Kalaupapa." *What had his wife told her?* "My wife....worked in a leprosarium in Korea....years ago." He almost said *trying to become a saint*.

She glanced at him. But he didn't see any sign that she knew any more. She said, "Leprosy got to Polynesia in the mid-1800's. It was unusually virulent in what was essentially a virgin population. In Samoan, the words for leprosy are *ma'i mutumutu*, 'the sickness of cutting off'. Both because fingers and ears and noses tend to scar off late in the disease process, but also because people were cut off from their families, sent away to Samoa's leprosarium on a distant island. The modern saints of leprosy were the people who brought dapsone, the first effective treatment for leprosy, to the leper colonies in the 1950's. Here, the medical officer who did that later became known as *tapuafuanua*: sacred of the land, in part, because he brought the people home."

"You worked with him?" Han's voice was distant, as if it belonged to someone else.

"The Tapuafanua? No. I was just getting to know him a little when...." She shook her head, as if to herself. "We're still diagnosing new cases here. And if you've got an active case now, you have the potential for transmission and new cases in the future."

Tell me about it, Han thought. What, in the end, his wife hadn't been able to handle. *Noblesse oblige* is one thing. Going to bed with it is something else.

"But organized case-finding is impossible in a democracy: the political repercussions of actually finding a case, when families are still terrified of the disease, are too great. At least for this government. But the Tapuafanua knew every family in Samoa that had ever had a case. And he was the Tapuafanua.."

"So if he had been willing to work with you...."

She smiled. "Maybe. This *is* Samoa."

"Tell me," he said harshly, yanking up the front of his shirt. "Is that leprosy?"

Glancing at his exposed belly and chest, she smiled. "No. I don't think so. And I've seen a lot of your skin in the last couple of days. Looks like the world's worse case of *Tinea versicolor*. A skin fungus. Annoying. But not dangerous. That why you wife left?"

Even if what you have been using to hold yourself together is something horrible, when it's taken away, you still fall apart. Finally he said, "Take your pick: leprosy in the family, being married to a cop, being married to a Korean."

She grinned at him, "Not much difference, hey?" Her face sobered. "Who in your family had leprosy?"

"My sister. At least that's what they said. It was all a long time ago. After the war and the partition. Both my parents were dead. The surviving kids got parceled out among the uncles. Except for my sister."

"She got put in the leprosarium. That how you met your wife?"

"She was volunteering there. She's Catholic." Ann nodded as if that explained everything. "I went back a couple of years ago. Finally got the story out of an aunt." His sister had been long dead by the time he went looking for her. But the stern young woman volunteer, half nun, half prisoner of some personal war, had helped him find the records. It had been no stretch to offer her whatever refuge he could provide. It hadn't been enough.

He tucked his shirt in. "So what will you do now?"

"I don't know. Mainly, I have to see how the government handles Neil Hutchinson. If they fire him, I'm not sure I can stay on. Politically or professionally. I told you Colonel Munro was due in this afternoon as a mediator. Mediation isn't what's going to happen."

"I know Begley's wife doesn't like Hutchinson, but is she that powerful?"

"Not...not in the palagi sense of being able to cause things to happen. But she does have the governor's ear, one way or another. And can be called a doctor, at least here. So if there's a deficit, or if one is created, I should say, she's certainly available to fill it."

"So what's to mediate?"

Ann smiled. "You sound like Neil. Neil thinks he can complain to Colonel Munro, get Gloriana out of his hair and get on with trying to get the health system working. But Gar Munro isn't a mediator. He just likes to play power games. The governor thinks Gar is like Neil's high chief; he'll order Neil to quit making trouble about Gloriana and everybody will live in peace."

"Where does Ray Begley fit in to all of that?"

"When he was alive, he was certainly an embarrassment. But, one, the damage was done, and, two, it wasn't going to be for much longer."

"Welly calls him the walking dead. Though...." Han remembered Hutchinson's assessment of Begley's illness. "...Hutchinson seems to think he could have held on for quite a while."

Ann shook her head and laughed. "Poor Neil. The operative word in internal medicine is *maybe*. Internists spend half their time trying to convince people who feel fine that they ought to spend money and feel bad taking medications because *maybe* they'll have a heart attack or stroke if they don't. And the other half trying to convince people who are half dead that if they stopped doing the few things left they still enjoy, *maybe* they won't die so soon. Ray drank like he had all the time in the world. He didn't. Believe me. Welly and I are right on this one."

"Is there any way the Tuna Pimp could have anything to do with Ray Begley?"

"Not that I know of. He was killed in the riot, yes?"

"No. Probably as part of a robbery. But that night. It's why we're here looking for this boy, Uli. He's connected with the Tuna Pimp's death."

"And with Ray?"

"I don't know. But that's another reason why we're here. To see what we can find out."

Upland scrub and trees gave back to taro fields, clusters of banana trees, and then the fales of a small village. She pulled up beside the guest fale just short of the village green.

"For now, we just wait," she said. "Someone will come."

The wind was hot. Banana fronds clattered in a down-slope grove. Otherwise, it was silent. Not even the sounds of a distant radio or children on this Sunday morning. Finally, a stocky, middle-aged man in white shirt and black lavalava strolled over and greeted them.

Ann replied. She didn't use the chiefly syntax and pronunciation. Han wondered if that was going to be okay. Would this—presumably—mid-level chief take offense and refuse to deal with them. But the chief was commenting on her good Samoan, and she was apologizing for knowing only the ordinary speech. Now she was introducing Han. The man's hand was like gnarled wood, his face suddenly broadly welcoming.

Ann turned to Han. "What do you want me to ask?"

"Does he know the boy Uli?" Han described him, the long hair, the attitude. As Ann translated, the chief's face hardened. His head jerked inland, toward the deep forest and distant mountain peaks. He spoke, his voice harsh. Ann asked him a few more short questions. He seemed to be saying no to all of them.

She turned to Han. "He says that Uli was from this village. But not any more."

"Since when?"

"An interesting question. Which we can discuss later. We are being offered tea."

An hour later, they were headed out of the village, back across the high ridge road. "You don't believe they were telling the truth about Uli?" The chief's story had been confirmed by the group of elders who had gathered in the guest fale with the impromptu meal.

"No. I mean, Samoans don't lie. At least not in the way palagis use the term, meaning deliberate deviation from truth and truth as an unbendable standard. And I went out of my way to ask the questions so that there wasn't any sense of what you wanted, of some socially obligatory tale they were expected to tell. They don't like the guy. They don't like his friends. What I couldn't tell really was how long he had been gone. And I can't tell you whether that's just a problem with my Samoan or something else. Gone as a direction? Gone as a time frame? Gone as an epistomologic statement: ringing changes on the nature and validity of truth...."

She glanced at him and smiled. "Not making much sense, am I? Samoa does that to palagis. For what it's worth, palagi culture does the same thing to Samoans. They run into western concepts of truth like stone walls."

"It's a problem," Han said, thinking about other people who run into cultural stone walls.

"Indeed. All that aside: I think, if we had a transcript made by a bilingual palagi of a recording of what these people said to me, the gist would tilt very strongly toward Uli's having been gone from the village for a long time. Weeks. Months, maybe. But having sat there—watched their faces, how they did or didn't look at us or at each other—I think he was actually there much more recently. Maybe even as recently as yesterday."

Han looked at her. She lifted both hands off the steering wheel, spreading her fingers in apology. "Don't ask. I can't tell you. They also mentioned people he hung out with. They wouldn't be specific, but there was someone they seemed to viewed as Uli's equal or slightly inferior. And then, someone who was giving him orders."

"Palagi or Samoan?"

"The equal/slightly inferior, definitely Samoan. The other...I'm not sure–I'm not sure of any of this–but maybe palagi."

14

Ann threaded the jeep through the crowd of people and vehicles at the airport and pulled up to the curb. "This okay?"

Han nodded. "Thanks." They both bowed slightly, and she drove away.

They had passed the last two hours almost in silence. Places along the way, quiet dells speckled with sunlight, he had almost asked her to stop and let him make love to her. Since he wasn't a leper. But he had other bodies to worry about besides his own, specifically, three dead ones he had to get onto an airplane. He had gotten Ann to make a quick detour to the hospital, where the guard in the security office had told him that Sarge and the TPD officer who had been on duty at the morgue were already on their way to the airport with the ambulance.

The airport was a hybrid of outsized Samoan fale and airplane hanger. Passengers flowed through high open doors into a wide pavilion cluttered with ticket desks and check-in and curio stands and Samoan families sitting on the floor among towering piles of luggage that always included rolls of mats and barrels of provisions sufficient for a long-distance canoe voyage. At the hospital yesterday with Hutchinson, Han had worked out how to keep the bodies of Begley, Sapatu, and the Tuna Pimp and the rest of Han's specimens as secure as the situation allowed and then get them all to the airport. But that was a hell of a lot different than actually seeing the stuff successfully loaded into the aircraft's holds.

Particularly as now it turned out that the Sierra Nevada of luggage he had observed in the airport lobby belonged to most of a village on their way to L.A. via Honolulu to a wedding. This included two dozen wooden casks of New Zealand bully beef and a dozen each hundred-pound plastic casks of sugar and sacks of flour. The rolls of palm-leaf mats took up the same volume, but they did weigh less. There wasn't much clothing.

The freight agent shrugged. "Well," he said, "They can't take anything fresh, like bananas or taro, because they can't take agricultural products into Hawai'i or California." He smiled. "They are a very important family. Their tickets pre-date your arrangement."

Fortunately, just as Han was considering reaching across the ticket counter to tie the agent's shirt collar into a knot, he heard a small sound and looked around. Old Sasa, the police chief, was standing beside him. Normally, you didn't see Sasa on Sundays. Sundays, Sasa was three hundred percent very high chief of Manu'a, church and state as one. But today he was here, looming beside Han, in uniform and looking exceptionally bland and serene, which usually meant that something exceptionally stupid was going on.

Also fortunately, the freight agent decided that if a high chief of Manu'a wished to exalt three third-rate coffins and a large metal shipping container with the dignity of his position, that was his right. The freight agent wasn't going to argue with him. Nor did the family involved argue but gracefully made arrangements with the agent to have ten of the barrels of salt beef, one roll of mats, and four each of the containers of sugar and flour to be forwarded on the Wednesday flight. They were still trading mellifluous speeches in the chiefly syntax with Sasa when Han climbed into the aircraft's hold to watch his cargo being secured.

Satisfied at last, he climbed out and hopped down onto the runway. The white concrete surface blazed in the afternoon sun. He shifted into the shade of the pavilion, looking around for Sasa or anyone else he could catch a lift up-island with.

Across the interior, where newly arrived passengers gathered, he noticed a parting of the crowd, the beginnings of a ceremonial space. In its center, a tiny, slender, elderly Korean male, draped in a cream colored linen suit, stood calmly as if waiting for trumpets. This had to be the Consul from

Honolulu. Beside him, radiating impatience even standing still, was a male palagi of medium height with perfectly cut short dark hair wearing a designer aloha shirt and khaki trousers in which, like the Korean, he still managed to look crisp. *That won't last*, Han thought. Behind them were a matched pair of huge Chinese-Hawaiian males, absurd in ill-fitting pale grey suits, presumably the Consul's bodyguards. And behind them were a matched pair of palagi males: tall, broad-shouldered, short pale hair, pink European faces, almost identical aloha shirts in one-color-on-white prints, and black shoes and socks.

"Holy shit," Han said aloud. "F.B.I.?"

He heard a grunt. Sasa had reappeared at his elbow. The official party was being joined by Leon Fischer, the Attorney General, and by the Korean fleet rep and sub-consul. Han guessed that Sasa was supposed to be with them. But whether the old man was resting on his supreme cultural dignity or what Han was beginning to suspect was a carefully disguised appreciation for the absurd, the two cops continued to stand together at parade rest outside the barrier.

Han said, "I've found the gun that wounded Sapatu." The old man glanced at him and then back at the official party. "And I've got preliminary evidence that it's the same gun that killed the Korean who was shot–the guy called the Tuna Pimp". He saw the recognition in the old chief's face. "And the name of a possible suspect that connects the two."

"But not the boy himself."

Han wondered how Sasa could have known about the boy, Uli. Then he realized that it was just the word, boy, an untitled man between the ages of eight and sixty, to use Welly's definition. And the implication: no titled man would do such things.

"No, sir. We haven't been able to lay hands on him yet."

"His family will protect him," the old chief said. But his tone said, *not for long*. Han felt one of those cultural tectonic shifts. Had Uli's family actually been covering up for him this morning? Did *not for long* mean that the family would now give him up, turn him in? Or was Sasa about to bend all the regal light of his position onto Uli's village, setting them on fire?

The old man grunted again, as if reading Han's mind. His voice as bland as his face, he said, "As you see, we are honored by the assistance of the Federal Bureau of Investigation." He glanced at Han again, but this time the light in his eyes was sharp and bright as a prism. "It appears that the civil rights of some of the fishermen may have been violated."

"You mean," Han said, watching the official group shift toward the exit gates, "The four dead ones?" The old man nodded. Matching his tone, Han went on: "This does happen, sir. From time to time."

The old man nodded again. "You do your job," he said. "And I'll do mine."

15

Ann changed into olive cargo pants and an old shirt that she saved for hikings and jammed a tiny camera and a map that claimed to outline the island's water systems into her pockets. She wasn't in the mood to be social. Within a few strides, she was out of sight of the last of the doctors' fales and climbing steeply.

The track led up to the chlorination shed in a last clearing before the forest took over. As far as Ann could tell, the chlorination process worked intermittently, if at all, but she had never been able to get her superior at the Public Health division to come look at it. The shed and the chlorine tank existed and so served their purposes. Ann left the clearing and began grappling up the tree-laddered red cliff behind it.

At the top of the first cliff, she stopped to pant and to look at her map. This was not her first such Sunday excursion, but she had never done this section right behind the hospital. The topographical lines on the map nested in a dauntingly tight pattern. She had done most of the lower down water systems, impelled, like now, by times when she felt like she was about ready to jump out of her skin. But the harder climb suited her mood.

She thought of Han's sudden retreat into himself at the airport, the squared shoulders and rolling stride as he walked away, an image out of Kurosawa movies and too much Honolulu Channel 13: cowboy Samurai, not Korean. There was no way he could find her attractive. She was too gawky and rude. Angry at herself and the stupidity of things in general, she thrust the map back into her pocket and started up through the trees.

Maybe fifty yards up the slope, the little stream that fed the hospital system emptied from the mouth of a narrow gully, hardly wider than her arm-span, maybe three times as deep as she was tall. She waded into the water. The stream bed was a natural water main worn out of the underlying lava, with only a scattering of free boulders. She worked her way up the slick rock, thinking of *Lorna Doone*. She climbed out into a park-like lawn of moss and fine grass, under the high forest canopy. The springs rose here. A length of exposed pipe, one small, forgotten bit of public health infrastructure, poked up. She pulled out the camera and took a few shots.

If she'd had any sense, she'd have stopped there. But she had a bad case rock fever. And the best way to deal with that was to get the landscape back into foot-traffic scale. Getting over the ridge that separated the Fagaalu valley, where the hospital was, from the Fagatogo valley, was no great goal, but she could drop in at Sa'ili's and cadge a warm soda and a little gossip. And so what if the police station was there too? It was Sunday, and Han wouldn't be there now anyway, and it was none of her damned business if he was.

Just to prove it, she stalked up the ridge angling off to the right in the general direction of Fagatogo. An old path led vaguely out across an open stretch overgrown with bushes twice her height and tangled with vines. Ten minutes later, festooned with leaves and other shreds of plant life, she guessed this route was not a good idea. Twenty minutes later, the tangle was probably thinning out–along with her temper–but she was also over the hump.

She was in the upper reaches of what had to be one of the high up-slope coconut plantations behind Fagatogo. The trees were very tall, spindly, many of them with their heads broken off, the grass and weeds around them rough and unkempt. Ann moved down one edge of the grove, watching where she was putting her feet. But she glanced ahead down the interface of forest and plantation. And saw something peculiar.

Her eyes said, it's a body, hanging from a tree at the edge of the forest.

Her brain said, you're always saying things like that. It can't be a body.

Her eyes said, it is too a body. A dead body.

Her brain said, it can't....

A young man was hung from the outstretched limb of a huge banyan tree by a length of bright cloth twisted around his neck. Ann's eyes sheered away from the bloated, purple face. Lavalava, she thought. He hanged himself with his lavalava.

She began to process details. The body was beginning to swell, legs spreading. The skin was shiny, mottled, purple-brown and grey. Where it wasn't tangled in the noose, the young man's hair fell to his shoulders.

Uli. The boy they were looking for.

She stood for what was probably a very long time. For a normal person. Staring at the ground, head bowed. But she wasn't a normal person. She was a physician. And healing had failed this guy. Healing and community. If Han was right, and he was a murderer. Or just a misfit. Feeling that she was doing something at once right, necessary, and damned odd, she photographed the body where it hung.

She turned and started down the edge of the old plantation. She realized that she was hardly breathing and that the feel of the rough ground and the way that the sunlight sparkled through the forest canopy were strangers, as if she had been, for a few minutes, a silent Orpheus, walking in the underworld.

She heard the sound, something between a cough and a shout. She whirled around in horror. But the body still hung, dead and inert, where she had left it. But now something was coming fast down through the undergrowth toward her.

She ran like a startled deer. She wasn't in great physical shape but she was light and agile and going down hill. At the bottom corner of the abandoned plantation, a rough track angled away, half screened by bushes, down to the right toward the plantations lower down and the nearest village. She burst through the bushes.

And all but into the arms of a young Samoan who appeared silently from the right. He grabbed her arm. She shrieked, an animal sound of fear and flashing rage, buried her teeth in his arm and flailed at him with knees and feet. He cried out in surprise and pain and let go. He fell back from her. For a moment they paused, in equilibrium. And then he went on falling, tumbling down a wooded bank, crashing through the undergrowth but still silent, until, with one small cry, he folded like a singed bug, and disappeared into the brush further down the slope. Ann clutched at a nearby sapling, righting herself. She heard something else behind her, a swish of branches, a near-silent footfall on the loam. She fled down the path.

16

Han waited at the airport until he saw the aircraft carrying his cargo actually lift off for Honolulu. Then he got Sarge to transport him and the officer who had been on guard at the morgue back to the station in the ambulance. There was no sign of the Chief's red Suburban, either at the airport or the station. How many of that official party the old man had loaded into his magic coach and where the hell he had transported them, Han didn't want to know.

He checked in the dispatch room, but there was no message from Derrick Lee in LA. Or no one had thought to write it down–stone age memory being more reliable than its literacy. If the person who is doing the remembering happens to be around.

He got himself a cup of warm water from the spigot out behind his office and glanced up the steep track toward the center of the village and Sa'ili Tua'ua's house. He probably had, at this point, a reasonable explanation for the death of the Tuna Pimp, even if he didn't have the likely perpetrator in hand. What were the chances that the Tuna Pimp's death had any connection with the other two? He thought about what little he knew about the boy, Uli. A known punk. Outcast from his family and no job. But partying at the Frigate even early in the evening, when the Tuna Pimp was still alive and whatever cash–as well as tuna–he might have had still in his possession. On the other hand, Begley was dead, or had been right about then, and they had never found his wallet. So had the dead doctor's cash funded the boy's earlier spree? Uli wouldn't have had the gun by then. But following a known palagi drunk down the road in the dark and bashing him over the head with a lump of concrete seemed a straightforward enough approach to cash flow. If you think that way. A possibility anyway. Welly said the boy was dressed palagi-style, in pants. He would have to ask Osgood if the man he had seen in the starlight on the road could have had shoulder length hair.

He went back into his office, but the heat was unbearable and he went back outside and leaned on the boardwalk railing, looking out at the village and sweating. What about Sapatu? Was there any possible connection between Sapatu and Uli? In general, wise punks don't kill cops. Also, if Uli was up on the mountainside robbing and then killing the Tuna Pimp, he would have a hard time being down on the mudflats of Pago shooting the assistant chief of police. The places where Sapatu and the Tuna Pimp had been shot were only about a thousand yards apart. But, given everything else going on at about that time, getting from the one place to the other wouldn't have been that easy. Which left the problem of the gun.

Just keep plugging, Han told himself. Just keep getting the times down closer and closer. Sooner or later, there won't be any space left and the pieces will have to fit together. Gotta go around and talk to all those people again: Osgood, the Frigate crowd, the Tongan settlement, the fishermen in the hospital.

He grunted to himself, conscious of an extreme lack of zeal. What *about* Sapatu? He had never really given Sapatu's death much thought. That kind of thing is so much the potential fate of police officers that he had just accepted it as that. That and bad coronaries. But if you put Sapatu's death back into the jar with the others and shake them all up, what do you get? Could Sapatu have any independent connection with any of this. What about with Begley? The punk Uli was certainly Han's favorite choice for double murderer, but what about the old feud with Sapatu's village? Where had Sapatu been at 8:50 Friday night? Or who had he been giving orders to? Han's Sapatu was not, of course, the Sapatu said to have threatened Begley–if there was a threat–but Han had no idea how deep Samoan vendettas ran. He needed a consultant.

He thought about going back out to the hospital to find Ann. But talking wasn't really what he wanted to do with her right now, and she didn't show any signs of interest in what he did want. Welly would say any damned thing that came to mind, depending on what about his native culture or his family was pissing him off most at the moment. Han walked up to Sa'ili's house.

Samoans don't have doors to knock on because they're not supposed to need the kind of privacy that requires warning of your arrival. Han walked around the back of Sa'ili's house, saying *Talofa?* from time to time and feeling foolish. He wiped the sweat off his face with the tail of his shirt. On the other hand, in a place where any barrier to a breeze is lunacy, having a culture evolve without privacy is probably not illogical. Finally, a stunningly beautiful girl with a voluptuously sleepy face appeared at one edge of the porch.

"Is Sa'ili here?"

The girl smiled at him, delicious and uncomprehending. He tried Samoan. The girl giggled. But she pointed up the mountainside. Han recognized the word for plantations.

"Thanks," he said. He had no interest in any more exercise in the afternoon heat. But whatever cooling was going to happen would start soon as the sun dropped behind the highest ridges. Stumping on up the dirt road, Han guessed it was something to look forward to.

Ahead, a bent tree stood picturesquely backlit against the afternoon sky. The tree shifted and became the figure of a tall, bulky man, and then the figure of Sa'ili Tua'ua. He wore only a ragged orange lavalava, tied at the waist. He was chopping at the ground with a stone-age digging stick. He lifted a massive tangle of taro roots, trimmed it with a couple of neat whacks with a bush knife, then began planting out the separated roots. At least, Han thought, the forty-five degree slope meant you didn't have to bend over so far.

The big man grinned, dropped his tools and wiped his hands on his lavalava. "It's one way to get away from the family. God knows, nobody else comes up here on a Sunday afternoon."

They shook hands and Han thought, so, is it just a Samoan thing, this keeping of the spaces so neatly between you different selves, individual and communal, without doing violence to any? They stood there silently together, looking out across the leeward island, laid out below them like a shaggy green carpet. The sky and the sea were blue, and a tiny, private breeze was working its way from somewhere cool across the backs of their necks. Or could a bright man get away with that in any culture, as long as you didn't scare the horses? No. Because there are Hitlers and the gulags, imperial Japan, slavery in America, apartheid. So maybe the trick is the no violence part. Han thought about his own life and gave that idea up for a lost cause.

They both heard the sound and looked up. But it wasn't the high-pitched cry of gulls, circling hopefully above them, or the clatter of palm fronds. The sound had been soft, visceral. And now there was an animal, moving fast down through the forest.

Suddenly, the sound transformed to a greeny-brown figure like a manic wood-sprite that rocketed through the brush at the top corner of the taro patch, tripped, fell and rolled down another dozen yards or so before coming to rest in a heap. Ann Maglynn lay looking at the sky as if it were a sign written in a foreign language. Han and Sa'ili scrambled up the slope towards her. She curled like an animal, preparing to spring away. Then recognition swept her face. It crumpled like a child's, and for a moment, Han thought that she was going to cry.

But she said, "I found Uli."

"Dead?" Sa'ili said.

"Why did you think it was Uli?" Han said.

She sat up, wrapping one arm around her knees, as if holding herself together. With her other hand, she drew the long hair. "He was naked, though. Hung. By a lavalava. Strips. Of a lavalava. Maybe it was someone else."

But they all must have been thinking the same thing. A boy with long hair that nobody's been able to find today. A boy in trouble.

"Suicide," Sa'ili pronounced. "Too common, unfortunately."

"Where did you find him? Can you take us back there?"

Her face was pinched and frightened. "It's an abandoned plantation." Her head moved fractionally, pointing back up slope.

Sa'ili nodded. "I know the place. Contested land." He had straightened up and was gesturing, drawing maps across the mountain spine with his hands. "Right where you could argue that the rights of Matagi-fou–Uli's village–and our village, Papasaa, come together. It was never really worth the struggle, either to work or between the villages. I don't suppose it's been worked for the last ten or fifteen years, but he may have known it as a little boy." He looked down at Ann. "What on earth were you doing up there?"

"Hiking", she said, with the abashed defiance of a child. "Following the waterlines. From the hospital." Her face pinched down again. "Somebody tried to stop me. After I had found the body and started down here. He grabbed at me. And I…" She moved her head as if she were having a hard time getting the words out. "Pushed him over a cliff."

Auxiliary units, Han thought. Lots of them. A helicopter would be nice. Radios.

Han looked at Ann. "Sa'ili' will walk you down to the village. You can stay at his house if that's all right with him. You can go to my office. You can go back to the hospital. But write down whatever it was that you saw. Whatever happened. I'll come and get your statement from you later." He looked at Sa'ili. "You'll need to notify the duty officer. If you can't find him–which is always possible–just call Sasa and let him handle it. He'll know what to do."

"The family must be notified."

"In this case, that may not be so easy. Also, remember, by this time we may have two bodies." Han looked down at Ann. She still sat clutching her knees tightly. He reached out for her, made her stand up. She stumbled against him. He wrapped an arm around her, knowing, as sensation poured down him like sweat, that it was what he had been trying to tell her all day. And her body responded. But then she stiffened and stood away.

"Thanks," she said, not looking at him.

"This cliff," Sa'ili said, "Where you pushed your attacker...." He looked at Han. "Do you suppose it's the other boy? The one they said was out in the truck?"

Han shrugged. "Maybe. It's the only explanation that fits with anything else."

"It wasn't really a cliff," Ann said. "I mean, you couldn't, like, see sky. I just shoved him away and he kept falling, like the ground had....disappeared or something."

Sa'ili nodded, looking at Han. "The trail that comes down from that plantation runs along a narrow ridge in places. But the undergrowth is thick enough, you wouldn't necessarily realize how steeply the ground falls away on either side."

"Okay," Han said. They seemed to take it as an order. Which is how he meant it.

He turned away and moved as quickly up the trail as the heat, the rough ground and his rubber thong slippers allowed. After about fifty yards, he gave up on the slippers and tucked them in his hip pockets. He moved on up the trail, toes gripping into the earth. People said there were no thorns in Samoa's jungles, no venomous snakes, no predators. Certainly nothing like Nam. Of course, there were always people. Of course, that had been the problem in Nam as well.

He found the place where Ann had shed her attacker. The trail was scuffed up enough to show fragmented prints from her athletic shoes. A couple of branches had been stripped from saplings, and down a short, sheer drop, the forest carpet of leaves and low bushes had been scored and disrupted. There was no body there now, but beyond a rough hedging of bushes, one of which was partially uprooted, the slope continued down almost as sharply.

"Hello," Han called. "Is anyone there?" He wasn't sure he was saying it right in Samoan, but if an injured man was down there, any voice would be worth a hail back. But there was nothing. Leaves rustled, but the afternoon breeze was stirring in the forest canopy.

He worked his way down the slope. He could hear water now. Further down, a streamlet rose in a tiny spring of lava boulders. There were no more signs of anyone.

He hunkered down in that quiet woodland bowl and listened. Listened to the water. Listened to the wind beginning to push harder through the tree tops. If he was right, and if Ann had told the truth, her attacker had fallen down the slope Han had just descended. And then he had gotten up and walked away. Or, if he was unconscious or his neck or back were broken, had been moved away. Or was waiting, watching, somewhere nearby in the bushes. Whatever the case, he probably didn't feel very well. Han stood up.

"If you're here," Han said in English, "And you need help, you need to let me know where you are. If you've cut yourself or broken anything, in this jungle, without help, you'll be as good as dead in forty-eight hours." If the man was still conscious, even if his neck was broken, he could see and he could shout. So if he could see the grey shirt and the black shorts of the Territorial PD or if he could hear Han's voice, he was hiding from him.

Han didn't have the time or the personnel to play hide and seek. The sun was gone over the mountain ridge now, firing through the tops of the trees but shadowing all below here on the eastern side of the island wall. He made one quick pass around the little dell where the spring rose, then clambered back up to the trail. He still had another body to account for.

Except that the body wasn't there.

He found the abandoned plantation just beyond a screen of undergrowth from the place where the footprints sketched Ann's struggle with her attacker. Halfway up this side of the rough quadrangle of spindly coconut trees, a giant banyan thrust out into the open space. Its growth would have long predated the attempt to clear and use this land and been too much trouble to remove. And the long thick branch elbowing out above the trail made an obvious place to hang yourself from, if you were thinking that way. But there certainly wasn't any body there now.

Han stood where he was. Ann hadn't imagined the attacker. The man's bare feet hadn't left the tracks she had, but Han didn't think she had thrown herself off that bank, rolled down the slope and then gotten up, climbed back up and run down the hill to tell them stories. But had she imagined something here? He walked slowly up the edge of the clearing. There was certainly nothing with the bulk of an adult human body lying under the tree. Or anywhere visible on the nearby ground. There were no trailing vines, no half-fallen branches that could have suggested a hanging body. He stopped again, pouring sweat. The wind was rolling the tops of the trees back and forth, but there wasn't much getting down to him. Maybe this wasn't the place. Maybe there was another plantation further up. He grunted disgustedly and gazed up at the big tree.

And saw how the body had been taken down.

Ten more minutes—five more minutes—and he wouldn't have seen it. The afternoon light would have been too far gone. If he had never watched an extraction team taking a body down, or heard the lectures on suspicious circumstances, he wouldn't have seen it. But he did see the scoring in the old tree's bark where somebody, working fast and not being careful, had cut loose whatever the boy had hung himself with. Whoever it was, if he was working alone, would have had to let the body drop. Han crouched down, looking at the ground. The light was failing, but the loam was thick and carpet-like here, mostly overgrown with low plants and grasses at this interface of old forest and disturbed ground. So he probably would not have found marks of impact anyway. He reached out and touched something that might have been a lump of mud. He raised his fingers to his nose and smiled grimly.

Shit.

He stood up, scrubbing his fingers on a leaf. He let his gaze work slowly around the edges of the darkening glade. So what had Ann see about that body that someone else hadn't want witnessed? Or at least not until the body was far enough decomposed that it wouldn't be obvious how the boy had really died. But did it have to be that? Maybe someone from the boy's family had gotten up here, found the body, taken him home for burial. Maybe Ann's attacker wasn't an attacker, just someone in the rescue party, and it was all a misunderstanding, the family party now struggling home with a rotting corpse and a wounded man. Han didn't have much use for conspiracy theories. He had far too much experience with the limits of human intelligence. On the other hand, he had yet to see the limits of human bad behavior.

Two more hours of full daylight, Han thought, and you could find out for sure. But he had maybe half an hour to get off this mountainside before he wouldn't be able to see to put one foot in front of the other. Overhead, the trees were seething in the wind, and clouds were stacking like folds of heavy drapery, cutting off the first stars. He turned and paced quickly down the edge of the plantation, looking for where the trail cut into the forest again.

The family explanation would have been a reasonable one in Samoa if the boy had a family. Which, everybody said, he didn't. There was the second kid, the village lad who had stayed in the truck. The explanation that he was Ann's attacker was obvious, but that didn't mean it wasn't as good an explanation as any. But Han didn't think he'd rolled down that slope, bounced back up and made off with the body in the fifteen or twenty minutes max it had taken Han to get up to the plantation.

Which meant that there was at least one more person. And that he, Han, had to talk to Ann as soon as he could.

17

"Papasaa," Ann said. She was sitting cross-legged on a mat on Sa'ili's front veranda bent over a mug of tea. Sa'ili and Welly looked at her with polite concern, as one does with sick friends who show signs of dementia. "It all has something to do with Papasaa." Her brain really was working, though the words were kind of falling over themselves.

"You need something to eat," Sa'ili said critically and went off to confer with his ladyfolk.

Welly said unhappily, "Munro's here. They're all closeted up at the governor's house."

Ann nodded, letting him shift the conversation if that was what he needed. "Well, we all knew it would be him. It's just as much Neil's doing as Gar's or the governor's. Everybody thinks Gar's going to fix things their way. And, of course, he encourages that." She twisted another slice of lemon into to the tea, as much comment as condiment. She looked up at Welly suddenly and laughed. "You too, huh? What'd he do? Promise you he'd get you back to New Zealand? I know he's got connections there." She was still smiling, watching Welly light another cigarette, dark brows pulled across his face.

"You know, we were never lovers." Welly looked at her sharply. "Oh, that's not true. Of course, we went to bed together a few times. It was actually fun. Which doesn't usually happen for me. I'd met his wife and pegged her for a hysterical personality disorder–too much gold jewelry and all the fashionable diseases. Made it easy to believe what he said about her, an excuse for doing her dirty. But then came the offer you can't refuse.

Come sail with me and some friends from New Zealand to Samoa. Dream of a lifetime. Always wanted to see New Zealand. Always wanted to sail long distance. Jesus. Got down there to meet him and it was him, two gay guys–thank God, they were great sailors and it made it a little easier for me–and his wife. Four weeks–but who's counting–of being a non-person."

She grinned, shaking her head. "Hey, man, just call me on the phone and tell me it's over. Or nothing. It doesn't worry me. I can live with this. Believe me, I've done it before."

Sa'ili came back out carrying a plate piled with cold baked sweet potatoes. Welly reached for the one shaped like a hard-on. Ann felt herself smiling again. She wanted to finish her story, but she thought of Sa'ili as a conventional Samoan and she didn't want to offend him.

"We had terrible weather the whole way up and Gar and his wife locked themselves in the forward cabin and did nothing. I wasn't strong enough to do the heavier work, but I could at least cook and clean up and share watch with the other two. Slept on a bench. When I could. I think I slept the first two weeks I was here." She watched Welly peel and eat the yam, biting off chunks like it was a banana. The vacancy in her mid-section might have been hunger, but she wasn't ready to chance it.

"You know, Gar's not really bad. He just makes promises. And then gets kind of confused when people expect him to live up to them. Like a lot of us. Running our mouths."

Sa'ili was too polite to say, *who?* He said, "What about Papasaa?"

"Sapatu," Ann said slowly, re-orienting herself to Sa'ili. "And the Tapuafanua and all that wahoo and where Uli's body was. *Entia non sunt multiplicandum prater necesitatum.*"

Welly laughed sourly. "Things don't multiply beyond necessity: look for the common solution. William of Occam: the original conspiracy theorist, AD 1349. Nah. There just isn't much room here for anything to happen. So of course it's connected. Doesn't mean it's causal." He reached for another sweet potato.

For a moment, there was something in Sa'ili's face. Ann thought he was going to say something to his cousin about being a pig. And then saw something else, some recognition. Some connection. But then he did suggest that Welly's manners reflected aspects of the legality and origins of his parentage. And whatever Ann might have seen disappeared into another cousinly wrangle, like puppies growling and chewing and rolling each other over in the dirt.

In the end, they put her in a taxi. At the hospital, she couldn't quite bring herself to walk alone across to her flat past all those deep shadows between the buildings. So she slunk off into the surgery suite to shower. Shedding her filthy clothes in the locker room, she pulled the little camera out of one cargo pocket. She hadn't even thought about the camera in the last hours. The back was shattered. It must have slammed against something in her tumble down the hill into Sa'ili's plantation. Too bad, but–she shivered–she didn't really want those pictures anyway.

Dressed in fresh scrubs and a spare pair of rubber slippers, she padded through the hospital to the ER. She still owed Neil four hours of ER duty for the Tapuafanua's funeral, and he and Adele usually did Sunday evenings. Neil wasn't there. But Adele was. Ann found her perched on a stool in the middle of the main room as if set to catch any possible breeze that might work its way through the space. She was bent over a chart, writing intently, looking small and fierce and alone among the big, cheerful Samoan nurses.

"He's still with the Inquisition," she answered in response to Ann's question. "It's been quiet, but I'm glad you're here. I never did like grown-ups."

"Any...sense of what's happening?"

"Oh, they'll find some way to blame it on him and fire him. But at least then they'll have to pay our way home. Up to now, they've been just trying to piss him off bad enough so that he'll resign, break contract. Then we'd have to pay our own way home."

It was an interesting wrinkle on conspiracy theories. Ann could imagine perhaps one person–the governor's buddy, the lawyer Leon

Fischer—who might be able to *conceive* of saving the government money by getting the Hutchinsons to pay their own way home. But neither Fischer or anyone else was capable of making it happen. And certainly not in Samoa. Ann tried to grunt companionably, something between sympathetic ear and reality check.

"There's a lot of *it* out there. But there's not much they can really blame on him."

"Oh," Adele looked up from her chart. A flash of humor crossed her face. "Mostly being in the wrong place at the wrong time."

"...There *is* certainly a lot of *that* going on...."

"...Now that Gloriana's gotten rid of Ray, there's nothing in her way but Neil." Adele bent back over her chart.

"She is certainly rid of him," Ann said cautiously. Adele snorted but didn't look up.

So angry, Ann thought, and so certain. So American. Suddenly, she was seeing Han's wife the night she was here, vomiting up the pills, cradled in Ann's arms, having failed at being a saint. And Ann knew that telling Welly about Gar and his wife were in some scrambled way supposed to make her feel okay about falling in love with Han. But it wasn't working. Han's wife wanted to be a saint. Ann just wanted to be a decent human being. Disconsolate, she wandered into one of the darkened clinic areas.

Could a Samoan be a saint? Certainly the dual nature of Christ wouldn't worry Samoans the way it does palagis. *Teo le va;* Keep the betweens. Divine and earthly. But what do you do if you live *in* the betweens, a rat in the walls of culture? She laughed at herself and wondered if she had enough time to get to the hospital kitchen and see if she could scare up something to eat.

There was a rumbling outside, then the snap and slam of the back door screen. Too late, she thought. From where she stood, she could see Adele on her stool but not the rear entrance. Adele looked up and then back to what she was doing with the serenity of clinicians who know that the next disaster is not theirs. One of the nurses peeked around the partition and grinned.

"One for you. Ankle."

The young man in the wheelchair was grunting and grimacing in pain, and he flinched when Ann approached him. His ankle was probably broken: swollen, purple, the lower leg with a distinct out-sprung angle. He also had the clear outlines of a human bite on his right forearm.

For a moment, she stood there in the bright overhead lights, looking down at him. Waiting, perhaps, for some acknowledgment that he knew who she was. *How many skinny little red-headed palagi women doctors are there this island?* But that was there and this was here. She had been something else on the mountain side. And so, perhaps, had he been. And now he was the patient, and she was the doctor. She guessed that her own mouth was as capable of producing a septic wound as anyone else's.

She knelt by his leg and inspected the abrasions made by her own athletic shoes, palpated the bones as best she could as he whimpered and pulled away from her. The words for *ice* and *x-ray* entered the Samoan language at about the same time, but she got the point across. A few minutes later, they had given his wounds a first scrub and one of the nurses was rolling him off down a corridor, the injured leg cantilevered out in front of him and wrapped in an ice bag.

She called the hospital operator. "Is Sarge around?" Almost before she had put the phone down, the old guard appeared, his face alert. She said, "There's a man in x-ray that's wanted by the police. He's not going anywhere without help, but I'd just as soon he didn't get any." Sarge grinned ferociously and headed off to the central block of the hospital.

She tried calling the police station. She was beginning to shake again. Dialing took a conscious effort. One of the nurses was signaling her about another patient. She had already been through three different voices on the other end of the line in an unhelpful mixture of English and Samoan when she thought she heard a basso grunt that might have been *Han.*

"Solo?" There was a bit of silence. *If this guy is Samoan, he's going to think I'm nuts.*

"Yes?"

And then she was babbling about the kid with the broken ankle. "I can't come get you," she finished. "I have patients."

"Don't worry about it," he said shortly. "I'll be there."

And ten minutes later, he was: no siren, maybe out of respect for the hospital, but certainly roof lights and attitude. How he had laid hands on a squad car, she never found out. But he was pushing the wheelchair when the kid came back from x-ray.

"I'd like to just take him to jail," he said succinctly.

Neil Hutchinson walked in the back door with Welly. "I'd like to take 'em all to jail. Who'd you have in mind?"

Welly held the boy's films up to the light. "Remind me not to go hiking with you."

Adele said, "Did they fire you?"

Han said, "Not yet."

Neil said, "Not exactly."

Welly said, "They didn't give it to Gloriana?"

Adele said, "Will they'll pay our way home?"

"No," Neil said. "Yes."

"That's what I like," said the visiting do-gooder orthopedist, who had just turned up. "Decisiveness."

Ann left.

The kid was still sitting in his wheelchair in the little crash room by the back door. Behind her, in the main room, Ann could hear Welly and the orthopedist arguing cheerfully about what to do with the boy's ankle. Whatever they decided, Han wasn't going to be happy, since surgery was sounding inevitable. Through the back door screen, Ann could see the flare of Sarge's cigarette as he stood guard. The boy's face wrenched in distress.

Should she hate him for attacking her or herself for injuring him? It didn't seem to matter. Maybe Samoans are right and it is just context: the *now* rather than the *was* or *should*. She checked the ice bag. The ice was melted. Without speaking, she took the bag to the sink and refilled it. As she wrapped it again around the ankle, she looked into the boy's face.

"Uli was your friend," she said gently in Samoan.

Surprise, pain, fear: the emotions passed like primary colors across his face.

"Why did he...." She didn't know how to say 'kill himself'. "Why did he die?"

As if squeezing the words out of himself, the boy said, "Shark."

The medical officer coming in for the midnight shift walked in from the back hall, and the orthopedic rescue party erupted from the treatment room. Adele and Neil were gone, probably to Neil's office where they could discuss their fate in privacy and, more important, air conditioning. Ann found herself standing outside the back door alone.

Han appeared, looking explosive.

"What did he tell you?" he demanded.

Ann shook her head. "Not much." Maybe he thought she needed to be walked home. Maybe it just happened, but they were walking together out across the front of the hospital grounds. "He said Uli was killed by sharks."

"Sharks."

"I've seen people mauled by sharks. That body hadn't been anywhere near sharks."

Han made a soft sound in the darkness, a growl or a snort or a soft laugh. "Though that's not a bad guess as to where it is now."

"What do you mean?"

"It was gone when I got there."

"Gone?"

"Gone."

At least, Ann thought in the silence that followed, with only the sound of their feet crunching on the gravel of the road making a small here-and-now out of the incomprehensible, at least he believes that the body was there, that I did see something.

As if reading her thoughts, he said, "I found where it was, all right. And I do think this kid...." Silhouetted against a light from the hospital, his head jerked back toward the ER. "...Tried to stop you because you had seen it. Did you write out that statement for me?"

"No." Hadn't even thought about it, she might have said. "But I did take pictures."

Han stopped, and she saw the edge of a flashing grin. "Well done. That also explains why they were trying to stop you. To get the camera. Doesn't make a lot of sense otherwise."

"But, the camera got smashed. Some of the film may be okay. What was already rolled back on the reel. But the pictures of the body would still be exposed. I mean, you know, still stretched across the back of the camera where the body broke. I mean, the body of the camera."

She hated sounding like a fool. She was glad she couldn't see his face. She might be trying to fabricate some honor toward Han's wife, but it was all damned hard work and she wasn't doing very well. They were walking now among the lower residential pavilions. He stopped and sat on one of the terrace walls, putting his hand down beside him as an invitation. A spear of light came across from the hospital, making it a tiny bit more proper, in Samoan terms. Ann though about Samoan night, private, and therefore sinful. A warm wind slid around them like a silky, dark quilt. She sat down beside him.

"Think about what you saw," he said patiently. "You're a doctor. You don't have the pictures, but you had to look at the body. You at least had to look through the camera to take the pictures. How long do you think it had been there?"

"Long enough," she said slowly, "That it didn't occur to me that there would be any point in trying to get him down myself, like to try to do CPR or anything."

"Why?" He walked her through the images in her head, the color of the legs, the swelling, the great banyan tree, witness and executioner. Finally, he made her look at Uli's face. "Was it grey, like it was drained of blood, or dark, like the blood had choked off there?" She tried to remember, not wanting to see again but curious at his choice of words, words which somehow suggested no preference, purely clinical, suggesting means to an effect.

"Dark," she said slowly. "As dark. Maybe darker. Than his legs."

His head nodded slowly and the light from across the road moved across his face. "Was his mouth open?"

"No. Yes. A little. As if his jaw was slack. But not gaping."

"His tongue wasn't sticking out, then?"

"No. Not obviously."

He nodded again.

"What does that tell you?"

He glanced at her. His mouth curled up at one corner. "What's it tell *you*?"

She thought about it. "Differential pressures of some kind? I don't know much about heads. With legs, if you have poor venous circulation, you get a swollen purple leg. If you cut off arterial circulation, you have a pale dead leg."

"So whatever happened to this guy, it probably didn't involve an injury that cut off the circulation to his head."

"But...."

"Don't worry about it. Like you said, seems unlikely we'll ever have a body to prove anything from." He stared silently across at the hospital. She followed his thoughts: into the operating room, to the bedside of a potential witness. He said, "But it's worth remembering. As a check on what other people remember."

"If they remember."

"Yeah." He looked at her. "You know, there's got to be at least one more person involved." She hadn't thought about it, actually. But he was right, of course. If the body was gone, the kid with the smashed leg hadn't taken it. She didn't know how he had gotten himself off of the mountainside. But people do sometimes do that sort of thing, particularly if they're strong and healthy to begin with. But they don't get themselves down off the side of a mountain with a smashed leg and a dead body they've cut down and stash the body somewhere or drop it off a cliff into the ocean *and* get themselves and their smashed leg to the hospital.

"Maybe...maybe that other person I thought the people in Uli's village were talking about? Presuming this guy...." She nodded toward the hospital. "...Is the other one."

"Most likely," he said. She wondered if he was thinking what she was, that the first two people who came to mind were the last two she wanted involved. She almost said something about Papasaa. But since the only two people Han knew from Papasaaa were those same two people, she didn't. He stood up. "But, do me a favor. Don't go hiking again any time soon."

She stood up as well. "And don't take candy from strangers."

"Yeah, well...." They walked up the terrace steps into the quad. She could see him sweep the area with a quick movement of head and eyes, always alert. "Like Welly says, the problem is, nobody's a stranger around here."

We are, she thought. You and I. Aliens, allies. She wanted to touch him, fold herself into comfort and safety. An illusion, but no less intoxicating for that.

The power went out.

They both stopped. The only light had been a single pole lamp in the middle of the quad. But without it, they were in some danger of stumbling up steps and falling off terrace walls. He grasped her arm just above the elbow.

"You all right?"

"Yes," she said. She stood absolutely still. She knew that she should pull away from him, but she didn't have the strength–she wanted him too much for that. But she was also too proud to do the other, to press herself forward into his embrace. Whatever happened next had to be a choice, not a defense.

His hand slid up her arm, wrapping over her shoulder. The rest was easy.

But they had less than ten seconds before the hospital generator came on. It wouldn't light the quad, but it would certainly silhouette them clearly enough for anybody's view. She heard the generator rumble, off on the other side of the hospital. She put her hand against his chest and skimmed her mouth back from his.

"Wait."

She led him up the terrace as the hospital lights came on behind them. The door to her flat swung open under her hand. She thought, he's going to lecture me about remembering to lock it. The lights came on.

Except that the light wasn't electric. It was the oil lamp on the table.

A cheerful voice said, "You always were good in a storm, I'll say that for you." Ann choked a scream and then, as her eyes adjusted to the light, Gar Munro's voice became Gar Munro's silhouette and then his figure, sitting at her kitchen table.

"What are you doing here?"

"I do have a key. It was my residence, after all." He looked expectantly at Han.

Her fury surprised her. She wanted to go for Gar with teeth and fists and feet. Like the poor kid on the mountainside. *Mauka* But this was *makai*, toward the sea. She pulled herself together. Like a duchess. Or kept things apart. Like a Samoan. "Lieutenant Han: this is Colonel Garfield Munro. He's here as the government's mediator in the hospital business." She looked coolly back to Gar. "Lieutenant Han was detailed here from the San Francisco Police Department several months ago. He's been working on Ray Begley's death, among other things."

Gar couldn't have seen anything, which was good. And the introduction had been weighted, Samoan style, as well as she could. They were still standing, Han in the doorway, she a few steps inside. Gar lounged at his ease at the table, eyeing them expectantly. Like a little boy, she thought–no, a little girl: determined to cause all the trouble she can. The thought amused her. Goodness: was *that* the problem? It would explain the boat.

Suddenly she wanted to laugh. Instead, she said aggressively, "Neil said you fired him."

"Certainly not," Gar said. "We just gave his job away."

"Not to Gloriana?" she said, echoing Welly.

He laughed. "No." He named the head of the public health division, a mid-level traditional chief, pleasant and ineffectual. Gar shook his head. "They never would have given it to Gloriana." His voice whipped the words with the scorn of the insider. He would do well in Washington. "Whatever her connections to the governor. And the mob connections in L.A. were a little much."

Ann snorted. Poor Gar. Always one remark too many. She wondered if Han would pick up on how much Gar was fabricating.

Han said, "What do you mean, mob connections?" The words brought out the British cadences of his voice. Ann caught the flash of curiosity in Gar's face. With Gar, though, curiosity was more apt to kill the thing that intrigued him than himself. But now his inside knowledge had been challenged, and he would have to show off. It wouldn't occur to him that Han might know more about what he was talking about than he did.

"There're more than a hundred thousand Samoans in L.A. And like Italians in the northeast, most of them are solid citizens. But close-knit extended families have a variety of uses. In L.A., mostly it's enforcing. Gloriana and Ray kind of orbited on the periphery, the part with the money, anyway, the parties, Vegas and the Springs. That's how they met."

"How do you know? Did you know them there?"

Gar's smile had an edge now. "No. Ray and I both went to U.C.L.A., but he was ten or fifteen years ahead of me. But he always liked to talk."

"Did he ever say anything specific? Names? Incidents?"

"No." Ann could tell Gar didn't like admitting that. He would have loved to provide the final clue, the tidbit that broke the case. And he would probably still tell the story that way.

"At the risk of being rude," Ann said, "I am going to invite you gentlemen to continue this discussion somewhere else. The doctors' lounge in the hospital might be a good place: the power's on there and Colonel Munro can use the bed and bath in the lounge if the governor hasn't arranged something more formally for him."

She didn't actually pick up Gar's duffle and throw it at him, but close. She locked the door behind them, then leaned against the door, letting frustration and amusement do battle across her body. All you have to do, she thought, is win one battle at a time. Hard, though, when you really don't want to win. She hooked a chair under the doorknob and went to bed.

18

Han disposed of Colonel Munro easily enough. The man really didn't know anything. Han left him wide open to be the star witness, but he couldn't come up with anything verifiable. They parted at the doorway to the doctors' lounge without shaking hands. As a Korean, this didn't bother Han. His native culture accepted differences in status as a matter of course, not requiring demonstration that the other guy didn't have a weapon in his dominant hand. As an American, it amused him. What was he supposed to do? Salute?

He avoided thinking about Ann. But he did have a powerful urge to take that kid apart. If Welly and his buddy had left him anything conscious to work on.

He found the surgical party in the prep area outside of the operating rooms. Welly and the other surgeon were scrubbing. The kid with the smashed ankle was lying on a stretcher.

"He awake?"

"Close enough," Welly said. His eyes glittered over the surgical mask. Han snorted but went over to the stretcher. The boy stared blankly at the ceiling.

"Anybody know his name?"

"Sikolisipimoalipaki. Call him Bert."

Han looked down at the boy on the stretcher. His hair wasn't as long as the description of Uli, but it was wild and full, his few facial hairs grown out in long strings.

Han said, "Bert." The boy's eyes flicked a little. Even if the boy told Han anything, it wouldn't be usable in court, not after pre-op meds. But, then, most of the information Han had collected in the last thirty-eight hours wasn't usable in court, so what the hell. "Dr. Maglynn says you told her Uli was killed by sharks. That right?" There was no response at all this time. He tried again in Samoan, but it probably wasn't much more than *what happen Uli?*

Welly said, "You just asked him something about his private parts."

"You want to do it for me?"

"Ask him about his private parts?"

"Translate. And not make it up as you go along."

"Not sure I could do any better than you–making it up I mean." Turning off the water with a lever at his knee and clasping his hands up in front of him, Welly walked over to the stretcher and began talking to the kid. From what Han could follow, it wasn't chiefly syntax. He also couldn't tell that it anything to do with what Han had been asking. The boy mumbled something. Welly leaned down to listen. Then he stood back and nodded to the nurse anesthetist, a short palagi male shaped like a fireplug. The man rolled the stretcher away into the O.R.

"Kid's a Jesus freak."

"What do you mean?" Han said, irritated that his witness had just been carted off.

Welly shook his head. The orthopedist had finished scrubbing too and was backing through the O.R. doors, his hands clasped like Welly's in front of him.

"Satan is the new high chief, *fa'a Amelika* taking over from *fa'a Samoa*. Complete bullshit." Welly headed to the OR doors. "Kid's from Papasaa. There's no new chief in Papasaa. There's a significant shortage of chiefs in Papasaa. And there won't be any new ones until the family gets its shit in gear. Also: first time I ever heard the Devil had any interest in tuna fish." He bumped through the doors, leaving Han standing, alone and fuming, outside.

But at least he had a car. So he drove back to the station. The midnight desk officer who slept on the floor behind the desk was sleeping on the floor behind the desk.

Like last night, at the critical moment, he woke up. "Sir: you got a telephone call."

Han waited. Part of him still expected telephone messages in writing, but he was learning.

"From L.A.," the desk officer said cheerfully.

Han broke first. "Message? Phone number?"

"Yes, sir. Derrick, sir." He rattled off a ten-digit number. The area code was certainly L.A. and Han had the rest of the number somewhere in his office.

"Thanks. Did you take the call yourself?"

"Yes, sir." So it had come in after midnight. Han nodded again and went off through the back hall. If Derrick had called after four in the morning L.A. time, he was probably still awake. Han dialed the number. And got Derrick's voice mail. But at least the telephone was working.

He yawned until his jaw threatened to unhinge. He felt like he'd been hit by a train. And for what it was worth, the floor of his office wasn't where he had hoped to spend the night. He considered being pissed at Munro again, but he was too tired. He got himself a drink of luke-warm water and pulled out the Tuna Pimp's journals.

Now that he knew what wahoo was, the first book was obviously a record of the Tuna Pimp's tuna transactions. Han flipped through the pages. If there was anything significant there, he was missing it. He opened the second book.

I am become the tiger, no longer to cry alone when the claw strikes. It was a lousy poem. And the Tuna Pimp hadn't been enough of a scholar to put it in Chinese characters. But you got the point. He had dated it, like a journal: about two years ago. And the date fit roughly with the opening dates of his tuna brokering.

The careless farmer comes to the field with his blade. I am the rock in the helpless barley. I am the rock. And so forth. The first half-dozen pages were fragments of poems, all pretty much like the first ones, declaring the Tuna Pimp's new-found power and freedom. Then the tone shifted to more overt threats against the powers that be. *Not even pieces of the game, which have some substance, but bubbles they think us, baubles of their luxurious bath. But we shall become a rain of steel....I am the thunderbolt. I will open the sky.*

Han thought about the Tuna Pimp, living up on the mountain side, brooding over his gun among his boxes of wahoo. The date in the journal was about a year and a half ago, maybe six months after he had jumped ship. From that point, there was less poetry and more rambling essays on power and injustice. But as the weeks went on, the entries got more and more specific: somebody needed to pay.

Han rubbed his eyes and sat looking out into the night. A bug had battered and singed itself into a twitching lump against the glass sides of Han's oil lamp and lay now on the surface of the desk. So what had happened? Han didn't think the Tuna Pimp had planned the riot. But the rumor about the assault on the fishermen had sparked up, and the rest must have had its own inevitable logic: *I am the tiger; I am the thunderbolt.* In a quieter moment, the Tuna Pimp would see Samoans as just another oppressed people. He seemed to have integrated himself into the little Tongan settlement on the mountainside in something of that spirit. But on the night of the riot, in the emotional epicenter of that crowd, he would have seen Sapatu standing up in front of the Koreans in his uniform and his arrogance as the essence of everything he hated most. And God knows, Sapatu was a hard target to miss.

Han had no proof of course. But the gun that had wounded Sapatu was connected in as straight a line as you could get around here to the Tuna Pimp. And the man's journals at least provided a background kind of motive. And if Han could have interviewed every surviving Korean who had been in the crowd that night, could he find someone who might admit to having seen the Tuna Pimp pull out his pistol and fire at Sapatu?

Maybe. Probably. People will admit to anything, particularly when they had nothing to do with it.

So then what had happened?

Han could see the Tuna Pimp, horrified and exultant, scrambling back up to his shack in the backwash of the riot to find Uli and Bert ripping him off. Did he confront them, breathless, waving his pistol like Eli Wallach or with a cold growl like Toshiro Mifune? It didn't matter. They were half his age and twice his size. It wasn't proof. Only little bits of hard evidence here and there. But science made a *Tyrannosaurus rex* out of less. But of course, science hadn't had to go to court with it. But, he probably wasn't going to get to court with it either.

The telephone woke him up. Derrick.

"Find something?"

"Yeah. I think maybe I did. First off: your four computer jocks all check out: one from down here; the other three from up in your neck of the woods, Silicon Valley types. But about your dead doc: I asked around. Not my usual level of society. Got big nothing. But I was out at my parents today—yesterday, Sunday, anyway—and I asked my dad, just by the way, if he'd ever known your guy, being they're in the same speciality. 'Sure,' he says. Right off the bat, no prompting. Says the guy not only lost his license but was ejected from the local medical society—something that, like, never happens."

"Why?"

"I'm getting to that. Because he had turned up in photos of a wedding reception that was widely viewed as a mob do. Says there had been accusations before, including a couple of guys claiming they'd had tires slashed, coupla muggings, after they'd challenged him about medical stuff. But these photos were viewed as, like, proof. And he didn't deny it. Was just like, 'so what?' My dad says after that, the society just like turned their back on him. Dates fit with the probationary licensure judgement and when you say he turned up there."

So it was true. Han permitted himself a small bit of pleasure that he would have found this out even without Munro.

"Have you seen the pictures yourself?"

"You are, like I always said, a lucky bastard. Unbelievably enough, yes. Being both an immigrant and a doc in a real high-risk specialty, he is like totally paranoid about the legal system. So he documents everything eight times over–minimum. He sat on the executive board of the medical society when they canned your man. He Xeroxed the pictures and saved them with his notes on the case."

"See anybody you recognize?"

Han heard Derrick's soft laugh. "You mean anybody Samoan."

"Just give me a connection. I don't care what color it is–or the shape of its eyes."

Derrick chuckled again. "Serious bad guy called Tani Tuaua."

"Tua'ua. You sure?"

"Sure I'm sure. You know him?"

"No. But I know some of the family. At least the family here."

"Well. Everybody Samoan is related to someone . Hard to know how important that is. But, this guy's interesting. Fact is, he's been a pet of mine for a long time. The old guys around here remember him turning up here in the early sixties, fresh off the boat, went to one of the local high schools. Grabbed up by the high school football scene, like a lot of those huge guys are. But he was different. Went from guard to quarterback in a single season. 'Tani the Terror Tuaua'. USC was slobbering scholarships all over him before he finished his junior year, buffed him up academically, took him for the big ride. But by his second year there, he'd already been up before the judge a couple of times, assault, date rape. Always got off, but when he was drafted–by the Army that is–nobody pulled any strings to keep him out."

"That was all a long time ago."

"Yeah, but the story goes on. I've never had reason enough to make tackling the Feds to verify it worth the time, but the rumor is Tani was one of those guys trained for the Phoenix Program during Viet Nam. You know." Han did. If Criminal Investigation was the last vestige of civil social order in the midst of war, the Phoenix Program had been the opposite: covert ops, assassination, the opening rounds of the new world order, war by terrorism.

"This is a long story. So: he's back on your turf and active?"

"You bet. Enforcement, mainly, muscle. They call him 'The Shark' now. Except that he doesn't even need the blood in the water." Tani, Han thought: *tanifa*, shark. "Funny thing though. When I saw him in my dad's photo, I realized I haven't seen his signature in a while. Street word is that he's retired, gone to the Springs or Vegas like all good aging hoods."

"What's his signature?"

Derrick laughed. "Spontaneous, creative, and doesn't give a shit. If you know a hit is too damned convenient not to be commercial but doesn't fit any known pattern and you can't pin it on anybody, it's probably Tani. Bright, personable. They say he plays the ukulele and dances the hula. Lots of money. Where ever he is, he's probably the life of the party."

"What about co-workers?"

"None known. In any organized sense. My guess is, from something I got from an informant a couple of years ago, he picks up odds and ends of street kids to run errands. But they don't seem to survive the experience long enough to rat on him."

Han thought about Bert, the kid on the stretcher with the smashed ankle. The kid was probably damned lucky he had run in to Ann first.

"Thanks, man. I owe you."

"Yeah, well, you always do. But I'd still rather be here than where you are."

"Me, too."

After Derrick rang off, Han sat for a time watching another bug that had blundered into the pool of yellow light from his lantern. And he knew that, up to now, he hadn't been taking any of this seriously. Oh, he had been doing his job. To the extent that was possible here. But he had been going about it like the ultimate bad joke: the street-wise cop working in a place with no streets. So there were seven dead people. Eight, if you counted Ann's Samoan saint. One died of old age, five in a riot, one killed in a robbery, and one dead of an excess of self-destructiveness. And one suicide. Okay, nine. So, maybe a very bad day in Black Rock.

But one has documented associations with a bad guy called 'Shark'. And the suicide is said to have been actually been killed by 'sharks.' But you have a reasonable witness who says that's not true nor does that witness's description of the dead body fit a picture of suicide by hanging. And this second guy had in his possession the gun that wounded number three and killed number four. And number four was the owner—or at least the original thief—of that gun. It had to be connected. But it didn't make a goddamned bit of sense.

The hair on the back of his neck stirred. If Derrick's serious bad guy was here, there was nothing in this society that could control him. An industrial society could create a killer like Derrick's Tani. But it also had the resources to run him down. A place like this, until and unless such a predator got bored and left, there wasn't a damn thing Han could do about him. Unless Han could get proof. And how many times had he been in court with proof and it hadn't done a damned bit of good? He yawned again and rested his head back against the wall.

"Hey! Thought I had you sleeping comfy tonight. No more desks."

Han lifted his head and looked out his open door. Welly was standing outside on the ground beyond the porch, his wild face floating like a balloon between the floor and the railing.

"Sleeping behind desks is part of the job description."

"Maybe. But not when you can sleep with a nice body." Welly swung himself up to sit on the railing like a cheerful gargoyle.

"Yeah, well. She had other ideas." Han told him about Munro.

"You got that all wrong. She'll be so grateful you got the son-of-bitch out of there, she'll be even more grateful."

Gratitude wasn't what Han wanted. At the moment, mostly what he wanted was sleep.

"When is that kid going to be awake enough to talk to me?"

"Not til tomorrow. Or at least, later today. Come on up to Sa'ili's. Time for a beer. Or at least a better place to sleep."

They padded silently up through the dark village. The power was still out, and starlight fell around them like snow. Welly marched into the open corridor that ran across the back of his cousin's house. Midway along, he stopped and pulled at something that made the sticky sound of a refrigerator door opening. Things clinked softly as he explored the interior.

"Damn," he said. "Something yucky."

A tall silhouette filled the silvery oblong of the far end of the hall. Sa'ili's voice hissed: *"What* are you doing?"

"Looking for beer," Welly said.

"Well, do it with a light," said his cousin, striking a match that revealed a kerosene lantern right above them. "Besides, we don't keep beer in there." From an ice chest at his feet, he pulled a quart of Vailima. As if recognizing the inevitable, he gathered up three glasses and herded his guests onto a side porch, away from the sleeping family.

Han guessed this was the palagi side of Sa'ili's house: three low white wicker chairs and a little round glass-topped table. Han decided that he was beyond even feeling sorry for himself and accepted the beer gratefully.

When Sai'ili came back with the second bottle, Han said, "You guys know a Tani Tua'ua?"

Welly nodded. "Our cousin. You met 'im the other night. Went with us to the Frigate."

Han remembered him: tall, fit, listening to every word. Han's insides turned over.

"His name isn't Tua'ua," Sa'ili was saying. "That's a chiefly name. His name is Palapala. Tanifa Palapala. But yes, he's our cousin."

Welly grinned sardonically. "Rotten to the core. Definitely wrong side of the tracks. Or the village. Like, totally *mauka*."

Han's face flamed from the beer. But he was stone cold sober. "He still over at Papasaa?"

"Sure," Welly said, pouring out the beer.

"Why?" Sa'ili's voice was soft. He had turned the lantern way down. There was a tiny pool of light on the table, just enough to pour by, but not enough to see each other's faces clearly. Neighbors waking on their sleeping porches to the gentle rumble of voices across the way and looking out indignantly might not be able to tell who was sitting there.

"I'd like to talk to him," Han said. "If he's the same Tani Tua'ua. Or whatever. Palapala."

Welly snorted. "There probably aren't two of them."

"What do you mean?"

"Oh, nothing. He was a pain in the ass when we were kids, but he hasn't been around for twenty years, so I guess I can't complain."

"But what is it that you want to talk to him about?" Sa'ili said again.

"You said he's been gone. Where was he?"

"Army," Welly said. "Special Forces or some such. You know. Then L.A. Hey, you find those guys that were in the hotel bar?"

"Yeah. Only one from L.A., though. The other three were from up near San Francisco."

"That's only four."

"You only told me four."

"Five," Welly corrected. Han was going to protest. And then he thought about it. He had gotten the four names from the hotel manager. And assumed that Welly had miscounted.

"Okay," Han said. "Describe them to me again."

"I told you. Two of 'em were palagis, I mean, like *white* white. I didn't get a good look at the others. It was half dark and they were over in the corner. But there was more than four.... was a bunch of 'em." Han still couldn't go to court with it, but it was starting to make sense.

"You were out in the middle?"

"Yeah, me and the mates I was with. Table under the windows right across from the bar."

"Would you have been visible to the party back in the corner?"

"Sure. And the lights are a lot brighter where we were."

"Was the group in the corner, the L.A. group, there when you got there?"

"Maybe. I don't remember. But the corner was full. That's why we sat by the windows."

"So you–and Begley, sitting at the bar–would have been spotlighted, while the people in the corner were half hidden."

"Yeah." Welly's voice was a shrug.

"Later, when you and Begley got into it out by the men's room, you said that was broken up by the bartender. Anybody else see that?"

"The bouncer." That tallied with what the bartender had told Han. "Maybe some others. Just a feeling. I didn't really see 'em."

Han wished his brain was clearer. He stumbled in to make use of Sa'ili's toilet. When he came back out, Sa'ili and Welly were laying out mats and mattresses and mosquito netting.

"You said there was a lot of wahoo at the old man's funeral."

"Sure. For the Tapuafanua? You bet."

"How did it get there?"

Welly stood up from tucking a mosquito netting from around one of the mattresses and put his hands on his hips. "Whaddyou mean how did it get there? People brought it."

"No. I mean: was it all there already by the time you got there? Were people still arriving with it? Did *you* bring any?" Welly looked at his cousin as if checking if Sa'ili also thought Han was losing his mind. But Sa'ili stood quietly looking at Han.

Sa'ili said, "Much of it was there. I arrived earlier than Welly and Ann did. Some families did bring cases. Some was being carried in from a pickup that had been wrecked on the road."

"Yeah," Welly said. "Truck made one hell of a traffic jam in the middle of nowhere."

"Did anyone say when the truck was wrecked?"

Sa'ili shook his head. "I don't know. It didn't really concern me. Other than having to walk the rest of the way to the village. I got the feeling from what people were saying it had been there at least all morning. They weren't talking like it was an accident that had just happened."

"Who's truck was it?"

"Belonged to a boy from another village. There was much shaking of heads: you know, too much *fa'aAmelika*, everything's going to come to a bad end and this is the proof."

"You know," Welly said. "I knew I'd seen that kid somewhere."

"Bert?"

"No. The other one. Well, him too, I think. But I mean the one with the long hair: Uli. No wonder they dodged away from me. But he had tied it back. The hair. When I saw him in the village." It took Han another few minutes to get Welly's mouth in sync with his brain. But by the time they were bedding down, Han had at least a sketch of where the Tuna Pimp's wahoo had gone and how it had gotten there: a few more pieces of *T. rex* backbone.

Han lay fighting sleep, knowing that there were things he should be able to fit together now, if he could just stay awake long enough. Welly had fallen asleep instantly.

Suddenly Han was bolt awake. He prodded Welly with his voice. "What did you do with that kid? Did you leave him under guard?"

Welly grunted. "He's in the ICU. Closed space. Center block of the hospital. Besides, Tani can't fly."

Han was very alert. "Why do you say Tani?"

"Tani. Tanifa Palapala. My cousin. Comes back here after twenty years and wants to be Nofonofo. My family is probably the only family in both Samoas where you could actually buy a major title if you really wanted it. Looks like he really wanted it."

Welly's breathing went deep and regular again. Han wanted to kick him. But he had a point: *Tani can't fly.* And: *first time I heard the Devil had any interest in tuna fish.* Okay: so the Tuna Pimp's wahoo had ended up at the Tapuafanua's funeral. But it hadn't been intended for the Tapuafanua's funeral. The Tapuafanua hadn't even been dead then. So was it all just a fuck-up? A couple of bad boys had fallen in with the slick new guy in town. One of them had a pickup. So they'd been sent off with a roll of money to buy some wahoo to grease the skids of family politics. But then the other had happened. Han went to sleep wondering if they had returned the money or if that was one of the reasons Uli had ended up dead.

19

Han woke at first light. Birds chattered in the tall trees almost loud enough to drown Welly's snoring. Han rolled up his bedding and looked around for Sa'ili, but the rest of the house seemed to be asleep. He took off for the police station, bathed under the spigot behind his office and changed into clean clothes. He could probably get through one more day without having to go nice talk Old Lady Nozaki again. He wanted tea but had to settle for water and a headache.

The patrol car he had used last night was gone. But he lucked into a village bus carrying what must have been half the day shift nurses out to the hospital. He thought about hitting Ann up for tea but headed straight for the ICU instead. He nodded to the guard sitting on a mat outside the door among the camped families of ICU patients. The boy, Bert, was actually there, lying in his bed, breathing and awake. The ICU door swung open and Welly stomped in. He nodded curtly to the male nurse on duty but spoke to Han. "You seen Sa'ili?"

Han shook his head. "No. But I just...."

"What about Ann?"

Han shook his head again. Welly looked at the nurse. "Dr. Ann been here?" He yanked the top sheet out from the foot of Bert's bed and pinched the toes sticking out of the cast.

The nurse was shaking his head. "But she doesn't have ICU patient right now."

The surgeon grunted. "Come on. Let's go over to her flat, see if she's there."

Han waited until they were jogging down a back hall. "What is it?"

"Sa'ili was gone when I woke up. Family don't know where. He's had his knickers in a twist about Tani, our cousin, Tanifa, for some time now. Just worries me."

"Like what?"

Outside, rain was blowing in fine curtains from the sea. They trotted across through the residence compound and Welly beat on Ann's door. There was no answer.

"Just...I don't know. You just can't trust Samoans about titles. But...he's always thought he'd end up with Nofonofo. Tani turning up's kind of put a stick in that." He thumped on the door again. So much for a surgeon's hands.

Han wasn't getting this.

"You think Sa'ili may have gone off to...like...challenge Tanifa about the Nofonofo title?"

"You don't believe me. Believe me. It happens."

Not only was Han not getting it, he was caught between Derrick Lee's portrait of a high tech professional killer and Welly being hysterical about stone age village politics.

"What's Ann got to do with it?"

"Sa'ili doesn't have a car, of course. Ann's got access to the public health jeeps. She'd jump at the chance to take Sa'ili to Papasaa to try to get the family to loan her the Tapuafanua's leprosy papers. They were talking about it on the way home from the old man's funeral."

Han stood for a moment, watching the silver curtains of rain drift across the quadrangle. A huge striped umbrella was marching across the road toward them from the hospital. What do you believe about what someone tells you about their own culture? Who was in danger here? The answer to that one was easy enough.

Don't go hiking....
And don't take candy from strangers.

Han was suddenly very tense. "I don't have a car either."

Someone was crossing from the hospital under a striped umbrella. "No. But he does."

At their voices, the umbrella rocked back, revealing Colonel Munro. "Morning gentlemen. Goodness. Quite the party. She's got to be there. She's not in the hospital and the Public Health offices aren't open yet. She does make very good biscuits."

"Fuck," Welly said. "We need your jeep."

Welly looked like he was going to jump Munro and wrestle the keys of his rented jeep from him. While they argued, Han checked with Sarge, who denied seeing Sa'ili but confirmed that Ann had signed out one of the Public Health jeeps just after six a.m.

Munro's jeep jerked to a stop outside of the security office. Welly flung open the passenger door. "More the merrier." Welly was grinning like a shark. "Anybody got a gun?"

"No," Han said, crawling in the back. "Jesus. That's all we'd need." Munro threw the jeep into forward and they rocketed down the lane toward the shore road, mortally endangering three chickens, a pig and two geese. "Better we do this Samoan style, superior numbers and bigger rocks." On the other hand, Han thought, if Derrick Lee is right about this guy, what I'd really like is tuna boat captain Dirty Harry Wanabe's S&W .357 Magnum.

Bracing himself against the jeep's bucking, Han said, "Sa'ili doesn't have a gun, does he?"

"Nah. Not that I know of. The problem is, Tani thinks he does."

"What do you mean?"

Welly grinned at him over the seat back. "Me and my big mouth of course. Teasing him about that pistol, the one I took off that kid Uli. The one you say belonged to the Tuna Pimp."

"*What about guns?*"

"*Got one of his own now.*"

"*From you. And I wish you'd stop telling everybody about it as if it were mine.*"

Munro was a good driver—at any rate better than Welly who was a disaster behind the wheel. But you can only go so fast in Samoa. Even with all forward gears functional, they crawled up the leeward escarpment, slipping and grinding on the slick wet red clay. And then crested the top and were sliding and bumping down through the forest on the other side. If they had bothered to get out and look, maybe there would have been signs of the recent passage of the other jeep. But mostly they just hung on to whatever they could hang on to and trusted to whatever people trust to when that's the only thing keeping their vehicle upright. And it took forever. You could run over the goddamned mountain in less time than it took to drive.

That was right. *Tani can't fly.*

No, but he could walk. Han thought about his trot up the mountainside looking for Uli's body. And Ann's Sunday afternoon expeditions. And neither of them were Special Forces trained. Had Tani just gotten bored with his South Seas idyl and hiked over the mountain to the city lights? The island was barely a mile wide here, straight across. If you were fit and not afraid of ghosts, it would be a piece of cake. Somehow, day or night, Han didn't think Tani was afraid of ghosts.

"That them?" Han had seen a flash of metal through the trees.

"No," Welly said. "But we're getting there." Now Han could see the abandoned pick-up, Uli's pickup. Munro got around the wreck without leaving more than a streak of paint. Han watched through the rear-view window as they left the wrecked pick-up behind. A good cop, he thought, would be there taking down the license number to verify that the truck was Uli's, collecting every speck of dirt from cab and truck-bed for analysis. The truck disappeared behind them through the trees. Well, at least he remembered what he should be doing.

"You want to arrive like the Seventh Cavalry?" Munro's eyes flashed at Han in the rear-view mirror. "Or like the Indians?"

"They all lost in the end," Han said, bracing with knees and elbows as they bounced through a rocky streamlet.

"Down around this cut," Welly said, "We'll come out into the open on the other side of the river from the village. We'll have to leave the jeep on this side. Especially after the rain."

The jeep slithered down the rocky slope through a tunnel of overarching trees. And suddenly, there was the blue Public Health jeep.

The rain was falling steadily on this side of the mountains. They got out of the jeep. The river had risen over its banks on the village side. It spread in a wide smooth pool toward the guest fale. Han, Welly, and Munro stood peering across into the grey-green curtain of rain and palm trees. The only sound was water: rain, river, ocean.

"There they are," Welly said. Across the village green, against the silvery ribbing of tall palms, they could see people gathered. Han made out Ann's slight form standing in the shelter under a fale roof next to the towering figure of Sa'ili. Beyond them, deeper back in the trees, the front door of a palagi-style house opened. The door framed another tall man, dressed in shorts and an aloha shirt. Han recognized him as the extra cousin.

"That's him."

There wasn't a hell of a lot they could do, other than be there. Welly and Munro weren't officers. For Sa'ili and the people of Papasaa, the two docs were part of the hospital, a recognized source of official status. But Tanifa was a different story. If he had a firearm, they were all going to be in a shitload of trouble. On the other hand, if the big shark kept his cool, they were all going to look really stupid. Because until and unless Han could get those four guys from California to identify Tanifa as having been in the hotel bar with them on the night of Begley's death, he had exactly nothing to go on. And even that wasn't proof, only a verification of opportunity.

"Stay here," Han said. "Until I get all the way across. Then come, but stay well behind me and away from each other. If I stop, you stop." They didn't argue. That surprised him. Doctors usually assumed that since they knew medicine, they knew everything else as well.

He stepped into the water. He didn't like doing that. But compared to mountain rivers he had known, this one was neither deep nor dangerous and was warm besides. When he slogged up the bank and into the shallow spreading pool on the green, the players had shifted a little. He could see more people now, faces and figures in the rainy half-shadows.

Sa'ili stepped away from the fale where he had been sheltering from the rain. He stopped, his white shirt shimmering in the watery light. His voice boomed in Samoan. Tanifa's face twitched mockingly. *He doesn't understand the Samoan*, Han thought. *Or maybe it doesn't matter*. Because the people of Papasaa did. And then Sa'ili said it again, in English.

"I accuse you of the murder of the Tapuafanua." Sa'ili stepped forward.

Tanifa pulled the gun and fired so quickly that all Han saw was the movement. But the sound was the Four Horsemen: boom, boom, boom, boom. Flinging himself to the ground a few yards away, Han was spattered with Sa'ili's blood as chunks of the man's flesh were exploded by the slugs.

Tanifa leaped away from the doorway, sprinting toward the forest. Han scrambled to his feet and sprinted after him, shedding his rubber thong slippers as he ran. Tanifa was probably faster, but he was hobbled by his Tevas. How many more shells in the clip: four? Six? Ten? Han didn't think Tanifa dared turn: he had to look where he was going. They dodged around an outhouse. Han was falling behind. There was a short stretch of muddy open ground and then dense forest. Tanifa checked, began to swing around, steadying the pistol to aim and fire.

And fell over a pig.

The gun went off and both the pig and the man screamed. Han threw himself at the melee on the ground but got the pig instead of the man. Tanifa staggered to his feet, spattering blood around him. Han launched himself toward Tanifa.

A hail of rocks pelted them. One hit Han between the shoulder blades and almost felled him. The entire village was running toward them, even the old ladies trotting behind and waving towels as if shooing off the

Devil. Tanifa swung around heavily and fled through the wall of undergrowth at the edge of the clearing. Hands reached out to hold Han back in safety. But, howling like an animal, he pulled away and sprinted after Tanifa up the slope and into the forest.

20

For the first five hundred yards up through the forest, Han could hear the Samoan crashing above him through the brush, turning small stones under his feet that clattered down the steep incline, grunting when he hit something tender. Barefoot, slighter, Han coursed almost silently behind him, avoiding the slap of the heavier branches, padding across a short carpet of moss.

Suddenly, it was quiet. Han crouched, his mouth open to damp the sound of his heaving breath. Like below in the village, all sound was water: the whisper of fine rain, the patter from wet leaves. Above and to the right, Han could hear something else, the gurgle of a mountain stream. Did Tanifa know Han was there? Or had the sound of the water covered him? How badly was Tanifa hurt? Would he need to drink? Wash the wound? Or was he waiting with his gun to see what would come out of the bushes at him. A stiffening breeze hissed in the canopy. More water clattered down through the layers of the forest. But the sounds were random, the pulse of the forest.

In a moment between wind and water, he heard a snap of breaking wood. Then, farther up the slope, another. Cautiously, he moved to follow the sound. He couldn't turn back. One alien sound, one flash of skin or movement and he would be the hunted and–unarmed–dead.

Above him, further away but now distinctly to his left, another stone clattered and rolled. He stopped, crouching. The sound was wrong: A slap of leaves, the crack of stone on rock and then the clatter as the stone fell. The slope was very steep, strata of lava rock poking out like stair-steps. Maybe a stone would fall like that. And maybe not.

Very slowly, Han crouched to the ground and moved crabwise to his right, slipping behind an outcrop of black rock, hoping the grey uniform shirt and black shorts would make up for the movement, groping like a lizard with hands and toes to avoid loose rocks and forest detritus.

He waited long enough for his legs to cramp. Long enough to feel the bruise on his shoulder where he had been hit by the villager's rock. The rain let up. The earth breathed clean.

But suddenly, there was a scent blowing into Han's face. The acrid smell of human sweat, strong and tainted with...cigarette. Not fresh. Tanifa wasn't that stupid. But there was no getting rid of the smell. Han waited, alert again, aches forgotten, face into the wind. The wind was picking up slightly, angling down the mountainside from right to left. Tanifa was there. Waiting. Had been waiting. Like Han. Trained by the same people.

Finally, Han heard him grunt, as if at his own foolishness, and move off up the mountainside.

He wasn't as noisy as he had been at first. Han followed even more cautiously, placing each footfall, each hand grip. The way eased a bit, angling off to the left, not a maintained trail, but as if people had tracked through here, before the road. Up ahead, a whoosh of bird flight told Han that Tanifa had taken the path. A wounded man could walk there, not have to grapple.

Han followed, wondering again how badly Tanifa was hurt and how much advantage that gave himself. The path was angling definitely to the left now, leveling off. Han had only a vague idea how the mountain backbone twisted through here, high ridges and a couple of peaks. The path would logically skirt the highest places, crossing at a saddle. Matafao, at twenty-one hundred feet the highest peak on the island, was in front of them somewhere, but there was no way to see through the forest and the low clouds. The road back to the leeward side was somewhere off to their left.

When the pistol went off, it could have been inside Han's head.

Before Tanifa fired again, Han was already diving for the forest floor, rolling behind a jumble of rocks, tumbling and scrambling further down the slope to better cover. He came to rest in thick brush behind a fallen tree and more rocks. He waited for the next rounds, the sounds of Tanifa coming down through the forest after him.

But the only sounds were his own breath, his own heart. The wind was still in his face. But there was no scent either. He picked up a rock and heaved it sideways through the bushes. The ruse hadn't worked for Tanifa. No reason why it should work for him. But his options were limited.

No response. From where he lay, he could see through a gap in the trees across the upper edge of a meadow, higher up the slope. Another rush of tiny birds exploded upwards out of the low trees just beyond the meadow. Nothing more. No other sign. The place where the birds went up was at least a quarter of a mile from his hiding place. Could Tanifa have gotten up there that quickly? Only if he had fired off a quick shot and run like hell. But why? Why not come in for the kill?

Because he didn't have enough rounds to play games. He couldn't afford to miss even once more and he knew enough not to play blind man's bluff with someone as clever as he was himself.

And he didn't know that Han wasn't armed.

Tanifa was from L.A. Of course a pursuer would be armed.

Han was up and moving, still very cautious but moving as fast as he could, following the trail. Where the path led out into the meadow, Han shifted to the right, straight up through the forest, skirting the open ground. Tanifa had spent an hour in Han's company Saturday evening as they tracked Uli through Fagatogo. (Had that sealed the boy's fate? The night before, the night of the riot, had Tanifa just driven off with Bert and the pickup full of wahoo? Only later finding out what had happened to the Tuna Pimp and, by the way, to his own money? And what the fuck did any of it have to do with Begley? Other than providing another set of witness that Tanifa was on the leeward side that night.) But Han hadn't been in uniform then. He had been wearing Welly's shirt, loose, easily covering a shoulder holster. If you think that way. Today, Han was in uniform. He still wasn't armed. But could Tanifa see what was obviously a police uniform, worn by someone he knew was a police officer, for the few seconds he could have seen Han clearly, and *not* assume that somewhere about his person was a gun? Tanifa couldn't afford to play gun battles. He could only fire a shot to scare Han back and take off.

But why? Just to lose him? Tanifa must guess that Han didn't have any kind of voice communication with him. Because he would have used it by now. So he couldn't organize any surprises for Tanifa on the other side of the mountain until he got down himself. And there was no way Han could know these mountain trails as well as Tanifa did. So where the hell was he going?

And he had to be going somewhere. Han found the trail where it came back into the forest beyond the meadow. He caught sight of Matafao through the trees, its sharp high peak rising into the clouds. But it was almost behind him. He slowed. Why behind him? He let his mind range.

He didn't know these trails. But he did know the map. He let his mind lift. He saw the map: green paper, tight brown contour lines. Paper became forest and mountain shoulders, a helicopter ride: sharp descents to narrow beaches, sea-side villages, ocean. They were crossing the island where the caldera had broken. The sea had poured in, almost splitting the island into two. But the northwest half of the volcano's rim held, making a sharp S-turn out of the island's mid-section.

They were at the mid-point of the S now, headed—if Matafao was behind them—northeast, pretty much straight for the village of Fagatogo. What was in Fagatogo for a wounded fugitive? Not family. Tanifa had just blown away the one person in Fagatogo who might have helped him get away to the airport, maybe catch a hop to Apia. Apia: that open door to the rest of the Pacific and from there, anywhere in the world. Fagatogo had no clinic–it was too close to the hospital at Fagaalu. There weren't even any boats in Fagatogo to speak of.

The trail crossed a tiny stream coming down from the left. Han drank like an animal, sipping, lifting his head to listen, water dripping from his chin, sipping again. He rose silently and paced on. For the next hundred yards or so, stream and trail ran together in the same straight, northeasterly direction. Then, the stream turned ninety degrees off to the right and fell delicately over a miniature lava cliff into a pool, while the trail led straight ahead. Han cast back and forth for a minute, looking for any sign that Tanifa had abandoned his course. But he didn't see anything. The sound of the little waterfall was too loud to hear anything else. And the forest cover was too dense for the movements of birds to help him again. He went on down the trail. But it didn't feel right. He knew he had lost.

The forest opened slightly. He was at the upper edge of an old plantation, the coconut trees overgrown by the wild. Halfway down the clearing was a huge banyan tree.

Han knew exactly where he was. And what Tanifa was doing. He took off running, down the mountainside.

21

Ann left Neil Hutchinson tinkering with Sa'ili's IVs in the ICU. Welly had disappeared for a cigarette. Maybe three. Munro and the do-gooder orthopedist had gone off to find food.

They had been in the OR surprisingly little time by disaster standards, Welly and Ann in the chest and Munro and the orthopedist doing the rest, but they had worked hard. All four shots had hit Sa'ili somewhere, just not where you'd expect. As Welly said, the pistol must have pulled up and to Tani's left. Because at that distance, he should have blown out Sa'ili's left side and killed him instantly. Instead, the first three shots had torn off his right ear, shattered the right forearm flung up in instinctive defense, and amputated chunks of the right deltoid. The fourth punched through his right chest, breaking ribs, tearing up the right upper lobe and dropping the lung–which is probably what saved him from bleeding to death during the nightmare trip back over the mountains in the back of the Public Health jeep–and cracked the scapula but somehow missed both the bigger blood vessels and the major neural plexus of the shoulder.

"He'll live," Welly said as his cousin was being wheeled to the ICU. "If the bugs don't get him. He may even use that arm again. Worth sayin' your prayers, I guess. Jesus."

Ann didn't want to talk to anybody and she didn't have any jokes left. The adrenalin high had worn off hours ago. She would be back. She would probably spend the night in the ICU. She wasn't clever, not like Neil who could calculate and write orders and then go off to sleep in his own bed, trusting to nurses to notice things and call and confident that he would know what they meant when they did. But she could sleep on a spare gurney, opening one eye from time to time to see if the urine bag was filling and pressures and temperatures were staying right. "You don't know shit," an attending physician had told her once, "But your patients don't fall through the cracks." Right now, though, she wanted her own clothes and fifteen minutes to herself.

Out in the breeze-ways, outside of the central block of the hospital, she could hear wind and rain. The storm had come in for real. She breathed a little prayer–of relief that the storm hadn't hit while they were trying to drive back from Papasaa and in hopes that the power would stay on. She found the little hallway down to the exit by the chapel. The lights went out.

"Shit," she said. She touched the wall with one hand while her eyes adjusted. Faint grey evening light showed rain billowing through the screens that made up the last twenty feet of passageway. She began counting, waiting for the generator to come on. It was supposed to take less than ten seconds. A ten second breath hold for anyone on a respirator. Ten seconds in a blacked-out ICU. Ten seconds of staff blundering around in the dark, dislodging catheters, making mistakes.

At the count of six, the lights came back on and a gun went off.

She screamed and jumped away from the chapel door, and the gun went off again. Except, it wasn't a gun. The chapel door slammed open again. She cursed again, sobbing and laughing. She pulled the chapel door tight and stepped through the screen door exit into the storm.

And was immediately soaked. She stalked around the end of the building and across the lumpy lawn toward the parking strip and the road. At least it was warm. The trees bent and tossed in the wind and the road was filling with water, the ruts on either side now parallel rivulets. You could be in Connecticut, she thought. This could be snow. At least this isn't going to kill you. Bent over against the wind, she waded across the road and sheltered for a moment in the overhang of the first of the residential quad buildings.

She was conscious of things being over. Of nothing more to do. Maybe she could get the Tapuafanua's papers and maybe she couldn't. If they survived the storm. Of all the things the old ladies would think to take to high ground, a heavy wooden trunk full of old papers didn't have much survival value. Had Sa'ili put her in danger by asking her to take him over there? Yes, but that was irrelevant. She had guessed why he was going. And she had wanted to be a hero, to witness with and for him. And so she turned out to be just another stupid jerk. She should have talked him out of it, or at least taken him to someone he would recognize as senior, like old Sasa, the police chief. She didn't know everything about Samoan culture by a long sight, but this didn't take an anthropologist to figure out.

She watched the grey curtains of rain move cross the open quad. Okay. So what was left to avoid fucking up, if possible. Han, of course. He was an interesting guy, possibly a good one, but the last thing in the world that man needed was one more needy female in his life. So: get out. Neil and Adele will be out of here in a couple of weeks. Just go on back to Honolulu and find something. Or somewhere else. You can always be a doc-in-a-box. You'll survive. You've done it before. She made a wry face and lifted her face into the rain.

The wind lessened a fraction. She trotted out across the quad to her flat. She lived in the *mauka* end of the building, hard up against the forested slopes. The trees swayed and creaked in the wind, and she wondered if one of them was going to fall over on the building. Sticking her key in the lock, she thought, at least the wind's blowing the other way.

Slipping through the door, she shivered. Maybe remembering last night, of opening the door and having Gar there.

"Fuckin' took you long enough." She would have screamed but a hand gripped her face, clamping her mouth and pinching her nose. "Don't struggle and I'll let you breathe." She froze. The fingers around her nose let up. Now she could feel something else pressed against her cheek, cold, rigid, alien. Gun barrel. The man groaned and shifted, thrusting her down into one of the kitchen chairs, the gun still jammed against her cheek. She had assumed, to the extent that she was thinking at all, that this was her final cultural experience in Samoa, *moetotolo*, sleep crawling, night rape. Now she knew who the man was.

"Found your doctor stuff. Mixed up the medicine. Now, tell me how much I can take without killing myself." The only thing he could possibly be talking about was the old pharmacist's case she carried out to the village clinics; the only medication that would be powdered and have instructions for adding water would be the amoxicillin she dispensed endlessly for ear infections.

"You mean the pink stuff."

He grunted in assent.

"You could probably drink the whole bottle and it wouldn't hurt you."

He shoved the gun deeper in her cheek. "Don't gimme that shit." The room was dark. The storm and the darkness and the power being out left only the staccato sound of his voice, the faintest silhouette perceptible against the floor-to-ceiling glass louver walls. And, of course, the feel of the gun barrel against her cheek.

"It's true." Her voice was calm, something they train into you in medical school, nothing to do with what was going on in her guts. "All I had left was the more dilute stuff I use for younger kids. On the other hand, it won't do you any good either. That antibiotic isn't particularly useful for skin bugs. Which is what your wound is contaminated with."

His hand bunched the back of her scrub top the way a cat would pick up a kitten, and he threw her onto the floor. She fell against something box-like that could only be the old case. She cried out and he hit her, the flat of his hand hitting her head and slapping her face down against the case. She lay still, afraid to move. She felt a tiny tickle in her nose, blood or tears. He plucked her out of the tangle of chair and case and wall and flicked on a tiny flashlight, blinding her.

"What else is in there? What can I use? I need something for pain."

Holding up one hand against the light, she moved her jaw and tried her voice.

"All I have for pain is ibuprofen—Motrin, Advil...."

"Get it."

"It's in the bathroom." He motioned with the gun. The tiny light was just enough to highlight the gun and interfere with her night vision, but she got him the pills and he gulped them down with cup after cup of water. Away from him, and getting used to the light from the little flashlight, she could see his wound, a blackened hole in the left side of his shirt at the center of a broad stain of blood. If he had gotten all the way over here from Papasaa on foot in less than six hours, he was either a superman or the wound was superficial. But, as he had clearly figured out, blood loss was not the mortal issue. He gestured to the case with the gun.

"If not the pink stuff, what do I need?"

"I'm not sure...."

"You're a doctor, goddamit, you better be sure!"

"I didn't mean that," she said, the doctor voice reasserting itself like divine ventriloquy. "I know what you need. I just don't think I've got any left."

She routinely carried dicloxacillin, another dirt-cheap antibiotic useful against the equally prevalent impetigo and mosquito bite abscesses, but she thought she had given away the last of it on her last visit to the clinic. He made another gesture with the gun. She righted the case. The top opened out into little shelves, their few remaining contents tumbled together. In the deep well of the case, she carried dressings and liter bottles of sterile water and normal saline. And for about the first time in the last fifteen minutes or so, she got lucky.

"Here, this'll do." She shook four of the last eight capsules out of a pharmacy vial into his hand. It had been somebody's left-over but too precious to waste.

"What is it?"

She held out the vial so that he could see the label.

"Cephalexin. Keflex. Best I can do on short notice. Without you being on IVs." He looked at the capsules and at her, but they both knew he didn't have a lot of choice. He swigged them down. *You didn't ask him if he's allergic to penicillins.* On the other hand, if he knew enough to recognize the amoxicillin, that suggested he had taken it before and it hadn't hurt him. *Why do you give a shit? Habit..*

"Okay, doc," he said. She could see his face now. Broad, handsome. She remembered him more as the urbane visitor, the potential village benefactor, than as the man who had tried to kill Sa'ili. "Now, clean the wound up." He never took his eyes or the gun off of her.

She couldn't move. She panicked, thinking that she was taking too long, and that he would kill her for it. At last, as if some deep part of her brain that was more attuned to survival had taken over, she reached down into the case and pulled out the jug of saline and some Betadyne and the dressings. Intensely conscious of the gun now pressed against the side of her neck, she unbuttoned his shirt. The wound was stuck to the cloth, and she had to soak it to work it free. The wound turned out to be a six inch gutter of crusted blood, torn skin, fat, and muscle gouged out of the man's left side. Somehow, he had managed both to create the wound in the first place, which was freaky enough, and not penetrate to the abdominal cavity, which was a miracle. The only sign he gave of how much she was hurting him was a continuous soft growl.

The moment she was finished taping the dressing, he flung her onto the floor again and pressed the gun into the back of her neck. She had no thoughts in words, only a moment of total consciousness, almost of comfort: cool floor against her cheek, the sound of wind and rain on the other side of the louvers a few feet from her ear.

"Thanks," he said, almost kindly. "Now we're going for a little boat ride. You just need to remember who's the captain."

22

Han hated boats. And he hated the police launch most of all. He gazed down from the dock into the back of the launch as two officers grunted over the engine. A blast of wet rain shifted him sideways. Over the noise of the storm, Han shouted at the three other officers standing under the awning behind the wheelhouse. "When you get it going, head for Fagaalu. You don't have to try go outside the reef. Just stop anything that tries to get out."

They grinned up at him and went back to what they were doing. They wouldn't have tried to cross the reef in this storm, even under direct orders. Nor did they think anyone else would try. Han turned away and trotted up the dock toward where Chief Sasa's red Suburban was parked. Han jumped into the driver's side and looked at the old man, who nodded.

"Good. You have satisfied the honor of the Department. Now we will go catch your bad man." Han started the Suburban and headed up the road past the hotel. He was beyond asking questions. Fifteen minutes ago, filthy, wet, and breathless, he had burst into the chief's office as the old man sat looking bland and obtuse in some kind of meeting with Leon Fischer and the two F.B.I. agents. The old man had excused himself, abandoning his visitors around the huge old desk, and descended with Han to the dispatch office. There he made a couple of telephone calls and gave a couple of soft-spoken orders that had sent people scurrying like roaches in a sudden light.

Now, on the far side of the village of Utulei, he ordered Han to stop. "Pull over," he said, gesturing to Begley's duplex. The power was out; street and building lights were dark. The late afternoon was dim with wind-driven rain and cloud. But a crowd had gathered at the end of the row of buildings, at least a couple of dozen men, tall, muscular, grim-faced. Han remembered the tuna boat captains. And the mob that had taken on the fishermen. Without explanation, Sasa got out and led Han through the crowd, greeting each of the men as he passed him. They closed behind him, following, sweeping Han along with them.

Suddenly, on the beach, the mob of Samoans became a team. From a shed beside the yacht club, they lifted out a Samoan longboat. Han had only slightly more knowledge about boats than he did affection for them. But he knew about Samoan longboats. Designed in the 1840's by an enterprising palagi married into a Samoan family and determined to shift the balance of power toward his new relatives, they were built on the model of Long Island double-ended whaleboats But expanded to 24 oars manned by 24 Samoans. Modern times meant that the bow of the boat was occupied a boy mascot instead of a nine pound naval gun and a gunner and the competition was racing, not war. But you got the idea. The oarsmen set the boat at the water's edge and looked at the Chief. The old man gave a short, rasping speech in formal Samoan, something, Han guessed, between a benediction and orders. He gestured out to the right, to the shallow point separating Utulei and Fagaalu.

Then he looked at Han. His head jerked toward the bow seat. "Go get 'em."

Han looked at the Chief. And at the boat. And the men. And the waves breaking on the beach. The bay wasn't supposed to have waves. Not like this, anyway. Wind-driven rain sheeted across the water. Off to the left, just beyond the hotel, a set of running lights were wallowing around the point. Maybe the running lights were attached to the police launch. And maybe they weren't. "We need a light. At least for a signal." One of the men grinned, pulled a chunky, nine volt flashlight from under the gunner's seat and flashed it on and off.

He nodded. They waved him into the bow seat. The next two minutes were Keystone Cops playing pick-up-sticks, people running back and forth with oars twice the length of a man. And then, somehow, they were set. The boat leaped into the water like a horse going over a fence, and the men leaped into the boat, two by two, front to back, rowers and pushers, until the last pair jumped in. Beyond the breakers, the boat shuddered. Then the man right ahead of the steersman in the stern began beating out the rhythm with a wooden slot gong: *thok, thok, thok.* The boat settled and scooted over the rolling water like a live thing. The steersman thrust the rudder to the left, angling the boat to the right to follow the shore and stay inside the protection of the reef. *Anywhere along in here,* Han thought to himself, *you can have some doubt about what the hell you're doing.* He turned and craned forward, trying to make out Fagaalu's cove.

For Fagaalu had three things for a wounded fugitive that Fagatogo didn't. It had doctors—and at least one who was small and, so, easy to overpower but savvy about boats. And it had a sheltered bay right at the exit of the main harbor that was anchorage for half a dozen sailing yachts, a least a couple of which were small enough to be handled by two people but big enough to make the forty mile journey across the straits to Western Samoa. Maybe even in a storm.

Han looked through the growing darkness of the afternoon toward the shore road. And realized that he was seeing the TPD's two squad cars, one after the other, roof lights blazing, winding along the shore road toward Fagaalu. They were led by what had to be the Chief's red Suburban. Han wondered who was driving.

The steersman shouted and pointed. At first, Han couldn't make out anything particular. Ahead of them, he could see the anchored boats. Minute by minute, as the longboat drew closer, they resolved into three smaller single hulled, single-masted boats and a big, sea-going catamaran. But then he saw movement, a nonsensical jumble of heads and limbs in the water that was suddenly a smaller figure, half climbing, half being thrown up onto the deck, followed, more slowly, by a big man using only one arm.

Han couldn't see the gun from this far away, but he knew it was there.

"Is good boat," said a voice in front of Han as if commenting on the superior equipment of one team over another. Surprised, Han recognized Jim-son-of-Jim, one of his constables from Saturday morning. No wonder he had known about tides. He grinned over his shoulder at Han. "Bad weather; very steady."

A shout came across the water. Han looked around. The police launch, still well behind them, was pigging through the heavy swell, falling farther behind with every stroke of the longboat's oars. He turned back to the catamaran. A small, loose-footed fore-sail was free now, fluttering in the wind. The main sail, brilliant white against the stormy afternoon, was sliding smoothly upward. Even across the quarter of a mile of water that still separated them, Han could hear the rattling sound, like a gun going off, as the big sail flapped in the wind.

Another shout came from the police launch and then the blast of a shotgun. Ahead, Tanifa's pistol went off, its muzzle a brief flame in the near dark. Han cursed. Why had Tanifa fired? He would know that the distances and the movements of the boats were too great for any effect. Had he been shooting at something nearer? Ann, perhaps, no longer useful to him now that the sails and the anchor were up. Han strained through the darkness to see her, but he couldn't.

The catamaran was moving now as Tanifa cranked in the mainsail and it cupped against the wind. The big cat skimmed away across the swell, more on the water than in it.

"Good boat," Jim said again. "But too much sail." The catamaran was flying toward the break in the reef. Han had never seen a sailboat move so fast. *"Ava,"* Jim said. "Water come ovah reef but no can go back. All water must go out t' *ava*." Han remembered Jim's explanation from the other morning. He meant the break in the reef. Even in the near dark they could see the waves, towering rollers crashing on the reef, and the single dark slit of clear water sucking the big sailboat to freedom. The cat was making straight for the break in the reef. From the longboat, they watched helplessly as the big cat slipped through the gap and skated up the huge wave on the far side like a water bug.

And flipped over.

"Too much sail," Jim said again. "Too much wind outside. Too much waves."

As they watched, the hull that had hung, suspended, in the air, propped momentarily by the structure of the deck and the brace of the mainsail on the water, reasserted its link to gravity and forced the boat completely over so that the cat's two silvery bellies shone against the dark sea. The next great roller picked up the whole thing and threw it against the reef.

As a single voice, the oarsmen moaned. Han was silent, gazing at the rolling water.

More cries came from behind them.

The police launch was sinking. Illuminated by its own spotlight and running lights, it was already half swamped, the five officers shouting and waving at the longboat.

Han gave no orders. The oarsmen waited, the slot gong holding, *thok*.... holding, *thok*.... Han pulled out the big flashlight, trying to train the beam on the open water beyond the break in the reef. Nothing. From behind them, in shore, Han could hear the roar of a couple of outboard motors, even over the thunder of the surf on the reef. He glanced back. The launch was gone, sunk, leaving five angry policemen bobbing around in the water like abandoned oil drums. A Boston whaler and a small pleasure craft were coming out across the intervening water. They carried lights; Han could see a couple of men in each boat.

He looked back to the opening in the reef. The storm had broken a little; enough light filtered from the clouds that they could see the rip tide of bubbles pulling back out to sea. On this side of the reef, one of the hulls of the cat was still afloat, upside down, but being pulled back toward the gap in the reef. And then a tiny light shone, just beyond the reef, a tiny red light winking on and off. Han thought he was hallucinating.

"Man overboard," said Jim. "Man-overboard light."

Han tried to train his light on it. The swells rocked the longboat and the tiny red light in different rhythms and Han kept losing it. He couldn't think. To think meant knowing he was risking thirty-five lives for the possible rescue of a murderer. To think meant to see the wall of water beyond the reef and to feel his own death. The longboat rose and fell with the swell, alive under him. Suddenly, in the beam of his light stabbing out across the water, he was seeing the man-overboard light, a round white life-preserver and a tiny white hand, waving at them.

"*There!*" He didn't mean to command. But the slot gong spurted sound like the rush of a heartbeat; the great oars dug the water and the longboat flew out into the current. It leapt at the wall of water beyond the break in the reef, soaring up and up the towering back-wave until Han was looking over the crest and out into the ocean that covers half the world.

For a moment, the boat flew, half-airborne, then crashed down into the trough beyond. *Jesus, we've killed her.* The oarsmen shouted, laughing and pointing. Han saw the life preserver and the man-overboard light and a little white face in the water like an oversized clump of foam.

He leapt toward her. The water rose to meet him liked a fist from the sea, punching him back into the boat. Or maybe that was hands, grabbing his legs, tumbling him and then another body, like fish, into the bottom of the longboat. The next wave half broke over them. Choking and coughing, Han tried to right himself, tried to grip Ann's body. But he was being lifted by the swing of powerful shoulders back into the bow of the boat. Hands shoved him into his seat and laid Ann's body into his arms. She stirred and coughed and vomited water over his knees and coughed some more as he held her against him. The oarsmen cheered as if Han and not they were the heroes, every other man tossing water out of the boat with hands and buckets and plastic scoops while the others maneuvered the boat around to start the journey home.

The current was too strong to get back through the break in the reef. They worked the longboat along the edges of the reef as it bent to the left, molding to the edge of the drowned caldera that was Pago Bay. They crossed the entrance of the deep cove at Fagaalu, then Utulei's broader, shallower cove, the villages dotted now with lights. Beyond the point where the hotel stood on its promontory, the reef had been cut away for the old coaling station and the island's main dock gave immediate access to the shore. As they slipped under the lights from the hotel, headed toward the dock, they could hear music, talk, laughter from the bar. Just like nothing had happened.

23

Han was dreaming of pigs and death in the jungle.

He jerked awake. He sat up and leaned his bare back against the painted cinder block wall of Ann's bedroom. On either side of him, dawn light, a sea breeze, and the cacophony of early morning birds sifted through floor-to-ceiling glass louver windows. His heart slowed and the sweat began to dry. So what's better, being eaten by pigs or by sharks? If Tanifa had been looking for social advancement in the idiom of his childhood, sharks must be a move up. *God*, Han thought, *I've been in Samoa too long.* He got up, tied a lavalava around himself, and went into the tiny kitchen to make tea. Ann was still in the hospital, but Hutchinson had told Han he would probably let her out today.

The weather hadn't been much better yesterday, but they had been able to get the wreckage of the big catamaran off the reef. The grisly chunks of flesh left by the sharks webbed into the tangle of fiberglass and aluminum weren't identifiably Tanifa in the usual sense. But they weren't Ann, and beyond that, Han wasn't sure he cared a whole lot. The weather had delayed the mid-week Hawaii flight until this evening, but the delay had allowed Han to put what was left of Tanifa on ice and make arrangements to send the lot on to the path lab in Honolulu. Welly reported that Munro and the two F.B.I. agents lined up like seagulls on a dock at the hotel bar each night, clearly counting the hours until they could fly out. Han didn't know what had become of the Korean Consul, and he didn't care.

Out in the world of functional electronics, Derrick had gotten a picture of Tanifa to a helpful Chief Superintendent in Auckland and to

Han's colleagues in San Francisco. They now had four people who said they thought the photo was the guy who had joined them in the hotel that night. The two who remembered anything about a fracas between two customers out near the men's room thought that Tanifa had been with them both before and well after that time. But they all remembered that he said he had diarrhea and was in and out from the group several times through the evening.

Han took his tea and stood in the doorway, watching morning move up through the trees from the sea. Han did now believe that Tanifa had killed Begley. All Han's evidence was circumstantial —you can't hang a man for being at the same party and then, two years later, in the same bar as a murdered man. But Tanifa fit Hank Osgood's description of the man he had seen walking up the shore road from where Begley had almost certainly died. And last night, the boy Bert, now swinging around the hospital on his crutches like a kid on a jungle gym, had confirmed that he and Uli had dropped Tanifa at the hotel about eight. The details in the middle were vague, but they certainly hadn't picked him up again until after the riot. Bert also said Uli's death was payback for stealing the money meant for the wahoo. But it could as well have been house-cleaning. And it fit Tanifa's Stateside M.O.

But *why?* Welly kept saying Tanifa had wanted to buy a title, buy his way to respectability. Maybe so, but even if he and Begley had known each other in L.A.–and Han still had no proof of that beyond the single photo–what could that have to do with a stone-age family title debate? Most of the mess, Han thought, was mess that came after, not before, Begley's death.

Sarge appeared across the quad on his early morning rounds. The old non-com worked third-world half-time: twelve hours a day, seven days a week. Han lifted his mug. The old man grinned and shifted course. Han handed him a mug of tea with a chunk of lemon in it, and they sat in silent communion on the terrace wall outside.

Sarge had helped Han with Bert last night, adding a useful 'bad cop' flavor to the interview. The story of the death of the Tuna Pimp had been simple enough and much as Han had thought. What blew Han away was the simplicity of the telling. Not even the 'so what' of a South-of-Mission street punk, who, in his very belligerence, betrays some sense of guilt. Sarge had shrugged. "He was low rank, doing what he was told." So, Han thought, if six million Jews died to transform the world's conscience from Agincourt to Nuremberg, somehow that skipped Samoa?

There were lots of other things Han needed to know from Bert. What time had Tanifa hooked up with the boys again and how? If Han was right, and Tanifa had killed Begley, Tanifa would have wanted to put as much distance between Begley's body, rolling by then in the gentle waves of Utulei bay, and himself as possible once he had laid down his alternative alibi with his drinking buddies at the hotel bar. When and how had Tanifa found out about the Tuna Pimp? And what had happened to his money. Had Tanifa and Bert killed Uli together and strung him up? Ann's description of the body sounded like it had been there maybe half a day at least, though not much more. So why would they have been back there in time to see Ann taking pictures of it? Volumes of questions Han would never have the answers to, mainly because he couldn't imagine how to frame the questions so that Sarge had a prayer of translating them.

He did ask, "Why did Tanifa ask you to come up on the mountain with him Sunday?"

For about five minutes, Sarge couldn't get the boy to say anything. Then the words began to tumble out. "He says, Tanifa say he's worried about Uli. Was angry but now very worried Uli may hurt himself out of shame. They must go look for him. They go, walk long time. Very hard. This boy can feel the ghosts all around. Why would Uli come to such a place? They come, they see Uli's body hanging there, and Uli's ghost very angry. This boy can see it in his face. He has seen boys who hang themselves. They are pale, sad. Not Uli–he is still red-faced, angry, even in death. And this boy knows that Tanifa has killed Uli, that he has brought him here to kill him as well. But then, they see the palagi doctor. Tanifa say catch her, take camera. He doesn't see camera or why this rich Tanifa needs to steal camera, but he thinks maybe he can get the palagi doctor to help him. But she attack him, push him off mountain." Sarge snorted editorially. "Saved his damn' life."

Han nodded. "Tanifa was savvy enough to know that he didn't have time to go after either of them. He just had to get that body out of there. Pick up the pieces later."

Bert had sat between them, cheerful and expectant as a large puppy, waiting to be given a treat. Han wasn't fooled for a minute. Was any of it true? Or was he looking at Tanifa twenty-five years ago? If there were any fingerprints but the Tuna Pimp's on the spent shell Han had found in the shack, they would surely be Uli's. Han had no other hard evidence linking either boy to the Tuna Pimp's death. Charges could be brought, but they'd never hold up. There was no one but Bert himself as witness to the robbery or the death. Bert was a very lucky boy indeed. They would all just have to hope no one else ever discovered that primal conscience or gave it any real skill.

Sarge left to finish his rounds. Han pulled on a uniform. He was becoming something of a fixture at the hospital himself, even without Hutchinson having lent him Ann's flat. He had now interviewed all the hospitalized fishermen and found one who remembered seeing the Tuna Pimp with a gun. No one wanted to rat on what he thought was a crewman off another boat. But Han had unearthed a picture of the Tuna Pimp, and the one guy had identified him. Han crossed the sandy road to the hospital building and went in through the door by Hutchinson's office. Through the director's open office door, Han saw Hutchinson behind his desk. They nodded to each other as Han opened the door to the central block of the building.

Within a few strides, Han realized that he was wading through a excess amount of Samoan family. The hallway to the ICU was lined with mats filled with people talking, eating, sleeping. Right outside of the ICU door, three monumental old ladies dressed in white sat reading their bibles. On the mats in front of them were three small plates with one slice each of taro, yam and banana as if they were icons to whom offerings had been made. Their mouths moved in silent prayer and their eyes never lifted from their bibles as Han passed into the ICU.

Sa'ili was propped up in the bed beside a grey metal U.S. government issue desk that served as the ICU nursing station. He was down to a single IV; Welly had said he might be moved to the surgical ward soon. He was still moored to a suction apparatus on the floor via a long tube into his chest and lots of tape. Welly was asleep, snoring in an armchair, his feet up on the end of his cousin's bed. He was also clean-shaven. Clean-shaven and his wild hair somewhat shorter than usual. Clean-shaven and wearing a charcoal grey with-pockets lavalava and a–relatively–sober madras print shirt. Both of which might have been pressed some time in the fairly recent past. Well, Han thought, the clothes aren't white. So he's not planning on a funeral.

Sa'ili's eyes opened, taking in Han standing at the end of his bed. And was *there* behind his eyes in a way Han had not seen in the last few days.

"So," Sa'ili said. Han could see that each word hurt. "He's dead."

Han nodded. "Did you really think he killed the old man? The Tapuafanua?" He shouldn't have been asking questions. But he had to know.

A thin smile moved across the Samoan's face. He took a painful breath. "No proof."

Welly woke up, yawning like a barracuda and levering himself upright in the chair.

Han nodded toward the door. "There's half a village out there. That you-all?"

"You bet," Welly said. "Big time *fa'a lavelave*. Big trouble." Sa'ili grunted warningly. Welly ignored him. "Surprised you haven't heard. Being it's your boss." As far as Han knew, Sasa had not been in to the station at all yesterday. But Han himself had been plenty busy and had no idea what the old man had been up to or where he had been. "He and the most important talking chief in the windward districts are rounding up all the senior chiefs from over there, gonna *discuss* the family's guilt leaving a major title like Nofonofo open so long, creating a situation ripe for greed and violence."

"That why you're dressed in a skirt and not smelling like last night's brew?"

"Hey, they decide to reward me for saving the family's golden boy, who am I to spit in their face?" Welly looked more like a barracuda than ever. "Me 'n Neil, that is. Notice there's suddenly not so much talk about a new Director of Health?"

Han couldn't say he had. But he remembered Hutchinson sitting behind his desk in his office and looking very much still in command. Looking at his friend, he felt himself smile. "So….when do I start calling you Sapatu?"

Welly's grin let out another notch. "D'ya see the three old toads sitting outside the door? Old ladies in white, praying, refusing food?"

"That like *sepuku*, Japanese ritual suicide?"

"Get a grip, man. This is Samoa. No. They're just pissed because the Nofonofo mess is being blamed on them. You know: *if you don't appreciate all I've done for you, I guess I'm just another old lady, waiting for Heaven.* Those three haven't missed a meal in the last decade. I'd be real surprised if it lasts through lunch."

In the surgical ward, a single bed was set up in an alcove near the nursing station. Ann sat propped up against the wall, cocooned in a thin, bright Hawaiian print quilt, her knees drawn up. She saw Han as soon as he came on to the ward. She smiled, shyly, he would have said, and her eyes were full of questions. He pulled a stool over and sat beside the bed.

"How're you doing?"

"Neil says I'm remarkably coherent for someone who had a serum sodium of one-sixty thirty six hours ago. He says he'll let me go if its normal this morning."

"You know he...Neil...gave me the key to your flat?"

"He told me we were two reasonable people and we should be able to deal with it."

Han felt himself smiling. She looked at him full in the face, but her smile was still puzzled. "Is that it? Just...being reasonable? No *right* and *duty* and *honor* and all that?"

"Whose?"

She laughed out loud. "Okay. I'll buy that." She looked at him again and her smile was quiet. "You know, it still feels odd to be alive. Some of it's the sedative Neil insists I take–and he's right, I wouldn't dare sleep otherwise. Because I'm dead when I sleep, in the water, deep under water. It's not frightening. I'm just dead. With the light coming down through the water." She shook her head. "That's not real: there was no light. I knew the boat would go over when the wind and the back-wave hit it. I jumped free. I hit the water. I had the feeling of going way deep. And then I realize I can't breathe and I begin to struggle....and then I wake up....."

Han didn't want to listen. It was his worst nightmare. So he slid up on the bed beside her and wrapped his arms around her so she was cradled against him instead of the wall.

"....I wouldn't be alive if it weren't for you."

"Me and twenty-five Samoan longboat men."

He felt her mouth move against his shirt. "They were there because of you."

Well, if she wanted to make him a hero, it was okay by him.

"You know, he let me put on a life jacket. That's very strange. I can't get over that. I suppose he just wanted to keep me alive until he was ready to kill me. But it's the other reason I survived. That and the man-overboard rig popping up out of the water when it did."

Han took a slow deep breath. Her body molded against him. A Samoan surgical ward has about as much privacy as anywhere else in Samoa, but he was considering chancing it when a broad and disapproving brown face appeared over the nursing station counter. He winked at it.

He shifted one arm and was rewarded with a small expanse of breast. Perhaps by way of diversion, he said, "Everybody keeps telling me that Tanifa did what he did because he wanted a title. Something that he didn't have a prayer of getting in the usual way of things." Han thought about Welly in the ICU. About the last person in Samoa Han would have expected to care about a title. "And since everybody keeps telling me that, I guess I have to believe it. But what I don't get, is why Sa'ili did what he did." He looked down at the top of Ann's head. "More of same? Or did he really believe Tanifa killed the Tapuafanua?"

"They're not mutually exclusive." She yawned hugely and shifted softly against him. The movement set off a whole new range of sensation, so that he wasn't paying a whole lot of attention to what she was saying. "Honor of the family and so forth. And, in fact, it's possible that Tanifa did kill the Tapuafanua. The Tapuafanua would never have agreed to Tanifa's being made Nofonofo. Never. And Welly and I both saw bruising on the Tapuafanua's neck, on his corpse, laid out at the funeral. We were arguing about it when Sa'ili and Tanifa came up to us. But I think Sa'ili was just way ahead of you. He didn't know anything about Begley and Tanifa in L.A. But he could make all the other connections. And he wasn't distracted by the riot or the Tuna Pimp. Or being injured."

"Or having to prove anything in court."

"Yes. But he was also willing to put himself at risk as a test. He put his concerns out to the village in a way that they could understand. They could always ignore him."

"On the other hand," Han said. "He made damn sure he had more than just village witnesses."

"And Tanifa, if he was innocent, could have just told Sa'ili to stop being an asshole. He might have done that anyway, innocent or no. God knows plenty of people do that in our culture, bluster it out, even seem to convince themselves. But he couldn't do it. Not on his home ground. Not *makai;* not by the side of the sea. Even after all the evil he had done." Her voice grew very soft. "Sa'ili had created a kind of cultural tension. Like pouring cold water on hot glass: I think Tanifa just kind of shattered. At least for that moment. And when it was over, Sa'ili was shot and the gun was in Tanifa's hand and all of us were standing there as witnesses. Whatever else he had or had not done or anyone could prove, *that* was irrefutable."

A police officer walked up to the nursing station. Not just any police officer but Jim-son-of-Jim, looking exceptionally spiffy in uniform shirt and dress with-pockets lavalava. The nurse nodded toward Ann's alcove and Jim marched over.

"Sir, the Chief wants you."

Han's personnel file in San Francisco contained the quote *The Chief can get stuffed.* Or words to that effect. But this was a different chief. Han looked down at Ann's face.

"You okay?"

She nodded.

He waited for the withdrawal, the accusation. But what he got was a wry smile and the twitch of an eyebrow, the recognition, as only maybe a soldier or a doctor could, of duty. He nodded in turn and slid away from her, feeling the cool empty spot as the air touched his side.

He followed Jim out of the hospital. He didn't bother trying to ask the kid what this was about. Even if Jim had known, in the palagi sense of knowing something, Han knew he wouldn't have answered. What Jim knew in Samoan was that it was none of his damned business.

The red Suburban was outside, purring, waiting for Han. Apparently also for Han to drive. Jim climbed into the back with two other young officers built in on the same heroic scale that he was. Sasa was sitting in the passenger seat.

"We are going to a meeting," the old man said. His white uniform shirt and black with-pockets lavalava were so clean and starched they could have marched away on their own. "In Papasaa." Han gazed at him. The old man jerked his head imperiously toward the road, very much the cultural icon about to re-engineer the major chieftainships of the windward districts. Han considered arguing about whether it was appropriate to deploy the TPD's only detective in an all-day side show as a chauffeur. And then decided against it. Even a cop can recognize a force of nature. He put the Suburban in gear and eased it back, turning down the drive toward the shore road.

The trip to Papasaa hadn't gotten any faster in the last forty-eight hours. In fact, Han discovered the rationale behind the three extra officers. And the chain saw that he had not observed earlier stashed into the far back compartment of the Suburban. The Territorial Police, among their other less obvious duties, were clearing the road to Papasaa.

The river hadn't gone down either. They left the Suburban, as usual, on the near shore and waddled across the waist-high water, arms lifted akimbo like wings, awkward as ducks and unable to swim or fly.

On the far side, Sasa was met by a delegation of older men led by a tall, leathery, figure draped in real tapa cloth and carrying what even Han recognized as an official staff. There was a brief exchange of words including all of them—Han got the picture that the local leader was politely thanking individuals of a far lower class for having delivered Sasa safely. But after that, having fulfilled their roles as driver and road crew, Han and the three patrolmen were clearly dismissed to their own devices. The official party strode away across the green toward the guest fale.

Like the rest of the island, Papasaa looked seriously tattered. One of the palagi-style houses had lost its roof. The ground was matted with downed palm fronds. A small levee of wet sand had been heaped up for a short way among the houses closest to the river to divert the overflow from the river away from the green. This last suggested a little more human assertion than Han was accustomed to see in Samoan village relations with the elements. But, along with the absence of efforts to clean up the village or replace the damaged roof, the action all seemed to focus on the guest fale on the beach and on the village green spreading back behind it.

The official party had ascended in to the guest fale where a number of lesser chiefs were already seated at or between or behind the main pillars of the fale, depending on their status. Sasa and the man with the tapa cloth and staff were seated with their backs to the two central poles. Younger chiefs were lowering the pandanus shutters. Privacy: always a bad sign in Samoa. Out on the green, what looked like half the village was seated on the grass—not even on mats—most of them bent forward, as if in supplication, many with a cloth or folded tapa on their heads. Jim looked at Han and his eyebrows went up and down, but he didn't say anything. He trailed off after his fellows.

Unenlightened, Han wandered up the length of the makeshift levee. It hadn't been particularly successful and water stood in pools through much of the village. Han wondered, slapping at his arms and legs and neck and killing a minimum of four mosquitos with each blow, if heaven to mosquitos was, as for at least human males, unlimited reproduction—or at least the acts associated with it. Part of him was aware that the storm had changed the look of Papasaa enough that he hadn't cued off the sight of it yet, wasn't really remembering what had happened here the last time he had been here.

And then he came around the end of one storm-swept fale and was looking at the palagi-style house where Tanifa had stood on the front steps and lifted his pistol and fired at Sa'ili.

The hollow boom of a big wave pounding on the reef rolled over him. He didn't drop to the ground, but the instinct was there and for a moment, the cold sweat.

Han snorted and walked up the steps. In Samoa, sweat is just sweat. He tried the door: open of course. The eyes in the back of his head registered a couple of children observing him half hidden behind the neighboring house. The rest of the village was far too concerned about what was going on in the guest fale to worry about a policeman wandering in and out of people's houses. He pulled the door to behind him and stood quietly for a moment.

The house was empty. He could see most of it. A partially closed back space looked like it was used for a kitchen. The rest of it, more like an enclosed porch, was open to view. In the right hand rear corner, the enclosure of the back room had created an alcove. A Samoan palate mattress lay there, draped like a royal dias with a mosquito net hung from the rafters. Just beyond the bed, a chest of red wood, its top carved in a geometric pattern like a tapa print-board, was pushed against the wall. All very high status. Worthy of a wealthy visitor, a family member made good. Han walked across the room and opened the lid of the chest.

Inside, with the folded lava-lavas and bed linens, was a black canvas suitcase, the kind with its own pull frame, just big enough to occupy an entire overhead bin in an aircraft so that no one else can get anything in.

The case did belong to Tanifa; the label bore his name and his airline tickets were zipped into an inner pocket. But if it had more secrets than the brand name of Tanifa's underwear, Han didn't find it, even separating the lining from the frame and exploring the slits with his fingers. Nor was the chest itself or the mattress or the little bookshelf against the third wall of the alcove any more revealing. Han stood back into the middle of the room and thought about being Samoan. Which wasn't terribly helpful. But he knew, in that moment, that it was no accident the old man had shanghaied him for this trip. So he thought about being an American of other than industrial-world, European, or even just born-there origins. About having more freedom than your upbringing presupposed, and more insight about the uses of that freedom than a native born American could dream of. Seeing through the cracks in the walls of culture.

Samoan houses don't have places to hide things because nothing is hidden. *But this isn't a Samoan house, it's a palagi-style house.* For some reason, Han thought about the Tuna Pimp and his little shack on the mountain side. His eyes moved up to the place where the walls met the down-slope of the tin roof. Tanifa had been very tall. But he would have wanted to see what he was doing. A pair of simple wooden kitchen chairs stood neatly side by side against the inner wall enclosing the back room. But in the interests of efficiency, Han went first and climbed up on the wooden chest.

Like in the Tuna Pimp's shack, the corner where the tin roof, the four-by-four framing, and the–in this house–vinyl siding walls met formed a neat pocket space not visible unless you were eyeball-to-eyeball with it. Even the people who had built the house, being Samoan, would not see this space, because they did not expect it to be there. Like a lot of things in life, you have to think that way.

At first, he thought the space was empty. And then, feeling with one hand, he found the thick envelope that had been wedged into the slit between the siding and the upright. Covering his hand with a pillow case as a make-shift glove and at least some padding against the razor edges of the vinyl, he worked the envelope out.

The envelope was marked with the logo of the Bank of American Samoa and contained fifty-seven hundred dollar bills.

Han reversed the pillow case over the envelope and folded it carefully. Then he went outside and sat on the front steps of the house. After a while, a small dog came over and sniffed him, then moved on and lifted its leg against the corner of the house, clearly inviting Han to follow suit. The children also emerged and stood watching him.

The older child, a boy, said, in very clear English, "Did you find the money?"

Han looked at him. "What money?"

"The money of the rich American." With this child, at least, Tanifa had not even made it to the status of local.

"You saw his money?"

"Yes. He hid it in the...." The child did not have words to describe the place. He waved his hands around, maybe drawing the roof and the uprights. But then he shrugged. "My mother says it's none of my business. Of course a rich man has money to share with the family and give to the church."

"And did Tanifa do that?"

The boy shrugged again. A sharp word sounded from the other side of the fale, and the two children disappeared like smoke in a breeze. The little dog sat and scratched itself with great energy, one back leg pounding the sand. Han sat looking out across the inlet cove, to where the mountains came down to the sea. The air was almost as full of water as the water and the green mountains glowed pink along their edges. A little breeze rattled in the palms and the music of the breakers on the reef became gradually calmer, less percussion and more strings.

Han sat there for much of the rest of the day. At some point, a young woman and a couple of children found him, gave him a plate of food and a warm soda, and brought him seconds when he finished the firsts. (At that point, he remembered that this would go on until he left something on the plate, which he did.) He spent about an hour walking up the beach and then another hour walking back and probably slept another hour on Tani's palate under the mosquito net. And then whatever had gone on all day in the guest fale broke up and there was another huge meal, mainly centered on the guest fale but with Han and the three other uniformed officers served in some honor in another fine traditional fale on the green. And then it was dark and everyone went to bed. As far as Han could tell. Except for the little dog. From where he lay on another palate under another voluminous mosquito net, Han could hear the thump of the little dog's foot as he scratched.

24

About noon the next day, Han pulled the Suburban into its usual spot in front of the police station and thought that if he ever drove the road to Papasaa again, it would be too soon. Jim jumped out and opened the chief's door as his fellow officers extracted themselves more slowly from the back. But the old man didn't move. He looked at Han.

"Drive me to the bank."

Han's first access to Sasa had been during the drive back. And the old man's first response to the money had been the same as the little boy's mother: paper money, preferably in large denominations, is the lubricant of status negotiation in Samoa. But in the end, Han had been able to get him to see it from an outsider's point of view, especially an outsider cop's point of view: twenty dollar bills may be yuppie foodstamps, but hundred dollar bills, particularly fist-fulls of them, are the ensigns of the drug trade.

"We have no drug trade."

"Maybe not. But you do have a murder we're trying to pin on someone who made his living as a specialist sub-contractor for the drug trade. And why did he get it here? Why didn't he bring it with him? It doesn't make any sense."

The old man grunted. The front door of the bank was roughly twenty yards from the front door of the police station. Mystified, but certainly not for the first time, Han started up the Suburban and rolled it the few car-lengths to the bank. The old man sat calmly. Eventually, Han got out, went around, and opened the chief's door.

"You stay here," the old man said.

Like chauffeurs across all time and cultures, Han leaned back against the Suburban and folded his arms across his chest. The old man strode toward the door. And Han watched the outside bank guard and the people inside the double glass doors and beyond the broad front windows have just enough time to have seen the Suburban and the regal entrance and leap to do the old man's bidding.

Which, in American banking terms, was probably not quite legal. But was sure as hell efficient. In just under twenty minutes, two guards flung back the heavy glass doors of the bank in unison, and Sasa strode out. Han opened the passenger door for him, closed him in carefully, and went around to climb in the driver's side. Han looked at the old man.

"I believe," said the chief, "That we need to go to the governor's house. I have made telephone calls." He handed Han two sheets of bank records. Their message was easy enough to decipher. Han gave them back to the old man and pulled out onto the road.

They drove in silence up the long hill toward the hotel, toward the place where Ray Begley had died, turning just short of the hotel into the entrance to the Governor's residence. At the top of the steep drive, Han pulled up to the front verandah and glanced at the Chief. If they were making an arrest, by Samoan standards, they were seriously underpowered. The arrests Han had been part of here had involved the arresting officer and least six others. At six foot six and two hundred fifty pounds each, who needs handcuffs?

"Are we making an arrest, sir?"

The old man looked at him, his face blank. "There are plenty of chiefs." A pretty young man with a hibiscus behind one ear trotted down the stairs and opened Sasa's door. Han followed them up the broad flagstones into the house.

The young aide conducted them through the house and out to a covered lanai that ran the length of a long south-side wing and was probably called the ball room. Beyond a low balustrade, the vista down the rain-swept mountainsides and out to sea unrolled like a painted scroll. Today, the lanai seemed to be serving as an impromptu office. Several older, traditionally dressed Samoan men sat cross-legged on a low dias with folders of paper spread around them. Neil Hutchinson, Colonel Munro, and the attorney general, Leon Fischer, sat on chairs pulled up to the dias. Several other Samoans dressed in palagi clothes were also sitting around on chairs. Han recognized at least two of them as something to do with Public Health. All looked up as Han and Sasa walked in and then looked to their right as the governor emerged from a side door. The governor wore a white shirt and with-pockets lavalava with a lei of bird-of-paradise flowers like a medieval European's chain of office around his neck. Han and Sasa were offered chairs. Everyone was being too polite to ask them what the hell they were doing there, but Han could see the question on every face.

Still standing, Sasa said, to the governor, "This is Lieutenant Han. Since the death of Sapatu, he has been my acting Assistant Chief of Police." This was a surprise to Han, but he kept his face flat. He did suspect that he had just been introduced as having equal rank with a senior Talking Chief. This was a little unnerving, particularly as it was still not exactly clear what the old man was up to. However, having provided himself with an orator, in good high chief fashion, he sat down on the dias and folded his legs under him. "Your group is not complete," he said blandly.

The governor looked puzzled, but just then, the same side door he had entered through swung open. Gloriana Shutz-Begley swept in wearing an ankle length two-piece dress in white Filipino cut-work lace and a hat. *'Without Ray' is dignified Samoan matron, often with a hat.* The hat was too big. Again, Han though of a vamp from a '30s movie. She glanced around the room and chose a white ironwork chair that looked like something left over from the days of admirals' wives.

Gloriana nodded to Sasa in the way of one thanking another of high rank who honors them with their presence. Then she looked at the governor. "Everything appears to be settled now," she said grandly. "I believe we should move ahead as planned." Han saw Neil Hutchinson's face tense. One nostril flared. The governor picked up his pen and nodded fractionally to Munro and one of the other Samoans.

Sasa held up one hand. "Before you go on, gentlemen, Lieutenant Han has some questions he wishes to ask." All six Samoan men, traditional or westernized, rocked back slightly in their seats. Two covered their mouths with one hand, clutching the elbow with the other hand in contained surprise. And Han recognized the traditional village quorum for judgement: *There are enough chiefs.*

So he looked at Gloriana and said, "Dr. Shutz-Begley, can you explain why you withdrew six thousand dollars in hundred dollar bills cash from your bank account two weeks ago? After having had to secure a loan in part to do so? And why nearly that same amount, in bills in the sequence of numbers issued to you, was found among the effects of Tanifa Palapala in the village of Papasaa. You may remember Tanifa better by the professional name he used when you knew him as a hired killer in Los Angeles: Tani Tua'ua."

Gloriana's eyes and mouth made three little circles as she gazed at him. And then she folded out of her chair onto the floor in a dead faint. A real one, for once.

Epilogue

"Everyone always said Gloriana was dumb about money," Han said. "But *she* didn't know she was dumb about money."

Han, Welly, and Ann sat on a mat on the floor of Sa'ili's hospital room drinking tea out of early nineteenth century Staffordshire china, relicts of long-gone missionaries. The title debates on Nofonofo and Sapatu had begun in Papasaa. The aunties, the Tapuafanua's daughters, had decamped from outside the ICU when Sa'ili was moved onto the regular surgery ward. But they had left the tea service behind them for Sa'ili's use, and the set had been part of the attributes of the Nofonofo for a hundred years. And the Nofonofo had had the final vote on the Sapatu for longer than that.

Sa'ili appeared to be feeling a good bit better and trying not to display un-high-chiefly temper about being still tied to the bed by IV and chest tube. The china appeared to be helping.

Han went on. "That was her whole problem: with Hutchinson, with the legislature, with everything else she took on. She did know enough not to write him a check...."

Welly put in: "Tanifa probably told her he'd only take cash...."

Ann shook her head. "I have visions of them meeting, of her picking him up in the old merc, you know, somewhere like half-way up the governor's driveway, which is about the only twenty yards of private space on the leeward side of the island...."

Han shrugged. "Why not? She could call, be up to the hotel to get him in five minutes."

Sa'ili took a deep breath in the manner of one demonstrating that he can and said, without rancor, "Leon will take care of her. Leon will get her off."

Han almost said, *the one goddamned thing I can go to court with this whole mess and you want her to get off?* But he didn't.

"Ray was a bad man," Sa'ili said. "He hurt Gloriana. He hurt Maria Theresa."

"Bullshit," Welly said. "Not that Ray wasn't a shit. He was a shit. But she wouldn'a' had to be in such a hurry if it wasn't for the mediation, Munro coming down here and all. She wanted to be ready to step into the magic shoes. Fa'atofi Jake always knows everything about everything. He says he figures Ray saw Tanifa when he was staying at the hotel first off, before he moved over to the village. Musta told Gloriana he'd seen Tanifa. Man, talk about deliver us from temptation. Him being family...." Sa'ili grimaced. "...Distant family–would make it even better."

Han didn't know about any family connection between Gloriana and Tanifa, but he did know that the dates of Gloriana's withdrawals from the bank matched Welly's scenario. But he didn't say anything.

"In the end," Sa'ili said, "She didn't get what she wanted."

Han looked at the two Samoans. Were they content with that? It was probably a better justice than most. He thought about the Tuna Pimp and Sapatu and Uli: would their spirits accept death and justice intertwined? Probably not. Why should a ghost be any more reasonable than a live person? Han sipped his tea and thought happily about the ghosts of Sapatu and Uli and the Tuna Pimp, fighting it out with the spirits of the four drowned fishermen, haunting the mountainsides above Pago until the end of days. Han looked at Ann. And her old saint, the Tapuafanua? Well, whether the old man died naturally or whether Tanifa helped him along, Sa'ili would be Nofonofo now, and on his own terms. So the Tapuafanua had gotten what he wanted. And most people call that justice.

About the Author

Lynn Stansbury practices medicine, motherhood, and writing where ever her husband's Army career takes them.